Son of Thunder

Son of Thunder

The Sequel to Rembrandt's Angel

by

Steven M. Moore

www.penmorepress.com

Son of Thunder by Steven M. Moore

This is a work of fiction. Names, characters, businesses, events and incidents are either the products of the author's imagination or used in a fictitious manner. Any resemblance to actual persons, living or dead, or actual events is purely coincidental.

ISBN-13: 978-1-950586-07-3(Paperback)
ISBN-13: 978-1-950586-08-0(e-book)

BISAC Subject Headings:

ART015080**ART** / History / Renaissance
FIC022060**FICTION** / Mystery & Detective / Historical
FIC022040**FICTION** / Mystery & Detective / Women Sleuths

Cover Illustration by The Book Cover Whisperer:
ProfessionalBookCoverDesign.com

Address all correspondence to:
Penmore Press LLC
920 N Javelina Pl
Tucson AZ 85748

What reviewers said about *Rembrandt's Angel*

"...a thrilling, globetrotting adventure that provides readers a glance into the world of art forgery, Neo-Nazi conspiracies and even links to ISIS. The duo of Brookstone and van Coevorden can be favorably compared with utmost respect to Agatha Christie's classic characters, Miss Marple and Hercule Poirot. Esther is a strong, well-liked character with a saucy disposition, while Bastiann, though he plays costar and lover to Esther, is able to hold his own with regards to likability. ...the character Esther Brookstone provides readers with an unusual female protagonist who is more than just a senior Scotland Yard Inspector, she is a memorable and tenacious dame who readers will undoubtedly enjoy throughout the novel and will look forward to reading any of her possible future exploits."

—Lynette Latzko, *Feathered Quill Book Reviews*

"A deftly crafted and consistently riveting read from beginning to end. 'Rembrandt's Angel' showcases author Steven Moore's genuine flair for originality and his impressive mastery of the Mystery/Suspense genre. While unreservedly recommended for community library collections, it should be noted for the personal reading lists of dedicated mystery buffs that 'Rembrandt's Angel' is also available in digital book format."

—*Midwest Book Review*

"...successfully couples history's fascination with the still-missing master artworks that disappeared under the Third Reich with a pair of intercontinental sleuths who are more than a match for the cast of neo-Nazis they choose to tangle with. I say choose because 60-something Esther Brookstone of Scotland Yard and her somewhat younger partner and paramour Bastiann van Coevorden (Interpol) are clearly in command as they pursue a missing Rembrandt canvas across borders, from London to Stuttgart and Oslo to Peru."

—Amazon reviewer

Introduction

Although the inimitable Esther Brookstone no longer works for me, she has continued to let me document her adventures, playing Watson to her Holmes. This adventure is unusual. Because of its delicate nature, I have obfuscated the account a bit at Esther's request. If readers desire more details, they will have to ask her for them.

During these adventures, you would almost swear the old girl became religious. Her father was a vicar, so she can move in those circles if she wants to do so. As usual, she finds more trouble than she expected. The Good Lord protects the innocents...even when they're not so innocent!

George Langston
London, 2025

"The first day of the week cometh Mary Magdalene early, when it was yet dark, unto the sepulchre, and seeth the stone taken away from the sepulchre. Then she runneth, and cometh to Simon Peter, and to the other disciple, whom Jesus loved, and saith unto them, They have taken away the Lord out of the sepulchre, and we know not where they have laid him. Peter therefore went forth, and that other disciple, and came to the sepulchre. So they ran both together: and that other disciple did outrun Peter, and came first to the sepulchre."—John 20:1-4.

Ode to St. John

Ephesian hills called you home
To the place you last saw her,
And you held her holy hand.

You left our world all alone
To rise up and be with her,
And to again hold her hand.

Yet you left us your blessed tome
Describing your life with Him,
A life we need to understand—

Its message that calls us home
So we'll all be with Him
When the clock runs out of sand.

—Esther Brookstone

Cast of Principal Characters

From the first and second century
John — one of the original twelve disciples
Mary Magdalene — the first female apostle

From the fifteenth and sixteenth century
Sandro Botticelli — Florentine artist
Bishop Leonardo da Padua — Florentine priest

From the twenty-first century
Esther Brookstone — ex-Scotland Yard Inspector
Bastiann van Coevorden — Interpol agent
Denise Prince (Sister Denise) — Gerald's free-spirit sister
Walther Beck — Munich museum's archaeologist
Bruno Toscano — descendant of Leonardo's brother

And others...
Androcles — Greek co-conspirator with Mary and John
Claudius — Roman patrician
Father Jean Laurent — Jesuit priest
George Langston — Esther's ex-boss at Scotland Yard
Stanley Miller — Esther's spy partner
Sergio Moretti — Esther's friend and SIS handler
Hal Leonard — another Interpol agent
Harry James — handyman at Esther's gallery
Anna French — employee in Esther's gallery
Oscar Willoughby — Oxford Classics professor
Kurt Geiszler — German federal police inspector
Ernesto Felipe Lopez Diaz — cartel leader
Inspector Erkan — Turkish cop
Aslan Remzi — Erkan's partner

Note: Several European security agencies are mentioned in this novel. Great Britain's MI5 and France's DGSI are approximate equivalents of the U.S. FBI and DHS, while Great Britain's MI6 and France's DGSE are approximate equivalents of the U.S. CIA. The "MI" for the British agencies stands for "Military Intelligence," and these agencies originated in World War II. The "DGS" for the French agencies translates to "Department of General Security" with the "I" and "S" standing for interior and exterior. Esther Brookstone was in MI6 during the Cold War.

Part One

The Parchment

"The wind bloweth where it listeth, and thou hearest the sound thereof, but canst not tell whence it cometh, and whither it goeth: so is everyone that is born of the Spirit."

—John 3:8

Chapter One

Fifteenth Century, Florence

Sandro Botticelli kept his face deferential as Lorenzo de' Medici scowled. The patron of the arts did not seem to like Sandro's most recent painting.

"It is not obvious who those people in the painting are meant to be!" Lorenzo said.

The patron was a plain man of average height, a somewhat comical figure with his broad frame and short legs. A swarthy complexion and a squished nose seemed to belie his importance. His anger had made his already harsh voice even raspier, besides turning his face beet-red.

Now that would make a portrait, thought Sandro.

As was the lot of many artists in Florence, Sandro depended on Lorenzo's circle of friends for patronage. The banker behaved as though he owned Botticelli. In a sense, he did.

The painter studied his new creation. *One figure looks like me, but he is supposed to be John.* He had used that tactic before. He was always the most convenient model. *I am not a bad-looking man. And who knows what John looked like?* He could have done better with perspective, though. He had to give that to da Vinci—the arrogant fellow had made great leaps in perspective.

"I can title the painting so everyone will know who they are," Sandro said.

The powerful man's red face turned even darker. "Paint something else. This one does nothing for me. And it will make me appear a fool in front of my friends if I say it does. You created a scandal with that painting of Venus. Everyone knew it was Simonetta Vespucci."

"A stylized Simonetta, I assure you. The Vespuccis did not seem to mind. Amerigo rather liked it, in fact." He paused a moment, then added, "I immortalized their daughter, after all.

Lorenzo's eyebrows arched and he stared at the ceiling as if praying for divine intervention. Then he frowned at Sandro. "Throw this out with the trash. It is unfit for anyone's eyes."

Even with his patron's angry critique and all the political unrest and squabbling between city-states, Sandro knew it was a good time for the arts in Florence. Lorenzo deserved some credit for that. He even pretended to be a poet. *But he also is a horse's ass.*

After the great man made his exit, Sandro paced the floor in front of the painting. His problem was that he liked it, even with its imperfections and even though his most important patron did not. *You cannot please him or his sycophants all the time. Maybe I can sell the painting on the sly to one of his fellow art patrons without him knowing it. Maybe to the Vespucci family?*

*****

There was a knock on the door. *Did Lorenzo rethink his decision?*

The artist opened to see Bishop Leonardo da Padua smiling up at him, his beady eyes shining with excitement between folds of fat. "I have great news!" He showed Sandro a rolled-up parchment. "Guess what this is!"

Sandro enjoyed Leo's company. A small man, almost as wide as he was tall, and with an effervescent personality, he kept his homilies short and often had a wink, a nod, and plenty of forgiveness for his parishioners. Sandro knew the odd little man had also sired some bastards. *Warrior popes and fornicating priests, yet everyone looks the other way!*

Now Leo was bouncing up and down on his toes in enthusiasm, which almost dislodged the hat he wore to hide his baldness. During mass, he cut a priestly figure, dressed in the jewels and rich satin robes of his office, complete with miter. The robes also made him appear much fatter, something many parishioners laughed about.

Sandro eyed what Leo was carrying with misgivings. The cleric was always searching for historical documents and relics. Although the painter was no expert in antiquities, most of them appeared to have a dubious provenance. *The poor fool wants to make church history by discovering something of great religious significance.*

"Come, my friend. Let's have some wine and fruit so you can tell me all about it. I am not good at playing guessing games. Knowing you, what you have could be a document recording a heretic's last oath as he burned at the stake."

"My good man, you are cynical today." Leo followed Sandro into the studio, a workshop in his brother's house. "What's the problem?"

Sandro gestured at the painting sitting on his easel. "Lorenzo does not like it. I have a hunch he does not like anything mythological or that's not forthrightly religious. Apparently this is not forthright enough. I have resisted the temptation to scrape everything off the panel and reuse the wood. It is good, thick poplar."

The bishop studied the painting a moment, then shook his head. "So, make the old man more obviously religious. I always like to see halos. You know the subject is religious in that case. No doubts at all." He reached up and patted Sandro on the shoulder. "And do not be despondent. He thinks he is an art connoisseur, but he is not. He throws money around and makes his allies do more of the same. I guess that is good for you and the other artists." He paused a moment, putting his index finger to his double chin as he studied the painting some more. "Maybe I will buy it from you, but let us leave that business for later. Read this."

He handed the parchment to Sandro, who unrolled it on top of a work table and read the Latin text. He then glanced from Bishop Leo to his painting. "This is an interesting and unusual coincidence, my old friend. In my painting, that's John on the right, between his brother James and the father, Zebedee."

The bishop glanced at the painting yet again. He jerked a well-manicured thumb toward the ceiling. "Stupendous! It is an omen sent from the Lord above!"

Sandro groaned. "Or from the Devil below, considering that Lorenzo raised hell when he saw the painting. And not even you recognized the religious significance. Maybe I should put Latin titles over all their heads as labels. St. John, St. James—um, is Zebedee a saint? Enough." He glanced at the parchment again. "Where did you find this?"

"A student from the medical school gave it to me. He said he bought it at a bazaar in Ephesus. Scholars say St. John died there, you know."

When Lorenzo had transferred the university to Pisa, he'd left the medical school intact. It became a center for science and attracted students from all over Italy, not just from the

Florentine Republic. They said da Vinci had secretly dissected cadavers there. Sandro could believe it. That other Leonardo was something of a ghoul. *Maybe he is more of a scientist than an artist?*

Sandro shook his head. "And you think this student has made a major find? Your parchment is most likely a fake. How much did you pay him for it?"

The bishop seemed embarrassed. "He did not ask for much."

Sandro figured his friend had been scammed and the parchment was not the wonderful historical discovery the priest wanted to make. He rolled up the parchment and handed it back to the bishop.

"And you think this proves St. John died there? I always heard he died in Patmos, not that I am a theological historian."

The bishop shrugged. "We do not know for sure that he did not die in Ephesus."

"Someone would have to go there to see if these directions make any sense. You are not asking me to do that, are you?"

Leo seemed crestfallen. "It did cross my mind."

"That expedition would require financing. Many florins. Lorenzo will not approve it. The bank is in trouble because Grandpa Medici treated money like it was cheap wine to give away to the rabble."

"But Lorenzo has connections. By the way, perhaps one of them would buy your painting. Maybe the Vespuccis? They are close allies of his."

"I thought of that. You know his friends as well as I do. They would not risk incurring his wrath by buying something he rejected. I tire of the painting anyway. What will you give me for it?" The bishop offered a meager sum in florins. "*Va bene*. It is yours. Take your painting and parchment and be gone. I have a headache from Lorenzo's visit alone, and you are not helping me recover."

The bishop finished his wine in two gulps. "I bid you farewell then and wish you a speedy recovery from both Lorenzo's wrath and your headache."

*****

When he returned to his church, Bishop Leo could not decide where to put the painting. He stared at it for a time, noting how John resembled Sandro. He did not think the painter's self-portrait captured the essence of the man, who he knew possessed a cynical humor that led to his mocking arrogant people, including Leo. That cynicism also led to disparaging wealth and property, although Sandro favored having enough of each to be comfortable.

Both the young painter and the saint in the painting had curly auburn hair, wide eyes, and pronounced cheekbones. He only lacked a laurel wreath to appear like a Roman emperor. A haughtiness in the expression added to that effect, but not as much as in the real man. *Maybe that was why Lorenzo hated the painting? But what to do with it?*

He was not about to donate it to the church. He had no love for Pope Sixtus IV after the papacy had sponsored the Pazzi uprising against the Medici family's power in Florence. Sandro's first fresco of the rebellion leaders' hanging had won Lorenzo's favor, but not the pope's. Even so, Lorenzo had offered Sixtus sponsorship of several Florentine painters, including Sandro, as a peace offering; they were to paint frescoes in the new Sistine Chapel.

Leo did not move in such exalted circles of political and religious intrigue. He had no desire to do so, but he valued his friendship with Sandro. That rascal da Vinci had scoffed at his friend's landscapes before he left for Milan in 1481.

Lorenzo had been both artists' patron, but Leonardo was no friend of Botticelli's. *What a shame politics and personal animosities affect art. Da Vinci was such an ass. A genius in many ways, but a pompous ass.*

Leo's service to God did not stop him from disparaging people or even his fellow clerics when they deserved it. Even popes were fallible, because they were only men chosen by other men—always lots of politics in that choice, too. But St. John the Divine had always seemed to be more than a man. *The beloved disciple.* That thought brought his mind back to the problem of what to do with the painting.

He decided to hide it in one corner of the armoire in his study with a sketch from one of Perugino's students he had recently purchased. He first folded and tucked the parchment in the back of the painting between frame and panel.

I will have to see about that expedition. Lorenzo is not mad at me. Lorenzo does not even know who I am! Only another priest among many, until I find the saint's burial place!

Chapter Two

First Century, Rome

"You have to flee," said Paul. "Nero has gone mad!"

"He already was mad," said John. The emperor had blamed Christians for the fire that had ravaged the city. Peter had been one of the victims of his ongoing purge. "The Church will survive."

"But maybe not the Church of Rome." Paul eyed the disciple. "To help spread his Word, you must leave, John. Peter would want that."

John nodded. Peter and he had had differences about the way forward at times, but that conflicted disciple had made great sacrifices. He had spent seven years in Antioch to stabilize the church there, and then left his family behind to come to Rome to confront the heretic Simon Magus. Now Peter had made the ultimate sacrifice.

"I would leave, but how? Nero's soldiers are all over the city."

"I have found a man who is leaving the city. A freeman who is well known to the soldiers. He is one of us and will keep you safe."

"I would be more concerned about keeping *him* safe. Simple folk with faith will become a solid foundation for our movement. Without them, we will be nothing."

"And so it has been since the Council of Jerusalem, when Peter, you, and others decided to embrace the Gentiles."

"Christ's message is for everyone, Jews and Gentiles. All men and women of any group who hear that message of love and embrace it are blessed. And we must temper our words of blame for his Crucifixion. He said on the cross, 'Forgive them, Father, for they do not know what they are doing.' In general, neither Romans nor Jews are to be blamed, according to His own words. It was all part of God's plan." He glanced out the open window to the quiet streets, silent now because citizens of Rome feared Nero's fury. "Where do I find this freeman?"

"Follow me, my brother. Be quick, yet stealthy. We must watch for the soldiers."

As he followed Paul, John wondered how the mad Nero's mind worked. *How can you celebrate your day of birth by murdering people?* he asked himself. He thought of Peter, who had inadvertently increased the Roman fondness for crucifying the Empire's enemies and common thieves in strange positions, by demanding he be crucified upside down on the inverted cross. *Yes, conflicted.* He had noticed that when Peter and he joined forces to preach to the Samarians.

John liked Silas when he met the old freeman and shook his hand. The handshake was still strong; John sensed his faith was too. *Keep him safe, Lord, as we journey away from Rome.*

*****

John popped his head out of the straw covering him and glanced around, seeing a dusty road in front and behind and low-lying hills in the distance. "I see we have lost the Roman soldiers," he said to the hay wagon's driver.

The slight breeze from the wagon's forward motion, while slow because of the two horses' ages, cooled his skin under the late summer sun. He looked away from the large ball of fire to the intense blue heavens above, interrupted by only a few clouds playing tag before they settled to sleep upon the hills. *Thank you, my Lord. I live to preach the Word yet again.*

The driver, a poor man with his clothes in tatters and worn sandals, had pieces of straw jutting from his beard, as if he and John were brothers. *As we are.* The remainder of the man's face was weathered and wrinkled, though, not that John did not feel tired.

The driver took pity on John. "You can come sit beside me for the time being, but be ready to hide again. This road is well traveled at times." He watched the disciple climb onto the seat beside him and then made an oft-heard request: "Tell me how you met Christ."

So long ago. John glanced at the blue sky again and smiled. He knew the driver was a simple man, but this believer was willing to risk his life to carry the disciple to safety. *Bless him, my Lord.*

"It is a long story. My father, brother, and I were fishermen and disciples of that other John who was called the Baptist. He baptized Christ, you know." The man nodded without taking his eyes off the road.

"So...when did you meet Him?"

John's voice deepened as he spoke, remembering. "We had heard about Him. I first met Him in a dream. A vision? My mind playing tricks on me? It does not matter. He had started a movement. We joined. I cannot remember when I actually met Him." He stared far down the road as if it led toward the future. "I see a new Heaven and a new Earth,

Silas. We are creating a revolution of love—God's love that came to Earth in the form of his only Son, Jesus Christ of Nazareth."

"I am not sure about that revolution. Take the Romans, for example. There's not much love there. I do not love them, that is certain. They are as barbarous as the barbarians from the north they fear so much."

John knew Silas was a freeman who had received his freedom from a patrician. But he still worked for the same man, feeling beholden to him. *Such a patrician might become one of us. We have to convert the nobles and rich merchants.*

He imagined the cypresses were Christ's soldiers lined up along the road to keep them safe from both Roman soldiers and barbarians. And patricians who feared the threat of the Christians. John knew he would have to preach to all of them in the future. *Why else am I here?*

"It will be a struggle, but His Church will endure and shed its light upon the world."

"I will take your word for it. To think otherwise is depressing. Where are we heading?"

"First, many thanks again for helping me escape." Silas smiled but said nothing. *A man of few words. He is more a listener.* "Two towns down this road there's a small inn. I must meet someone there."

"The Boar's Head? That's frequented by thieves and ruffians. You must be crazy!"

"I am not meeting *them*, Silas. And we must pray for those who steal and fight. Our Christ was crucified with two thieves."

"I heard that, but I would be wary about trying to make converts there if I were you."

"That's not the main goal of my journey. I did not plan to make it today. The person I intend to meet might not even be there."

Although John trusted this man, the less he knew, the less he could divulge.

Silas laughed. "So they told me when they asked if you could ride with me. Fortunately, the soldiers often try to use a boulder to crack a nut."

"Meaning the Romans warned us by sending in all those soldiers, their armor and weapons clanking and sounding an alarm?"

"Precisely. It often is easy to avoid them. They are so used to employing overwhelming force in battles that they have forgotten how to be stealthy."

"Lucky for me."

They fell into silence as John remembered when, not long ago, he had started in earnest on his dangerous mission to preach the gospel, a decade after the Crucifixion...

*****

John knelt by Mary's bed and grasped her hand. She awoke, her eyes finally focusing on him.

"I dreamed of better times," she said in a whisper. "He loved you very much, John."

There was weariness in the still beautiful face. Her nights were no longer peaceful. He was happy to see the Holy Mother's smile, though. He straightened her hair and kissed her forehead. *I wish I could have had more time to talk with her. We were so busy following her Son.*

"And I loved him," he said. "That is why I came to take care of you, Mother Mary. How are you this morning?"

Her eyes, that for a moment had seemed to be drilling through the house's thatched ceiling to the blue

Mediterranean skies above, returned to Earth and again focused on him. "Not so well. My time is near. I wonder what it will be like."

"We mere mortals always wonder about that. Some fear it, but He has taken away the fear, has He not?"

She thought for a moment. "When I am gone, find the other Mary. You have much work to do, John, as does she, and you can work together. She is competent and will be a great help to you. The world must know about His teachings, about his life here among us. They must also learn to conquer fear."

"I make you that promise," he said. "Shall I prepare a little breakfast for you?"

"I would like that. For us. Maybe I can sit on the edge of the bed today."

John left her room to prepare a meager breakfast for both of them....

So many years, but it seems like yesterday!

*****

"I am so glad you escaped," that other Mary said, after glancing around to make sure no one was listening. "Do you have His sandals?"

The driver's warning about the inn had been exaggerated. John had seen much worse establishments, and everyone there had minded their own business as he'd joined Mary at a table toward the rear. *Possibly the men would be working if there were work to be had.* The Romans' slaves did most of the hard labor, an economic system that favored patricians but not free workers. Like Silas, these men were not slaves, but they were poor, the city's outcasts for the most part. *Maybe Silas was smart to stay with his ex-owner?*

The Magdalene was a tall woman. *A tower in both physique and faith*, thought John. She had been there with him at the Crucifixion and discovered the empty tomb before any of the disciples. Before that, she had financed a lot of Christ's preaching but, as a result, she was no longer wealthy except in spirit. Many disciples thought she had been His lover, but John doubted that. The Savior had had little time to spend on carnal affairs.

John knew the two had been close. So much so that some disciples had become jealous, particularly Peter. Christ would make plans; she would refine them, adding brilliant embellishments—more choices in venue, accompanying persons, and so forth. John knew Christ's miracles and wisdom made that easy, but the result appealed to people and annoyed the priests who feared the movement. *She is as smart as she is beautiful!*

The quarrel between Peter and Mary had come to a head several times. John often thought the man did not want women to have a say in the Church's future organization. Levi had said, "Surely the Savior knows her very well. That is why he loved her more than us." Peter had never reconciled with Mary.

The Magdalene was like a sister to John. He drew strength from her. He feared for his life as well as hers, but he knew they would both accept whatever God had in store for them. His promise to the Mother kept him motivated, but the Magdalene's strength came from love. John was always humbled in her presence.

She spoke so softly that John strained to hear her against the inn's background noise. *Drunks tend to speak loudly and babble nonsense.* But he answered her question with a few nods and a pat to his belly where he had the sandals tucked into his belt and under his shirt.

Mary looked sad. "I cannot receive them, for I am too much under surveillance. I am putting you in danger. But we need to deliver them to Androcles."

"I do not see the point. They are just old sandals. He wore out many pairs as He moved around Galilee to preach. They do not appear to have any magical powers."

"It is what they represent. We have spread holy relics across the Roman Empire and its territories. The shroud, the chalice, and other relics. Now the sandals. They will help us spread His message."

"Yes, because of what they represent. I understand. But they are only symbols. His ideas are much more important than mere symbols. Those ideas are the only things that matter."

"And the relics will help to spread those ideas."

He decided to change the subject. "This Androcles is obviously Greek, but who is he?"

"A true believer. He leads a congregation in Gortyna. Please take the sandals there."

"A believer, you say? I heard he is a bit crazy. He believes the lion is Christ and Christ is the lion! Does he not know lions eat sheep? Christ called himself a shepherd of men. No lions involved."

Mary shrugged and smiled. "You would have to talk to him about that. Perhaps he only thinks Christ protected him from the lion. And perhaps that story contains no truth at all, a mere fable. I have never met the man, but I have heard about his good work. In any case, he is now doing Christ's work."

"All right, then, I will take the sandals to Androcles, but it will be dangerous. I have heard authorities are searching for him and his congregation. The occupying Romans feel threatened."

"That's what motivates them to search for us." Mary took his hand and squeezed it with a force that surprised him. "Go with God, John."

"I surely hope so. As old as I am, I believe my work for Christ is only beginning, but my life is in His hands."

"We will start small, and conquer the world."

Chapter Three

Twenty-First Century, Scotland

Esther Brookstone's blue Jaguar was making the trip back to Edinburgh in record time. The ex-Scotland Yard Inspector's fast driving did a good job of keeping paramour and Interpol agent, Bastiann van Coevorden, awake as she droned on and on about construction and refurbishing plans for her castle. He had to admit he had enjoyed a nice week there with her, in spite of the construction and lack of privacy.

Now retired from Scotland Yard's Art and Antiques Division, Esther kept busy between spending time with Bastiann, repairing her castle, and tending to her art gallery in London. She said she was busier than ever before. He was wondering if there would be more time for him if he retired. He enjoyed spending time with her, although it was hard to keep up with her sometimes.

Wags at the Yard had given them nicknames; she was Miss Marple and he was Hercule Poirot. She was sprier and a bit younger than Agatha Christie's famous character, while he was a less rotund than the actor who had played Poirot, although he sported a similar mustache. Nevertheless, the nicknames had stuck. He always wondered whether the monikers were caused by jealousy and envy about their successes or were only the creations of spiteful gossips. *Possibly not an exclusive or*, he thought, *because both could be true.*

Esther had inherited her Scottish castle from a distant relative and taken a fancy to it, despite Bastiann's objections. He had never known her to be less than a city dweller. Basic improvements had turned the ruins into a charming, livable edification with a beautiful view of a small lake. The roof no longer leaked either. *The castle even has acceptable plumbing now!*

He was never much of an outdoorsman or lover of the Scottish countryside. His colleagues still teased him about having aristocratic inclinations, although Esther was the aristocrat since her third and last husband had been a count. But Bastiann also liked the castle now because he could be alone with her. At least that was his hope for the future after the construction work was done—having the crew going in and out didn't encourage a lot of daytime intimacy. Consequently, he valued their long walks together far from the castle, romantic interludes of peace and tranquility although the Scottish moors were often bleak bastions of misty silence.

He was happy she'd retired. Danger had found her all too often. *She became obsessed with that Rembrandt and almost got us both killed!* His own work was also dangerous, but infrequently, and at least he no longer had to worry about her.

"Do be careful on the road back to London," he told her at the entrance to the Edinburgh Airport's main terminal. "You drive like a mad woman. It's not at all safe, you know."

She grabbed his cheeks and kissed him. "You be careful too, love. Ring me in London. I'll be bored without you, I'm sure. I should have never retired."

He straightened his mustache and grinned. "You're doing just fine with your castle and gallery. But what about me?"

"Yes, they do keep me busy, and I don't see enough of you. I'm going to have to find another Dutchman, I'm afraid. Or maybe that retired MI5 scientist my old school chum Natalie talked about when I last visited her." She winked at him. "We can make it a *ménage- à-trois*, dear Bastiann."

"You never told me much about him. Should I be jealous? And isn't your old school chum a widow? Maybe she'll go after him. MI5? The bloke must have a lot to talk about."

He knew Esther had a previous history with MI6 during the Cold War, not MI5. Although she still had contacts in both organizations, she had never gone into details. *I suppose it's all classified still.* He suspected she'd been a good spy, but he also knew spying could be boring work, requiring patience and stealth and not entertaining for the most part. *Do we expect life to entertain us more as we age?*

"Not likely for either of your suppositions," she said. "That MI5 scientist most likely can't chat about any of his work, and my old school chum was trying to set me up with him before all the trouble over that missing Rembrandt started. I never followed up on it. Maybe I will now because you're never around, if she hasn't co-opted his attention."

"Oh, please. You can't make me feel guilty about leaving you alone. If I have a free weekend, I'm available to party, wherever you or I might find ourselves."

She smiled and nodded. After kissing her again, he entered the airport.

I don't see enough of her either.

*****

Esther found her way to the M6 highway and was cruising along in her Jaguar, thinking about that last visit to her castle. Bastiann had been there to help, but Rodney Billings, a handyman from Edinburgh, was doing a marvelous job leading his ragtag construction crew. She had learned he met Sylvia Bassett, the thief of the Bernini bust Esther had recovered, but not by that woman's name. Esther had let the abused woman go so she could find herself. That woman was a bit confused. She smiled upon remembering their meeting. *A bit confusing for her and me!*

"Have you heard from her, Rodney?" she said to the handyman when he had mentioned Sylvia.

"No, mum. Nor seen her since. She was a bit of a mystery, she was."

That's one way to put it, thought Esther with another smile.

She had put the young girl out of her mind to enjoy the time with Bastiann. The getaway had been going swimmingly, even with the construction, until that documentary producer from BBC made his appearance.

"Someone to see you, mum," said one of Rodney's working men after she'd opened her new front door in response to his knock. She peered around him to see a small man dressed in a business suit. He looked like a banker. *Or a reporter?* No, while they had become a plague that had bothered Bastiann and her to no end, a reporter wouldn't be in a striped suit with matching vest and pocket watch. The chap held an Irish-style hat in his hands. *Most likely not from Edinburgh either.*

"Fine. Let's see what he wants." She waited for the construction worker to return to his work and then gave the stranger a more complete inspection right down to his shoes, now muddied a bit from the construction project. She also spotted his Range Rover parked next to her Jaguar. "Are you lost?"

The man flashed an embarrassed grin and offered a hand. "No, ma'am. Gerald Prince, ma'am. I am from the BBC's documentary production office. I'd like to talk to you about making one for us."

She'd been dusting inside—the construction always left all sorts of dust and debris about—so Esther wiped her hand off on her apron before shaking the visitor's. She wasn't surprised her grip was stronger than his. *A bloody bureaucrat! Probably votes Conservative.*

"Esther Brookstone. So, you aren't lost, but you do have the wrong person. I don't have money to finance a documentary for the BBC. As you can see, this castle isn't Buckingham Palace, and what extra pounds I receive from my government pension are going toward its reconstruction."

"Can I come in? It's noisy out here."

"Wipe your feet." She motioned him to enter and he followed her into the dark hallway. "I apologize for the mess. I would offer you a spot of tea, but we're in a rationing program right now, you see. No grocery delivers here, as you can well imagine." He followed her into a sitting room where wallpaper had been partially stripped from the walls, and the furniture was covered with old sheets with dried paint and plaster on them. Prince took a seat on a couch after examining its cover sheet; she sat opposite him in a wingchair. Both pieces of furniture made protesting noises when they sat. "Now, what's this about?"

"Would you like to have a bit more funding to finance your project here?" Prince said.

"Ha! You're not from the BBC. You *are* a banker."

"No, ma'am, I'm from the BBC. I want to buy rights to a documentary about the adventures you had thwarting those terrorists and neo-Nazis. We must strike while the iron is hot, as they say. People will soon forget about your heroics, and it is quite a tale, if I may say so."

She stared at him. "You may, but people have already forgotten, Mr. Prince. Most people forget by the next scandalous post on Facebook or the next insulting tweet on Twitter, both going viral in seconds these days. I know the BBC is trying to crawl into the 21st century, resisting all the way, but you have to study modern audiences better. I'd venture that *Downton Abbey* was more popular in the U.S. than here in Great Britain. Besides, no one is interested in an old and retired inspector from Scotland Yard." She frowned as she thought a bit. "Out of simple curiosity, what would my role be in this enterprise?"

"You would be a consultant, particularly to the actor who will play you, but our budget is limited. I'm sure you have no camera experience, so we'll have to hire actors to play you and that Belgian agent. Maybe do voiceovers. You do have a nice English accent and voice."

"Thank you, and he's Dutch. Again, out of curiosity, what would buying rights to our story entail? In other words, how much money are you offering, Mr. Prince?"

"I'm prepared to start at ten thousand pounds sterling, Mrs. Brookstone."

She raised her eyebrows at the mentioned sum. About to make a comment, she acknowledged Bastiann's presence as he joined them. After introductions, the Interpol agent took a seat next to Prince.

*****

Bastiann's hair had plaster dust in it. He even had a piece of dry plaster stuck on the tip of his nose. Three-day stubble surrounded his dirty and drooping mustache, which completed the appearance of a working man. Esther knew he enjoyed laboring and joking with the crew, particularly with

Rodney. A plus for her, but more so for him because he no longer complained much about the castle. *Fixing the plumbing first helped achieve that more positive attitude.*

"What do you think, Bastiann?"

He shrugged. "Up to you. Count me out. I still work for Interpol. I can never participate in something like that, not even as a consultant."

Esther slapped her knees, sending aloft two small clouds of dust from her apron. She stood. "Then that's the end of it. I'm sorry you came this far, Mr. Prince. If there's a next time, please ring me on my mobile so you can avoid a trip."

Prince shrugged and also stood. "You needn't make a decision right now, ma'am. Why don't I give you a week to think it over? What's your mobile number?"

"I prefer you ring me at another location. If I'm not there, someone can take a message if it's during business hours."

She went to a table at the room's entrance and returned. She gave him the business card corresponding to her gallery. He slipped it into his pocket. "You two have a good day now."

"Pompous little twerp, isn't he?" Bastiann said after their visitor left.

Esther refrained from telling him he could be pompous too, but he didn't appear that way in overalls.

Chapter Four

Twenty-First Century, Edinburgh to London

On the way back to London, Esther went a bit out of her way to stop at an artist's studio in Manchester. She didn't like the rundown neighborhood where the studio was found, but she had promised the artist she would collect another of his paintings for consignment.

She didn't mind that industrial city so much, but it had two football teams, each one having rowdy, fanatical fans. She didn't mind football either, but she thought those fans got carried away at times. It was a working-class city. *I suppose they need to let off steam from time to time. Life is hard.*

Her own family had only been comfortable, neither poor nor wealthy. Her father, a vicar, would be shocked that she often voted for Labour candidates. Maybe her last husband would be too. *I wonder what my count saw in me.* In working family's terms, she had married up and well, but her upbringing had taught her to be frugal. Even though she indulged herself at times, three marriages had left her well off and she wanted to keep it that way. *They're always inventing new taxes, no matter which party is in charge!*

Both of her parents had also been frugal. It was no wonder the family was surprised when her father announced a family holiday trip to Rome. Thinking more about it, she could understand her father's motivation. The ancient city had seen centuries of art history with a lot of it being religious art. Her father had focused on that to the extent that they never saw any other tourist venues like the Colosseum or catacombs. However, she remembered two places tourists often flocked to. They had thrown some coins into the Trevi Fountain and visited the Sistine Chapel. For a long time, as a child, Esther thought the fountain's statuary was Bernini's, and she couldn't imagine how Michelangelo had managed to paint that entire high ceiling on his back without plaster and paint falling into his eyes. The first allowed her to recognize the sculptor's name when it was associated with the stolen sculpture she had recovered. The second made her dizzy just thinking about the height. *Thank goodness I'm past those fears now.*

She had become both an art connoisseur, specializing in paintings, and an expert on the authentication of artworks and tracing their provenance. Somewhat self-taught–if one can call making a nuisance of herself among art experts at Oxford University self-taught–she had lived in Oxford with another husband, a professor.

She preferred 19th century art, although she liked some 20th century pieces as well. She even liked Picasso, but before he invented cubism. She didn't know what to call Ricardo Silva's paintings, but he was becoming more popular.

The artist could pass for a Renaissance portrayal of Christ —no halo, of course. His curly blond hair hung down to his shoulders, helping an equally blond beard to frame a youthful face that had dreamy blue eyes as its main feature. Esther always suspected Silva's trancelike behavior was caused more by smoking cannabis than any saintly communion with the Almighty. The entire package belied his Portuguese heritage. *Only shows stereotypes can be so wrong.*

"You'll have to help me put it into the back seat," she told him, sizing up his monstrosity. *Not my cup o' tea.*

"Do you like it?"

"I'll admit it's colorful." She couldn't tell which way the painting was supposed to hang, but she had sold his two previous ones for much more than the painter had asked, making him happy and providing nice commissions for her gallery. It wasn't that she disliked modern art—it was about all she could afford for herself—but a lot of it left her mystified. *And I'm supposed to be the art expert!* "Does it have a title?"

"It's on the back. I call it 'Horse without a Rider.'"

She moved her head from side to side, trying to see a horse. "I'll take your word for it. Wrap it in something so it's protected, and I'll be on my way." He found some sheets of plastic and did as she requested. They then carried it to her car, where it blocked the rear window view. *I hope a copper doesn't stop me.* "You behave now, Ricardo." She gave him a peck on the cheek.

"That's no fun, Esther."

I'll second that! Bastiann, hurry back to me, my dear.

*****

Esther's next stop was her gallery in London. Her two employees, artists themselves, fussed over the new painting after welcoming her back. Harry James, the Jamaican, who did all the heavy lifting and opened and closed the gallery every day, said nothing but looked at the gallery's ceiling. He was probably thinking the two girls were like magpies, squawking about something.

"It's beautiful," said Anna. "I wish I could buy it."

Esther also glanced skyward as if asking for divine intervention, thereby agreeing with her handyman. Anna was a tall, thin redhead who rarely smiled. The other employee, Dorothy, was short, stout, and always bubbly, and nearly blind without her thick glasses. Esther considered them to be female versions of two old Yankee comedians, Laurel and Hardy, except the girls weren't hilarious and were far too serious about art at the expense of having a social life.

Thank goodness they understand some of the modern works!

Harry took the painting inside and started to look around the gallery's walls.

Most likely wondering where to hang it. She was fond of Harry. He'd almost been deported by the government when it created an anti-immigrant program. Esther thought the woman who created it possibly won a lot of votes with the program because of the anti-immigrant sentiment in the U.K., but as PM she'd been saddled with negotiating BREXIT with the E.U., so Esther had a bit of revenge. Britain's leaving the E.U. had even complicated her relationship with Bastiann. Visiting him on the continent was now like visiting a foreign country.

Young Harry had come to Britain long ago as part of a program the government had established so non-British citizens from the Commonwealth could help rebuild and cleanup after the war. It was ironic that years later the woman who became PM declared many of those post-war immigrants to be illegal. Esther had never asked Harry how he had avoided deportation—she figured it was none of her business—but she knew he had married a younger white woman and they had three kids, two still in school. *Times have changed, and that particular change is promising.*

Harry had a side business of sorts where he played an electric piano and sang ska, reggae, and calypso on weekends. That appeared contradictory since he was the silent type at the gallery, doing what needed to be done, whether she or the girls asked him to do it or not. She had never attended a club where he played and sang. *I must do that sometime with Bastiann.* The clubs were in bad areas of the city, so she feared she needed more defenses than she could muster alone, but she loved the music. It was often sad and joyful at the same time, as was much music having a folk origin. She had tried to play some of her favorite songs from that genre, but she'd failed. *If my castle were only in Jamaica!* She imagined Harry James's singing as a hybrid between Harry Belafonte and Bob Marley.

She watched him pick the perfect place for Ricardo's painting, but he had to relocate a small piece in order to hang it.

"I want you two girls to sell it. The artist needs another cash infusion." She eyed the two with suspicion. "Anything of consequence happen this last week?"

"A wizened old elf stopped by to see you," Anna handed Esther a business card, "a larger version of the one with the axe in *Lord of the Rings.*"

Now that's funny, Esther thought. *But I remember Tolkien calling him a dwarf.* As a child, those books, along with Lewis's *Narnia* books, were among the few adventure stories approved by her father. She glanced skyward and grinned. *Forgive me, Papa, for disobeying you and reading Fanny Hill. And for corrupting my old school chum by suggesting she also read it.*

"He said you'd know who he was."

The card was discreet and displayed only the name Sergio Moretti and a telephone number in raised black letters on white stock. She turned it over and found a scrawled message in blue ink: *Call me.*

Presumptive old fool, she thought. Sergio, an old friend of her late husband, had been a great comfort when her count had passed on. He wasn't much for looks, but he had a good heart. She hadn't seen him since then. *We'll have a lot of catching up to do!*

"Thank you. I'll take care of this. Now let's list this new painting in our email newsletter. You never know when some rich recipient will read it and be encouraged to pop in to buy it."

"Is there a suggested price?" asked Dorothy, the older girl.

"Ricardo wants at least three thousand pounds. We won't put a price on it yet. Just say it's a wonderful piece by a new master, or something like that. We could get lucky, as we did with the first two. By the way, thank you, Harry, for hanging it. At least it's far enough away from the religious paintings."

*****

Although she was famished that evening home in her flat, Esther postponed dinner for a moment and tried to ring Sergio. The call went to voicemail, so she left a message. *Even the elderly use mobile phones now.*

Sergio had always liked technology. He had been a VIP at Grundig and was also a radio amateur. *That name always seems to be an oxymoron to me because most of them are skilled and anything but amateurs.* She had known some back when she worked for MI6 and met Sergio. *Useful blokes at times.* She remembered one harrowing experience where they had tried to help her get a scientist who wanted to defect out of East Berlin; they had helped her escape instead. *Exciting times!*

She then took a peek into her fridge and shook her head. *I need to make a trip to the market.* But she decided to postpone that chore and visit a nearby curry house instead. The one near her did a great job with tikka masala, and she loved their mango lassis. After her bland repasts with Bastiann in Scotland, dining there would be a welcome change.

As she prepared to leave, she eyed her baby grand and sighed. She loved to play it—mostly light classical and some show tunes as well—but she'd been neglecting the poor instrument lately. Music not only was good for her mental health, but playing it also helped her hands fight osteoarthritis. *You're not getting any younger, old woman!*

She missed Scotland Yard too. She didn't miss the Metropolitan Police's politics and bureaucracy, only the daily ritual of rising every day to go to work. The gallery was a partial substitute, and her old boss, Langston, called her in occasionally for consulting, but it wasn't the same.

It would help, Bastiann, if you retired, damn you! She would like to see a bit more of the world with him, traveling to India and the orient, in particular. *The only India I see is in a London curry house.*

She closed the door behind her and headed for that Indian dinner, ravenous because of the hour, but knackered from the trip and stops.

Chapter Five

Twenty-First Century, Lyon

Bastiann landed at the Lyon-St. Exupéry Airport, picked up his own auto in long-term parking, and drove the twenty-plus kilometers to Interpol HQ via the hook beneath the park. During the taxiing to the plane's gate after landing, his colleague, Hal Leonard, had called him on his mobile. They agreed to meet at the home office, even though Hal was in downtown Lyon.

In a sense, Paris would be more convenient for his work because there were more international airline routes to and from the City of Lights. He had no idea why Interpol, or whoever was responsible for the decision, had picked Lyon for HQ's home base and the National Central Bureau, or NCB. There were some advantages: Lyon was still in France, it had somewhat less traffic than the capital, and rent wasn't as high in the areas where he would consider living. He still maintained his old apartment in Amsterdam; however, it was a bit of a financial balancing act to do so. Amsterdam was home; Lyon was work.

His mother had worked for Sûreté, the French agency that had split into DGSI and DGSE, the interior and exterior versions of current French security. He often wondered what his life would be like in either of those agencies. For the DGSE, there was a good chance he wouldn't be living in Paris either, maybe not even in France. He had no regrets about his choices, and he was too old to change.

Bastiann sat at his small desk, twirling his mustache, waiting for Hal to saunter in. When he arrived, Bastiann said, "They don't allow me to catch my breath. I've just returned from vacation."

Hal scratched the salt-and-pepper stubble that made him look like a slumming tele star. "You do look a bit tired. Did *la grande dame* wear you out?"

Bastiann didn't react to the taunt. "She's in construction mode at her castle. We're whipping it into shape."

"And pretending you're living the life of an aristocrat. I have no sympathies. Shall we go see what the old man wants? He told me it's urgent."

Both men seemed out of place. Bastiann was too well-dressed in his three-piece suit; Hal was underdressed in khakis and a Hawaiian shirt. The two had teamed up before. Both men had a history with the NYPD homicide cop, Rolando Castilblanco. Bastiann didn't consider that a curious coincidence. *Rollie gets around.*

"I hope the case doesn't turn into something deadly. I would have joined DGSE or the gendarmes if I wanted to be a target. We're supposed to be consultants to the local police."

"I'm sure our next case will be labeled as such, report-wise. Doesn't mean it won't be dangerous. What's the matter? You finally find yourself in a serious relationship and decide you have to stay healthy for the old woman?"

Bastiann flashed a grin at Hal. "At least I have a serious relationship."

"*Chacun* à *son goût*. C'mon. Let's go."

Hal had used the French version of "To each his own taste." *Now he speaks French!* Bastiann's maternal language was French; he found English a bit tiresome and sometimes hard to understand.

*****

Sr. Agent III Karl Schuster, who Hal often called boss, welcomed them both to the small conference room and then shut the door. Bastiann was closer to him than Hal. The two often played tennis together, meeting at courts near Bastiann's flat in the early morning on good-weather days. Karl's house, Bastiann's flat, and Interpol HQ weren't too far apart from each other.

"This comes under the category of public safety," Schuster said, handing them each a folder. "I don't know who's doing it, gentlemen, but someone is making a lot of euros off small arms and ammunition shipments."

"Automatic or semi-automatic weapons?" Hal asked.

Their superior propped his chin on his right fist, flattening his goatee. He was a bit overweight and the room was warm, so he was perspiring. He wiped his brow with his handkerchief, eyed the two as if to say they had made him perspire, and then continued.

"Automatics, and lots of ammo. Chinese copies of other models, but lethal all the same."

"What ports are involved?" inquired Bastiann.

"That's one question. There are two others: if not from China, where are the weapons coming from, and who are the middlemen?"

"There are always middlemen," said Hal. He raised the thick folder. "I'll peruse this in good time, but where do you suggest we start?"

"Northern Italy? Old Yugoslavia? Hell, I don't know. Like I said, small shipments have been turning up all over. And those are only the ones customs finds."

"Arms smuggling is big business these days," said Bastiann. "Compared to Americans, Europeans have stricter gun control, yet it still goes on. It's all about greed."

"And the smugglers don't care how many people are killed with smuggled weapons as long as they make money," said Schuster. "Study the files and come back to me with some kind of plan. I have a lot to do, and most of it is bureaucratic nonsense. We pay the price for being the central HQ as well as an NCB. It could only be worse if we actually worked for the U.N."

Bastiann showed he agreed in part. *But the U.N. still doesn't leave us alone!*

*****

Bastiann and Hal took their folders back to their desks. By 7 p.m., they had a tentative plan, but Schuster had already left for the day. Bastiann thought that wasn't a bad idea and suggested they follow his lead.

"At least he has a life," said Hal.

"I have a life," said Bastiann.

"Tough luck, pal. She's in Scotland and no fun while you're here."

"Esther is in London by now. I should call her."

"Do that, and then we should find some beers."

"Make mine white wine and a vegetable sandwich. I've been eating heavy food the last few days."

"No haggis, I hope."

Bastiann made a face.

When Hal went to the restroom in the small café near HQ, Bastiann thought about where he would be next if

Schuster approved their plan. At least he liked the food in Northern Italy. The southern cuisine was a bit spicy at times. However, the best meal he ever had in his life was in a small restaurant in Grado, south of Trieste. He had accompanied it with a local red that was excellent. But that night's vegetable sandwich and white wine weren't bad. *Or maybe I'm too tired to care?*

He made the usual offer to Hal for him to sleep on the couch.

"Are you kidding? Almost any hotel bed is better than your old couch. And, who knows? I could get some action."

Bastiann smiled. *Ever the playboy.*

Chapter Six

Twenty-First Century, London

His half-sister, Denise, always embarrassed Gerald, but he still met with her for lunch from time to time. This time he had chosen a pub nearer to her work than to his to avoid his coworkers chancing upon them. He also chose a booth tucked into a dark, back corner.

She slid into the booth opposite him and snapped her fingers to call the waiter. "*Ça va, mon frère?*"

Prince hated his sister's French greeting. Three months ago, she had returned from a six-month whirlwind relationship with a French painter. He hated that she had learned the language so fast; he wasn't good at languages. He supposed she had experienced what they called "total immersion." The phrase probably had a double meaning in her case.

"What are you drinking, Gerry?"

"A martini," he said.

"I'll have the same," she told the waiter when he arrived. "And your beet salad."

"I'll have the fish and chips," said Gerald.

"He probably thinks you're stepping out on your wife," she said to him after the waiter left. "Thinks I'm the young, lithesome mistress you keep on the side for your lunchtime frolicking."

Snakes tattooed on each side of her neck writhed as she laughed, most likely more at his red face than her own joke—she always tried to make him blush. At least the snakes were color-coordinated with the lime-green streaks in her spiked hairdo. To complete the theme, he offered her his olive. She loved them; he hated them. He had forgotten to tell the waiter to hold that horrible Spanish import. With the tariffs, it probably increased the price of the martini by fifty percent.

Their most common discussion topic was as good a way as any to make small talk and pay her back for the taunt. "What's your latest conspiracy theory?"

"I have it on the best authority that the new American duchess will next have an extraterrestrial's child, not Prince Harry's."

He smiled. "Sounds like you believe in MI7, that fictitious agency that keeps us safe from ETs. Will the baby be as green as you are today?"

She frowned. "MI7 doesn't exist, and I never pay attention to the color of anyone's skin. Or anything else, for that matter, besides what's in my paintings. I'm an enlightened woman, unlike some relatives I have." She tapped the table top with her index finger; her nail polish as green as the rest of her. "You're making fun of me, big brother. That rumor is all over the internet. You'll see."

"No one has seen a baby bump yet, so let's change the topic. Remember that woman from Scotland Yard?"

"Vaguely. The one BBC wants to feature in a documentary?"

"Precisely. Esther Brookstone. I couldn't convince her to sign." He showed her the business card. "Perhaps you can sell one of your awful paintings at her gallery."

She examined the card. "You poor bastard. You don't know anything about art galleries, do you?"

"Not the business end, no."

"Her gallery's address shows it's a bit out of my league, love. I'm not that well-known."

"Really? Well, in my case, you're better known for your conspiracy theories than your art."

"That hurts! I'm a specialist, you know. My website focuses on religious superstition and legends, with some things about the royal family thrown in at times."

"And you create more conspiracies than debunking them. I'll admit you're not the only one I know who manages to confuse the sacred texts from the world's main religions, but you do a lot of it. Our old man would be so proud."

Her father–his stepfather–had done the Beatles one better by hitchhiking through Asia when he was young, "searching for the Truth." He always added "with a capital T." His work had become hard labor as a skilled mechanic who specialized in pasta-making machines. He met Gerald's widowed mother at a rock concert in Amsterdam where they became stoned out of their brains and woke up married. He became a conspiracy theorist later in life.

"I learned a lot from Daddy," Denise said. "And he respected my ideas."

The arrival of their lunches saved Gerald from another long litany of theories from Denise. As usual, she stole some of his chips.

*****

Son of Thunder

Diana Moretti, Sergio Moretti's wife, was a bit of an auction addict. She loved old furniture. When she saw the old armoire, she knew she had to have it.

The auctioneer had piqued her interest. He announced, "Renaissance-style armoire, another piece from the *Via Borgo Ognissanti* lot. Bidding starts at five hundred euros."

The auctioneer's boredom contrasted with her excitement. She was lucky her husband tolerated her addiction to old furniture and other relics. Even as a young girl, she'd been fascinated with "old things." Not so much the item itself, but the idea someone long ago had used the piece. Owning it was like hopping into a time machine to go and see how they lived in ancient times.

She had met Sergio in Athens and found him charming. Her parents jumped at the opportunity of her "marrying up" in status, mainly because there would be one less mouth to feed. All of their children, the exception and oldest being Diana, still lived at home. The recent economic downturn in Greece had left the family poor and lucky even to own their house.

She found her parents' reasons for encouraging the nuptials shallow, but she truly loved Sergio. He was funny, caring, and a lover who saw to her needs as much as his. She had much younger boyfriends in the past, many more handsome than Sergio, but they couldn't begin to compare with her husband's intelligence and joy of living. For her, that outweighed all else.

She was surprised when someone placed a bid higher than hers of five-hundred euros. As the bids increased in price, she studied the shabby man with the thick wire-frame glasses who was trying to outbid her. *Whatever can he want with this old armoire?* In the end, she bought the armoire for eleven hundred euros and thought nothing more of her competitor in the bidding.

*****

Walther Beck, who purchased antiquities for a Munich museum, had attended the same auction where Diana Moretti had bid on the armoire on the chance he could find some relic there at a bargain price. He too was surprised by the small bidding war for an old piece of furniture. *That Frau has become attached to a piece of junk*, he thought. *But what's that Italian Mr. Magoo's interest?* He wondered if the two had inside information about something valuable to be found within the armoire. *That might explain it!*

He checked the auction program. The armoire appeared to be only what the auctioneer had said it was, a non-descript period piece. There was no chance that its age was faked; the small auction house was a reputable one specializing in estate sales. Like everywhere else, people died in Florence all the time without close surviving relatives. For whatever reason, their most valuable worldly possessions, sometimes handed down through centuries, would go on the auction block.

Now the jeweled cross from circa 1350 CE is more interesting. He thought he might try bidding on that. In spite of the few inlaid jewels, he could be lucky because there was no provenance for the piece. They had found it in a church that had to be demolished. *Only the Church will benefit from the sale. As if the Vatican needs more money!*

Chapter Seven

First Century, Crete

Androcles gazed upon the sandals in his hands with reverence. "To think He once wore them."

With dark hair that had a touch of gray around the ears, the Greek could be a sculptor's model for the Greeks' Ares or the Romans' Mars. His piercing blue eyes bore into John, making the disciple feel uncomfortable. *Here is a strong soldier of God who is also a preacher.*

"And he once rode on an ass. Let's not worship either the sandals or the animal, only Christ," said John. He was about to mention the business about the lion but bit his tongue. *Maybe Androcles will take the hint?* He eyed the man. "You are not going to wear them, are you? That would be sacrilegious."

"Of course not. They will be kept safe and we will guard them with our lives. They will bring new hope to my congregation. They will reaffirm Christ's message for them."

"That message is more important than any religious relic. Do you understand that?" John waited for his host's response. *Is he up to the test?*

Androcles pondered the question before answering. "Yes, of course, I do. Many of my congregation will think the same way. But others are poor, simple people. They need symbols to buoy up their faith so they can ride upon the troubled seas of persecution."

Yes, a preacher! "I think it is a mistake for them to pin their faith to symbols and rituals. His words and work should be the foundations for our faith, not old sandals."

"Not everyone thinks like you, John," Androcles said to the disciple. "And why were you baptized, then, if rituals are not important?"

John looked caught out. "You win for now. Yes, it is a ritual, and it has a profound meaning for the faithful. But you cannot deny that the importance of baptism rests with the spirit, not the water."

Androcles shrugged. "Haw can spirit be understood, save through experience? Baptism is an experience. We do what we can do to spread His word to all nations." He gestured toward the door of the small room that was little more than a closet. "Are you ready to preach and share communion with my congregation?"

John followed Androcles out and waited as his host introduced him, a bit embarrassed by his effusive introductory remarks. The disciple started his sermon with the story about Habib the Carpenter.

"Jude, Peter, and I visited Antioch because people there had returned to worshipping idols." *I will put a halt to this insane affection for religious icons like the sandals!* "Habib Al-Najjar, a carpenter, met us there. He said to the people of Antioch, 'O my people! Follow those who have been sent. Obey those who ask no reward of you for themselves, and who themselves received guidance.' An auspicious start. You see, my friends, Christ's message cannot be found in icons, no matter how holy they are, or even in the words of holy men who were lucky enough to live with Him and hear his teachings in person. Christ's message is found in here." John pounded his chest over his heart. "You must absorb it and become one with it to become enlightened and earn His promise of everlasting life."

John went on for another five minutes until he saw stirrings, which indicated they had heard enough of his preaching and their attentions were failing. *Did my words have any effect?* He always had that doubt. Men and women who had not been there at His resurrection had trouble believing. Even one of the disciples had doubted.

They had just started communion when Roman soldiers from the garrison arrived.

*****

The Roman soldiers were not a match for the larger group of Greek Christians, but they did their damage. Rejecting a sword offered to him, John defended the congregation, and himself, with fists and headlocks, rendering soldiers unconscious instead of killing them. He often had to shake the pain from his fists after it landed on a steely jaw. His wounds were only minor as he fought beside the men in Androcles' group. Toward the mêlée's end, Androcles hustled John out a backdoor of the old house they used as a church.

"I had better move on," John told him. "They could have been searching for me, you know."

Androcles grabbed him by his shoulders and gave him a kiss on each cheek. "Be careful, my brother. The empire feels threatened. There are always more soldiers looking for us."

"And more Christians for them to persecute. It is a question of attrition, it seems. But, for now, they have the advantage of numbers, and we only fight on the defensive. The empire could win."

"What you saw there cannot be called fighting. We are completely untrained. We practice desperate survival here. Secrecy is our only real weapon."

"And your faith in the Son of God. Farewell."

"Godspeed."

As John watched him disappear into the old city, he could still hear yells from the Roman soldiers, rushing to reinforce their brethren. *If the attacking soldiers did not run, they are either dead or dying, and Androcles and his congregation will have fled with their dead and wounded.* John shook his head and glanced at the dusky sky. *It is a huge burden on my soul, my Lord.*

He found his way to the port and used his remaining funds to book passage to the Greek mainland. *The adventure continues,* he said to himself as the old ship moved across the amethyst surface under cloudy skies. *More storms await us.*

He missed Mary. *She is my rock, next to Christ.* He was looking forward to their next reunion.

*****

John met Mary again in a small house at the outskirts of Athens three weeks later. He had been checking to see if anyone followed him during the whole trip. From across the sea and into the city and more carefully as he approached their meeting place. The good people who provided lodging for the Magdalene would give their lives for Christ, but John did not want to endanger them.

His checks for pursuers were not at all obvious to the casual onlooker. Even with Christ—especially with Him—he had learned to protect the Son of God and all the disciples and apostles who were with Him by using his peripheral vision for surveillance and detection of those who wanted to do them harm. Now he was protecting Mary, her hosts, and himself. Being careless and being caught would not allow him to continue his work of carrying the Word to the people. Mary would be doing the same. Both of them were convinced their work was important, and He would want them to continue doing it as long as they could.

It helped that in this part of the world, most people hated Rome. *Makes it easier to stir up the rebellion,* he thought with a smile. He knew Christ had taught them to love their enemies, but many ordinary people saw the Church as an organization that would end Rome's evil grip across the lands they had conquered. *Onward Christian soldiers!* He shook his head. *If only we were many soldiers who could fight for the minds of men by carrying the Word to those eager to receive it!*

"Have you been fishing today?" said the old man at the door.

"On the Sea of Galilee," John said.

He opened the door wider, peered up and down the narrow street, and gestured for John to enter. He led the disciple to the back of the house where Mary waited.

"I have one more solo mission for you, if you do not mind," she said, not wasting time getting down to business.

"If it is God's work, why would I mind?" he said, hugging her and kissing her on each cheek. He clasped her shoulders and held her at arm's length. "Are you all right?" She seemed a bit sad, but she finally smiled. "For my part, I have to confess my last mission was a bit harrowing." He told her what had happened when he visited Androcles.

"Are the sandals safe?"

"Androcles and his congregation will guard them with their lives." His sad face beat hers. "Some have already done so."

Her brow wrinkled. "I have had similar experiences. Roman soldiers are brutal thugs and their leaders are worse. But history is on our side."

With her, optimism always wins. "What is my mission?"

"A lifelong one." She held up a simple gold ring.

"A wedding band? His?"

"The ring was His; however, it is not a wedding band. Consider it a friendship ring. I gave it to Him, and I have worn it on a necklace since He left us, but that's no longer wise." She looked at him again, her sad countenance betraying intense feeling. "Our love was never consummated, John. Please do not believe the rumors. He calmed me and ended my torment. That was all. There never was time. Sometimes I thought there was something there, but He was always so dedicated to His mission of love and peace."

"They knew you were financing our movement. You had to flee for your life. We all did. I am sorry about the rumors, Mary, but I never believed them." He frowned. If anyone was a loose woman, it had to be Mary of Bethany. *Did Peter go beyond a simple exchange of angry words and help spread the rumors?* "Did someone bully you during your journey?" She shrugged. He frowned. "But the ring is yours now. It is not like the sandals. It was your gift to Him. Keep it as a memento of our time with Him."

"I originally thought that way, but, like the chalice, it is a relic that should belong to all Christians down through the ages."

"I disagree. You can keep it as safe as I can. Maybe safer. I will not deliver it to another group."

"No, that's not my intention. I want you to guard it with your life until you die. It is too big for my finger, so I am afraid I will lose it. And a necklace can easily break. If there's an opportunity to keep it safe in a church with Christ's followers in a holy city sometime in the future, please do so. I am afraid that could take centuries. I am not sure the other relics will survive either, so this one must."

"The sandals and shroud are a bit questionable, I will admit, but certainly the communion chalice will survive. Where is it, by the way?"

"In a safe place." He frowned at her secrecy and she saw it. "The fewer people who know its location, the safer it is."

His frown changed to a smile as he nodded. "I agree. The same goes for this ring. Only you and I will ever know whose finger it graces."

*****

Before leaving, Mary and John joined in communion with the host family. Their hosts were simple but devout folk. *The hope of the Church*, John thought as he wound through the streets back towards the pier. Mary had given him money for his next trip to consecrate a church in central Greece north of Patras. He would take a ship north and then go inland.

He figured he was living on borrowed time. Sooner or later, the Romans would capture him, and he would be martyred like his brother, James. He shuddered to think that could also happen to Mary. *These are dangerous days for Christians.* His years in Judea had never prepared him for Roman brutality.

He glanced at His ring. *It is safe to wear it. The inscription is noncommittal.* It fit tightly on his finger; he would not lose it. Mary had put it on using soap, but he doubted he would be able to remove it so easily.

Maybe she is right. We will have a grand church in Rome and there will be no more Roman Empire, just a

Christian one. He hoped to see that day and find a fitting place for the ring and all the other relics. *Only the entire Roman Empire stands in our way!*

He recalled when he and Peter had gone to prepare for the Last Supper. As he sat next to Jesus, he felt safe. That feeling was still strong as he thought about the Son of God, but it was a feeling of spiritual safety now, not physical. *When my time comes, I must be strong like He was!*

Chapter Eight

Twenty-First Century, London

It was late when Esther returned to her flat after dinner. She decided not to turn in, but instead relax a bit and play her piano. She played a Chopin nocturne and was already into the more leisurely and stately Satie's first *Gymnopedie* when her mobile on the dining room table interrupted her tranquil mood with its incessant ringtone. She stopped her playing, went over, and hit the talk icon.

The caller was Sergio Moretti. "Esther, how are you, my dear? I'm sorry I missed your call. I need you here in Vienna."

The old fellow always gets to the point. "And I need a bit more explanation as to why. What are you doing in Vienna, by the way?"

"I live here now. Germany was becoming a big bore."

"I honestly thought you would have moved back to Florence then—old home town, more culture, and all that."

"I've always loved Vienna too. Consider it a compromise between Teutonic stodginess and Florentine *joie de vivre.*" There was a pause. "I trust you've recovered from your loss."

"You truly are behind the times, aren't you? I became an international celebrity for a brief while last year, and I was also in Italy. I was honored at an art function in Rome for recovering a Bernini bust."

"I'm sorry. I didn't know. We could have met and reminisced. Rome is only a hop away by plane or train, assuming the unions aren't on strike."

She read between the lines. "You always were romantically interested, you old dog, to no avail. I was always afraid my count would challenge you to a duel for being so flirtatious. Now you're also a bit late. I'm in a steady relationship with a Dutchman."

"Good for you. I've found someone else too. Married her, in fact. A lovely Greek woman. You'll like her." He laughed. "But that's all a bit beside the point. And I didn't stop in at your gallery to chat about our romantic escapades. I need you to authenticate a painting. I'll pay you for it, including all travel expenses. Do you have time for me?"

"I'm retired now, but, as you know, I run an art gallery, so I do have obligations. Let me try to arrange a visit. I'll let you know my travel itinerary by tomorrow if I can make the journey."

"That will be fine."

She heard the dial tone. *He didn't say what painting he wanted to authenticate. Typical.* She hoped it wasn't some modern painting like Ricardo's. *Why would anyone want to copy something like that? And how would I ever determine if it's a copy?*

*****

The girls assured Esther they could run the gallery for a few days. She wasn't so certain, but they had done a good job while she was in Scotland. And she was intrigued with Sergio's request.

She supposed whatever painting her old friend wanted to authenticate wouldn't bring her as many adventures as she and Bastiann had when they tried to chase down that nicked Rembrandt. They had received more than Andy Warhol's fifteen minutes of fame for those adventures. But the media attention had been fleeting, as she'd told that BBC chap. Fatigue from those hectic weeks was the major factor hastening her retirement from Scotland Yard. That, and the opportunity to own a gallery that had come her way. She smiled. *And to spend more time with Bastiann!*

The romance wasn't going so well. She knew the media attention couldn't disappear fast enough for the Interpol agent as he thought it could hamper his work, and the media had lost their interest in him more quickly than in her because he hadn't been involved in recovering the Bernini bust. She did encourage him to retire along with her, telling him he could become a private detective like Hercule Poirot. *But Bastiann has a mind of his own.*

She often imagined him being her fourth husband. *I'm willing, but is he?* She was a bit old-fashioned. She expected him to propose. She ignored the difference in their ages, but gossipers didn't. Some even said she demanded too much of her men, likening her to various Hollywood stars. But she'd always been faithful, nary a divorce. Of course, more feminist gossip applauded her. *Strange times!*

She spent the remainder of the day organizing the girls' work and helping them tidy the gallery a bit. Harry also found a better place to hang the new painting, moving others around a bit. *He does have an eye for that.* She left in the middle of the afternoon, ringing Sergio after arriving at her flat.

"I freed up my schedule," she told him. "I need to know more about the painting. Perhaps I'm not the right person to authenticate it." *It would have been nice if I had more information before having to adjust my schedule.* She blamed Sergio for that, wondering how he had been so successful in the corporate world.

"The painter is from the Italian Renaissance. I would like you to confirm it's one of Sandro Botticelli's paintings."

"Absurd! You most likely have been scammed."

"I also know something about art," Sergio said. He sounded a bit huffy. "I'm careful about what I purchase, but I'll admit the provenance is a bit obscure. That often happens, you know. It's not like there are computer records from that time. Botticelli didn't keep notebooks like da Vinci and the Florentine School was quite productive."

"With young painters copying older masters all the time." *But a new Botticelli? I'll have to see it!* "You might not like my appraisal."

"I'm prepared for that. I trust your judgement completely." Sergio coughed. "Most of the time, anyway. Picking the count over me was something of a blow to my ego, I must say. It made me question that famous judgement of yours."

"Oh, please. I'll come visit, if only to prove your judgement about art is waning. I have yet to arrange my flights. I'll confirm them later."

*****

First, Esther rang Bastiann. The call went to voicemail. She planned to leave an hour after she made airline reservations, but she was concentrating on her travel wardrobe when he returned the call.

"I've received the most curious invitation," she told him. "An old art collector and connoisseur I know in Vienna wants me to authenticate a painting he's discovered. He thinks it's a Botticelli."

"Discovered? In a museum's basement, I suppose. Does he think it could be a fraud?"

Bastiann's mobile signal dropped because of interference. She stepped out onto her balcony to improve the signal. *Are there too many pipes in the old building?*

"On the contrary. I need to add some objectivity, I fear. He's a bit too excited about it. I suspect he thinks his purchase was a bargain."

"Vienna? I'm not far from there. I'm finishing up here. I wonder..."

The signal faded again. She glanced at the buildings around her and cursed. *Maybe not the pipes.*

"I thought it would be a lovely place to spend a few days with you," she said.

"Sorry, your signal dropped. I didn't understand the first part of that."

She plowed on. "Maybe you could pick me up at the airport tomorrow? I've already purchased my ticket. I also have a hotel reservation. We'll share the room. I hope to see you there."

She disconnected and then remembered she hadn't told him which airport if he did manage to get free to pick her up. She hit redial. The call went again to voicemail. She left him the airport flight information and the hotel's name in the message.

She then realized she had no idea where he was, although he said he was near Vienna. *You're growing senile, Esther!*

That was one of her constant worries. Her father had suffered from dementia and often thought he was conversing with angels after he entered the nursing home. And then there was Alzheimer's, although back then they just called that dementia too.

She could still take care of herself and would often ride the Tube, knowing she could handle any mugger. She worked out, after all. However, she knew her youth was long gone. *What do they call them? Twilight years?* She made a face. *I'll go down fighting the Grim Reaper if he tries to grab me!*

Chapter Nine

Twenty-First Century, Trieste

Bastiann was able to decipher Esther's travel plans. He decided he could drive from Trieste to Vienna and be there in time for the landing of her flight. As he walked along the street toward the piers, he grasped the iron chains placed beside the sidewalk for citizens to grab onto to protect themselves from *La Borra,* the ferocious wind that often blew in from the port.

Like many cities in Europe, Trieste had a varied past. Long after the Romans, it had become the most important port of the Austro-Hungarian Empire. Some houses still flew both flags. It was still an important city in modern Italy, although Bastiann preferred Florence to the west, all of Tuscany, and Venice to the south, but his official duties took him all over Europe.

The American, Hal Leonard, and he had organized the arrest of gun smugglers who were shipping guns in from the old Yugoslavia. He was sure Italian courts would be too lenient with them. The lamentable turn to the far right in Italy could be a possible remedy for that, but his dissatisfaction with the arrests stemmed more from the gang's VIPs not being in custody. *We chip away at organized crime one thug at a time.*

His disillusion led him to thoughts about retirement. Esther wanted him to retire. Every day he came nearer to making that decision. He had put in his time. His only problem was that his life centered more on continental Europe while she was an English woman at heart. *Scottish too,* he thought with a grin, thinking of her castle.

Interpol had treated him well during his time as an international cop. Like any occupation, it had its ups and downs. But the tradition of staying out of the fray and letting locals make the arrests kept Interpol agents safe for the most part. However, now they could make the arrests on their own and there was never a lack of crimes or criminals. *Crime keeps me employed.*

Esther had nearly been killed during her obsession with tracking down that Rembrandt stolen by the Nazis in World War II. Most of her recent Scotland Yard cases weren't all that dangerous. Smugglers of stolen art weren't usually as dangerous as gun smugglers.

Maybe I can ease into retirement like she did? But where would we live? Esther had lived in Switzerland with her last husband, so perhaps she could live on the continent again. *Maybe we can do both. She has a castle!*

His thoughts were interrupted as uneasy sensations flooded his mind. He didn't have special ops experience per se like his American cop friend, Castilblanco, but he could sense when he was being followed unless the tail was excellent. This one wasn't. He stopped at a store window as if to admire some fishing gear.

The reflection of a small man wearing a long overcoat and holding on to his homburg in the stiff breeze was a parody of a character from a John Le Carré spy novel. With the other hand, he pretended to study a folded map. That made

Bastiann think of Esther again and some of her brief stories about working abroad for MI6. She carefully edited them "to protect the guilty," as she put it, making them more enticing hints about a past he would never know.

Maybe a tourist. He's certainly not a local. He continued on toward the port where he had left his hire-car. By the time he stopped beside it to fetch his keys, the little man had disappeared. *This old city makes me paranoid.*

He knew it was conceivable for leaders of the gun smuggling ring to decide to exact revenge. But the easiest way to achieve that was via a drive-by assassination. They wouldn't send someone to follow him.

As he drove off, his mind was already lingering on how pleasant it would be to see Esther again. It would also be pleasant to arrest the remaining gun smugglers. *They say patience is a virtue, but I'm losing it as I age!*

*****

Bastiann made the ride from Trieste to Vienna in about five hours via highways A1/E57 and A2. His route passed through Slovenia, which made him a bit uncomfortable since their best guess for the smuggler's HQ was somewhere in that area. He pulled into a short-term parking spot at the *Wien-Flughafen* with time to spare.

His smile broadened into a grin as he saw her leave security. He waved. After collecting her baggage, they sped away from *Wien-Flughafen* toward city center along the Danube via A4. They checked into a hotel not far from the *Ringstrasse,* one he knew from his business travels. He had recommended it to her, feeling Sergio wouldn't dare complain about paying for the modest room. Bastiann had heard the desk clerk's litany many times.

"*Herr* van Coevorden, Countess Sartini," he said, "your room awaits you." He handed Bastiann the key. "The bellhop can help you with your luggage. Consult the concierge for help with any tourist details." He handed back their passports. "Please use your room safe to guard your valuables. Have a pleasant stay and welcome to Vienna, the city of history and tradition."

Without needing a bellhop, they took the lift to the third floor and found their room.

"This is quite luxurious for the price, don't you think?" Esther said, bouncing on the bed.

"You're on a fixed income. Interpol pays for my stays here." He decided not to mention the real reason for his choice. He put her luggage, a suitcase and carry-on for toiletries, on the two available racks. His travel bag went on a third. "The restaurant isn't too bad either if the weather becomes nasty, which it can."

"Clear with a nip in the air is our forecast. How have you been, dear Bastiann?"

They didn't talk much during the trip from the airport. Bastiann had been listening to a CD of some concert Bruce Springsteen had given in Dublin some years ago. Hal Leonard had lent it to him.

"It's only been a week, but Hal and I made some good progress. He sends you his regards."

"Never met the man, but he sounds nice. I'm ready for some nice Strauss. It's Vienna, after all. Hal's taste in music is a bit extreme. 'My old mule?' 'Erie Canal?' I suppose that's American folk." She frowned. "Since you can't talk much about your case, let me tell you about mine. I'm prepared to be disappointed, but I'll admit the possibility Sergio has found a new Botticelli is exciting."

"I suppose. I am fond of his 'The Birth of Venus,' but I can only take so much of his religious paintings. Any idea what the subject matter is?"

"Mythological or religious? That is the question."

"A choice between seductive and mythological nudes versus old saints with halos and Madonna with Child. I prefer van Gogh, if you don't mind."

"You would. Sandro was a bit beyond the halo era. The most important question: is it real or fake? By the way, keep your receipts from your hire-car rental. Sergio will pay, or I'll have his old hide."

"Interpol already paid for the car, but I bet you neglected to tell your Sergio I'm part of the package."

"My Sergio? Hardly! He lost to my count. And I believe I mentioned I had a serious relationship with a Dutchman to stop him from pursuing me yet again. I didn't want him to get any ideas. But there's no need, as it turns out; he's married."

"Is that a disappointment?"

"Yes. I'll not be able to flirt with him very much, especially if his wife is mindful of his behavior, the old lecherous beast."

He went to the bed and sat by her. "You don't have to flirt with me, you know."

"Your implied activity shall be our just dessert, I think. Right now, I'm famished. These cheap airlines don't give their passengers much to eat, although that's insignificant compared to how they often give their passengers DVTs."

"For a short flight, less or no food is the norm. I'm also famished. Five hours in an Italian vehicle can do that to any driver. I was tempted by some strudel at the airport, but I figured it was stale and didn't want to ruin our dinner. Besides, airport food is so blasé. Not an apple in the strudel to be found, I bet."

"Let me tidy up a bit. Why don't you find us some ice for a little pre-dinner cocktail after we dress? That little fridge has some of those nice little bottles that now cost a fortune on the plane, and I saw two of them were white wine. I also saw cheese, sausage, and crackers, but I'm a bit wary of the sausage. Vienna's sausage can pack a punch. Not as bad as Munich, though."

Bastiann only drank the wine to save his appetite for dinner while Esther added some cheese and crackers. They dressed and headed for dinner.

They found a lovely, quiet restaurant they shared with three other couples. Esther settled for the tourists' standard, *Wiener schnitzel,* with *sachertorte* for dessert. Bastiann was more adventurous and tried the *Selchfleisch,* complete with cabbage. His dessert was the conventional *Apfelstrudel.* He was sure it was at least ten times better than what the airport offered. The main meal was accompanied by a bottle of fine, local wine they shared—white, considering the nature of the meat dishes they ate.

They returned to their hotel happy, but tired from their night out.

*****

Esther awoke. *What a strange dream!* She glanced at Bastiann, asleep beside her. *I can't see any blood.* She pulled the covers up to her neck.

She had dreamed he had been sprayed by an automatic weapon. With wounds bleeding, he staggered toward her, arms reaching out for help. She could see his assailant through the large bullet holes; Sergio Moretti was loading another magazine into the weapon. Then a huge eagle swooped down and grabbed Sergio in its talons and flew off into the night sky. The bird had the face of Alberto Sartini, her count.

She slipped into the bathroom to drink some water. She was shaking as she sipped it, looking into the mirror at her frightened face. *That was just too real! Must be indigestion.* She emptied the glass and gripped the edges of the sink. *I'm definitely not taking Bastiann along with me tomorrow!*

She had no idea what the dream meant. She figured not even Freud could make sense of it, although he might understand Viennese indigestion. She wasn't superstitious nor did she believe in ESP. She still wasn't about to take any chances. *Sergio can have a temper!*

She had met him in West Berlin before she met Alberto. He was her MI6 handler for a while before Jeremy Brand, who was now in MI5, the organization that only handled internal security in Britain. Her relationship with Sergio started like the one with Bastiann—dinners and concerts and the like—but she had always pegged him as a dedicated bachelor, so they never became intimate. She didn't know his true feelings until Alberto had passed on.

I'm glad he's found someone. I wonder if he's told his wife anything about MI6?

The British had always been clever about recruiting non-citizens to work in the field for them. Many didn't have a fondness for the U.K., but they thought the people and organizations they spied on were much worse. Such was the case with Sergio Moretti, who had no love for the East German state. Except for people who worked with them or searched through MI6 records, no one knew of these people's service. *And some of them, unlike Sergio, are very much dead!*

*****

The next morning Bastiann awoke to find Esther gone. She'd left a note: *Bastiann, I thought it would be more efficient if I go see Sergio alone. Make dinner reservations for two at Die Metzgerei for 6 p.m. I'll meet you there. Esther.*

While in the shower, he tried to decide what to do with his free day. He thought about calling the local Interpol office. It would be worthwhile to follow-up on the gun smuggling case. *Perhaps the carabinieri had made one of them talk?* He doubted it. He would also call Hal Leonard.

He wrote a note to himself to buy a bouquet of roses for Esther. He wanted to cancel out any feelings she'd experience meeting her old boyfriend, Sergio Moretti, once again. Of course, maybe Moretti's new wife would have that all under control. He smiled. *Nothing like eliminating the competition!*

He trusted Esther, but she was a bit wild at times, and not only in bed. She had gone through a few husbands, after all, and outlasted every one of them. He thought he'd outlast her, but that made him want her in his life as much as possible. *I need to work on that!*

He checked himself in the mirror before leaving the room, a personal quirk instead of vanity. Both Esther and he always placed more importance on the inner person and not on outer appearance. He looked like David Suchet, the famous actor who had portrayed Agatha Christie's Hercule Poirot, but he was still a bit dissatisfied with his appearance. She knew enough not to try to change those looks, and he respected her choices too. At functions, he thought they were a good-looking couple, but she tended to be less formal, in general.

Is marriage in our future? He shrugged. *Is it necessary?* She's been married three times. He had never been married.

He thought he was more eager to try it than she was to repeat it. *It must be terrible to lose a spouse. And she lost three.*

He collected his credentials and firearm and left the room.

Chapter Ten

Twenty-First Century, Vienna

Esther's taxi driver had no trouble finding Sergio Moretti's home. Vienna was an old city, so her friend's house in Grinzing was old too. On the way to it, she spotted some lovely wine cafes she would like to visit with Bastiann in the spring since, on that cold day, outside tables were without chairs and the parasols had been put away. There were no elderly couples dancing their waltzes and few tourists to watch them either. *Can Bastiann dance a Viennese waltz?* She had plenty of practice with her late husband, the count, but thought she might be a bit rusty by now. *Maybe we should take some refresher lessons together, Bastiann and I!*

A young maid came to the door.

"*Herr* Moretti is expecting me," Esther said in German.

"He informed me of that, Countess," she said in perfect English followed by a curtsy. *Leave it to Sergio to rub it in!* "Please, follow me."

Esther followed her through the stately house, noting, as they passed, the ornate library with old books and sculptures lining wall shelves, continuing to a large back workroom. She first spotted Sergio perched atop a work table like some wingless, prehistoric bird—he had a Roman beak like Alberto's—and then she noticed the painting.

"I inspect purchases here," he said by way of explanation, "and sometimes do a bit of restoration. You'll find that the workshop's quite complete."

"You're now an art dealer?"

"I buy and sometimes I sell. I don't have a gallery downtown like you do. It would be a drain of money I can ill afford with all the competition in this city. Consider me a broker." He stood, approached her, and smiled. The hug was unavoidable. "It's so good to see you."

She hugged him back. "Likewise."

Sergio Moretti was a short, barrel-chested man who could be everyone's image of an eighteenth-century English baron. But he reminded her of several actors who had played old Mr. Fezziwig, Scrooge's cheerful boss in Dickens's *The Christmas Carol.* He even had long sideburns and slouching shoulders. The twinkle in his eyes above his prominent nose seemed to warm the cold room; however, a flowing mustache destroyed that illusion a bit. *Yes, noting the resemblance to the Rings' dwarf king, a member of the Fellowship, was appropriate too. The girls had it about right.*

She gestured to the painting. "It appears to be a Botticelli, but is it? Looks can be deceiving. And his students made good copies."

"It's a painting on wood, good poplar, so they say, of the disciples James, John, and their father, Zebedee. In a fit of narcissism, Botticelli used himself as the model for John. I have no idea who the model for James is, if anyone."

"Perhaps Botticelli's brother. They lived in the same house. I suppose you're going by the supposed self-portrait of Botticelli found in his 'Adoration of the Magi.' Same model, I'd say, but who knows if either was truly Botticelli."

"Duly noted, but I think that's one clue that says this is his painting, right?"

"Or a painting made by some assistant or another painter using the 'Magi' painting as his model. Botticelli's shop produced religious paintings as if Sandro were the inventor of Henry Ford's assembly line. That was common practice back then. There are many copies of Leonardo's 'Mona Lisa,' for example. I don't even know if the *Louvre* has the best one." She paused a moment. "*La Gioconda*'s smile is easy to explain if you consider da Vinci dissected human bodies and studied anatomy. He knew what muscles were used to make a smile, even a slight, mysterious one. To change the topic a bit, has anyone else authenticated this painting? I mean, besides you?"

"Three other local experts. I'm not going to bias you in any way by passing on their conclusions before you examine it."

"I'm guessing you already told me their opinion about the wood, but thank you for that consideration. Let's suppose the painting's authentic for the sake of argument. Did he paint it on commission? If so, a commission from whom? In those days, painters had patrons who were rich, powerful men. All of Botticelli's fellow artists, Leonardo and Michelangelo among them, painted on commission."

"And competed for commissions," said Sergio. "I don't think Sandro, Leonardo, and Michelangelo particularly liked each other. Wasn't Michelangelo angry because Leonardo was a member of the civic commission that decided where to place his statue of David?"

"Being a Florentine, you know the history, but that's putting it mildly. I think they hated each other. I'm not sure about Botticelli and Leonardo, who spent a lot of time in Milan. Despite all that, none of it matters for authenticating the painting beyond offering evidence for our limited knowledge of art history. However, I am curious about the provenance. That can help with the authentication."

"Shall we retire to my study, have some wine and cheese, and discuss it before you begin your work? Maybe catch up a bit?"

"A bit early for all of that, although we are in Vienna. Have that iconic old man's maid you employ bring me a cup of tea instead. We'll have some wine and cheese at lunch, I presume."

"Among fruit and other delights," he said. "I assume you want to study the painting alone. I shall not distract you. I have some calls to make anyway."

*****

Sergio retreated to his library. His "calls" were an excuse. *I still find Esther's intensity troublesome after all these years.* He made himself a vodka tonic and sunk into his favorite chair, a recliner that allowed him to put his feet up while he read.

But the book remained opened on his lap. He had worked with Esther in more difficult circumstances. The year was 1978, and he'd been living in West Germany...

"Sergio, we have a problem."

The call had come in from the British Consulate in East Germany. His phone rang three times and then stopped. When it rang again, he was waiting for it, and received those dire words again.

"You'd better have a good reason to ring me at this hour. I'm entertaining someone."

"We have a package that needs to be delivered."

Not a good reason to call! "Arrangements have been made. You know the schedule."

"We need an express delivery. Can your package service ship tomorrow?"

"I'll have to make the inquiry and get back to you. Give me an hour."

"I'll ring in an hour." The line went dead.

Sergio put the phone down. He wondered why there was such a rush to get the old man out. Haste made people careless; carelessness could be deadly. He went to his closet and opened the door to reveal his transceiver. He patted the unit on its black top. "Are you ready to do the British Queen's chores yet again, my dear?" He turned on the radio, put on the headphones that would restrict the sounds of dots and dashes to his ears, and started keying.

The next night two West German agents drove him to the border. Knowing the route well, they had traveled the last few kilometers without headlights. One agent stayed with the black Mercedes while Sergio and the other agent moved closer to the checkpoint on foot.

"The lorry should arrive in five minutes or so," Sergio's companion whispered.

Tell me something I don't know! Sergio was functioning on adrenalin—it had been a hectic twenty hours—but he wasn't stressed. What they were doing had become an old habit by then, but lack of sleep and its resulting weariness upset his system.

They heard the old lorry downshift and come to a stop on the East German side. Sleepy guards would inspect the vehicle, find it empty, and wave it on. The guards knew those lorries. They wouldn't be too thorough because that shipping company did a good business hauling luxury goods to the fat East German elites. It also occasionally carried human cargo on return trips, something the guards did not know.

Two guards on the West German side stopped the lorry again and began to go through the motions of checking papers and routing slips. Sergio and his German friend moved toward the vehicle, running in a crouch. They slid under the lorry, opened the false bottom, and removed "the package."

"*Guten Morgen, Herr* Moretti," Esther whispered as she fell into his arms.

"What happened to the professor?" he asked.

"Mission failure three days ago. I had to kill someone."

"I expect you to explain that. No one ever tells me anything."

"I will in good time over a good drink."

They crawled out from under the lorry and disappeared into the tall grass...

Sergio raised his glass in the general direction of his workshop. He had become Esther's handler in West Berlin six months later when they sent her over the border again with a new identity.

*****

After Sergio left the workshop, Esther first examined the tools available. Satisfied, she started to examine the painting. She carefully removed the painting's wood panel from the frame, which she figured copied the old style and was possibly of more recent vintage. She then began her lab work by walking around Sergio's little lab to select her tools and materials.

She first analyzed a miniscule paint chip from the border by performing mass spectrometry and comparing the data with notes on her mobile. The paint was consistent with other Botticelli masterworks. So was the ancient wood panel and the frame; she hadn't been sure about the frame. The former was old poplar, as Sergio had stated. She then compared color choices and styles.

Her analysis took three hours. About halfway through, the young maid brought her tea and scones, her only refreshment. When she finished, she used the WC off to one side of the laboratory for a second time and then gave the painting a final once-over. When she turned it back over to put it back in the frame, she noticed what appeared to be a document tucked into the frame's upper left corner. *It must have been between the frame and the painting.*

She found her tweezers by the mass spectrometer and removed the parchment.

Intriguing. She unfolded the brittle document still using the tweezers. *What's this all about?* The calligraphy was hard to read, but she thought it might be in Latin. *From Botticelli's time?* Hard to tell. She had no reference data for parchment from that time to compare to, but she took a small sample and performed a mass spectrometry anyway, writing down the results. She then copied the text the best she could, folded the document carefully, and slipped it back into its hiding place.

She tossed her rubber gloves into the waste bin as if she were a doctor leaving surgery and left the lab to find Sergio.

*****

"I'm 95% certain the painting is real, not fake," Esther told Sergio at lunch after recovering her composure upon seeing the other lunch companions.

Sergio sat at one end of the long table, his lovely wife, Diana, to his left, and Esther at the other end. Perched on Diana's shoulder was a cockatiel that studied Esther with suspicion. She had already spotted the white Persian cat sleeping in a window sill enjoying the sun.

"Diana's fond of pets," said Sergio. "The bird's name is Anthony. The cat's name is Cleopatra."

"And I bet they're best friends," Esther said.

"But of course," said Diana with a smile. She handed a morsel of fruit to Anthony. "And well trained. If you're allergic to Cleopatra, I can have Elise take them out. But they usually have the run of the house." She grinned at Sergio. "Except in the workshop."

Esther had guessed Diana was about twenty years younger than Sergio. That didn't bother her because she and Bastiann had about the same age difference. However, she thought it was more appropriate doing it her way, the opposite of Diana and Sergio. Old men wore out faster than old women.

"Do you want to tell me where you found the painting?" she asked.

Sergio gestured toward his wife. "Diana found it. She loves to go antiquing and bought some old bishop's armoire on a trip to Florence. The Church was selling it at an auction. Can you believe that someone reversed the painting and used it to patch a hole in the armoire's left side?"

Diana laughed. To Esther, she appeared to be an older version of Simonetta Vespucci, the woman who had possibly served as a model for Botticelli's "The Birth of Venus." The laugh was a bit like the refreshing sounds from a wind chime. She was a mature woman who didn't show her age, so it was hard to tell how old she was. Esther was a bit jealous, but she couldn't help liking Sergio's new wife. *He's lucky to have her*.

But Esther's mind soon spun around to how fateful random events in the art world lead to awesome discoveries. *Imagine, a new Botticelli! How extraordinary is that!* She took a sip of wine, even though her hand was trembling. "So you paid next to nothing for an undiscovered Botticelli?"

"Someone tried to outbid me," said Diana, "so afterwards I thought I had overpaid for the armoire."

"We were going to replace that entire panel of the armoire," said Sergio. "It could be a period piece, but it is rather plain. I was thinking of reselling it."

"Quite a find. You can tell me your other experts' opinions now."

"All quite in agreement with yours, my dear. I trust yours more."

He would say that. "But they weren't thorough. They missed the document."

She reached into her purse, found her mobile, and screened the pictures she had taken of the parchment. She stood, walked along the ornate dining table, and handed the phone to Sergio. Diana peered over one shoulder, Esther over the other.

"You can also examine the original. It's in the back upper left-hand corner between the frame and painting. It's in Latin, not Florentine Italian."

Sergio scrolled through her pictures of the document. "It's some kind of word-map. Do you think it's the same age as the painting?" Esther shrugged. He turned to Diana. "How did those old fools miss this?" It was Diana's turn to shrug.

Esther saw humor in Sergio calling someone else old. "In their defense, I always try to test the pigments by taking a sample from the edge covered by the frame. They might not have done that, being too excited with appraising a possibly new Botticelli. My jiggling of the frame and removing the painting from it probably exposed the document. It could be it wasn't even visible to them."

"But what does it say?" inquired Diana.

"I'll have to verify my poor attempt at a translation, but it appears to be directions to the tomb of St. John the Divine, one of the subjects in the painting."

"On Patmos, I presume," said Sergio. He kept peering at the mobile's screen.

"I think it mentions the Temple of Artemis," said Esther.

"Ephesus? That's where that church honoring John's burial place is found. Where it's said he wrote his gospel. I thought all of that was in doubt—only legends, you know."

"If this parchment is of the same vintage as the painting, everything still is in doubt. Yet, it's interesting." Esther returned to her chair. "Take a look at the document when you have a moment. We could have something interesting. I have mass spectroscopy results of a small piece from the parchment. I'll use that and these images to consult with a Latin expert I know when I return home."

Sergio frowned. "We have a museum here in Vienna with artifacts from the Ephesian ruins. I don't remember anything about a crypt or urns with cremation ashes. There are a lot of Greek artifacts and a bronze statue of an athlete recreated from 234 fragments of some marble statue. Boring, I dare say. Besides, I'm not interested in St. John's burial place. Not at all. If you want to use your detective skills to find it, have fun. Maybe you can have that Interpol agent help you."

"Indeed." *But would Bastiann think I am once again becoming obsessed?*

Chapter Eleven

First Century, Agrinio

John's trip by sea from Athens to Patras was not difficult, but the overland trip to Agrinio was unsettling. Upon arrival, he could not tell who was in charge in the old town. There were signs of Roman patrols, but they did not appear to give the place much importance. He was still careful, but became worried when he was told the man he was to meet was dead. He managed to obtain directions to the man's home from a street vendor.

A heavy-set old woman was sitting in the front patio fanning herself. She watched him approach like she was a mouse and he was a hawk circling for prey. The disciple hesitated, but then continued with firm, deliberate steps toward her. "I look for Demetrius."

The woman eyed John with more suspicion now that he stood in front of her. "Not Roman, but still a foreigner. What is your name, stranger?" He told her. She jumped up from her bench, ran to him, and knelt to kiss his dusty feet. "Bless me, sweet disciple, for I have sinned."

"Stand, woman. Do not make a scene. We must always be wary of Roman spies."

She stood and brushed away her tears. “They killed my handsome Demetrius, you know. My sin is not giving him a proper burial. My son, also named Demetrius, says it is too dangerous. Let us go inside.”

He smiled. *No sin for not recognizing the guest they were expecting.* He excused that because, while a foreigner, he did not have many distinguishing features to set him apart from other men. *And perhaps, considering her recent history, she thought I was a Roman spy or a local who sought Rome’s favor?*

The woman was an imposing figure. He saw strength in her physique and detected an inner steeliness that made her a good disciple of Christ. *Especially if she derives it from Him!*

She led John to the kitchen. She made him sit at the rustic table and placed wine and bread in front of him. “It is all I have. We are poor. Proud but poor.”

“But your husband must have been one of the Christian leaders around here. My invitation to preach the gospel came from him.”

“Our poverty is not self-inflicted. The Romans have made everyone poor. They take what they want. Beatings and murders await people who resist. They invent more taxes and expect bribes. It is so bad that many locals have become collaborators if only to survive. And people are drifting away from the Church, fearful the soldiers will come for them.” She sat opposite him. “I am exhausted. Every day we resist seems more futile.”

“How many legions are here? I did not see many soldiers in the streets.”

“No legions. Merely one century. The centurion who leads them is a mean, old bastard who would as soon kill you as look at you.”

"Eighty soldiers then, more or less. You outnumber them. Why not run them out of town? Nothing violent, of course."

She shuddered. "And risk vengeance from a full legion?" She put a finger to her lips. "Do not even whisper such treason. They will kill you. They will kill us all!"

"They will do the former if they find out who I am." He paused to collect his thoughts. "Did this centurion order your husband's death?"

"He felt he had to do so, I suppose. One of the local spies informed him how important Demetrius was to our congregation, which Romans consider a subversive group."

"The Lord's grace and goodness will always be considered subversive to despots, even though I can imagine them using Christianity, in the future, to further their own agendas, including all sorts of evil behavior. We need to organize a meeting so I can give Christ's followers here some hope."

*****

The congregation, those who dared attend, met in what remained of the woods near the town. Romans had cut down many trees. Some were used for crucifixions. Some gave their lives to make fires where the Romans roasted the livestock they plundered from the town's citizens. What remained of the forest still provided a peaceful place to have a service and communion. John gave his sermon in Greek. After communion he moved among the frightened Christians and comforted them.

"You give us hope," said one man named Lukas, who seemed to have inherited Demetrius's place in the small group. "And we are humbled Christ's beloved disciple has come to pray with us."

John hugged the man. "We are not finished, my brother. Is there a stream nearby?"

"We have all been sprinkled with holy water."

"Of course. But Christ went to that other John to be baptized, the one who baptized my brother and I. He was baptizing at Aenon near Salem because there was plenty of water, and people were coming to be baptized. There is nothing wrong with renewing your allegiance to the Lord."

"We might have to carry some of the old and infirm."

"I can help with that."

It took several hours. Afterward they left in twos and threes and in different directions until only Lukas and John were left.

"I need to discuss a problem," the Greek said to John. He pulled on his scraggly beard and glanced about him as if he were expecting soldiers to jump upon them from behind the trees. John understood this fear. They would be helpless against Roman swords.

John took a seat on a boulder in the sun so his clothes would dry. "Personal or group-related?"

"Both," said Lukas, standing before him. "Christ did not resist the Romans when everyone told him to do so, but many in my congregation want to resist them here. Too many of them have become captives of the soldiers who torture them before killing them."

John stared at the blue sky he could see between the treetops. *What should I tell him, Lord?* But he already knew the answer to the man's question. "Jesus said, 'My kingdom is not of this world. If it were, my servants would fight to prevent my arrest by the Jewish leaders. But now my kingdom is from another place.' When the Sanhedrin tried to arraign Peter and I, we defied them but with words. I cannot recommend you attack the Romans, but when they attack you, fight back. Christ was crucified to save man and blessed us with the promise of eternal life. He made that sacrifice for that purpose, but you must resist so the number of Christ's followers on Earth can increase and carry to present future generations that same wonderful message. I forbid hunting the Romans, but resistance is needed and that includes freeing your companions from the soldiers. Does that make sense?"

Lukas grinned. "Absolutely. You truly are the Son of Thunder."

It was John's time to smile. Christ had called him and James the "sons of thunder," but John did not speak in anger. These people were good and deserved to survive the evil laid upon them by the Roman Empire.

*****

The old woman shared her simple breakfast with John the next morning. They finished with a strong brew made from boiling roots. It was a quiet moment of relaxation.

After some moments, she broke the silence. "Do angels exist, John?"

"My friend, Mary, claims to have seen one at His empty tomb. Such events are described throughout the scriptures. I have never seen an angel, but after seeing Him walk among us after the Crucifixion, it is easy to believe in them. Are angels only like the visions of people, or of entire groups, who have eaten bad fish? Mere creations of our minds? That's for each man and woman to decide. What do you believe, my sister?"

"I believe we need prophets and angels. Life is too hard otherwise."

"Not belief but fact. Be comforted in that more prophets will come, as will He at the end of the world. But now I must prepare for my journey."

He was packing his few belongings when the centurion came. The burly man barged onto the patio at Demetrius's home and confronted the old woman. She shrank away from him in fear.

"Hag, where is the foreigner?"

John debated going out a back window, but not for long. The centurion had to know he was staying there. *Spies? Surely not someone I baptized!* He decided either fighting the giant or turning himself in would protect his host. She did not deserve to die. He had to prevent that if at all possible. She had already suffered plenty with the death of her husband.

After studying the brute a bit more, he made his choice. It would not do to fight him and lose, for the woman could still die. *In other circumstances I would fight, but in these times it is too risky for her.*

He exited the house onto the patio and faced the brute. "I am no foreigner, but a citizen of God's world and protector of all that's in it. My name is John. What name do you go by, good sir?"

"His name is Brutus," said the old woman in a whisper.

The centurion turned to her. "Speak only when I command you to do so," he said.

"Brutus you say? Not the man who assassinated Julius Caesar, I hope. That would imply a very long life, but not as long as the one my Father and His Son can give him."

The centurion's gaze passed over John from head to foot. "You speak our language as if you were a high priest from the Roman shrine to Mars, the guardian of Rome. But you look like a country bumpkin."

John laughed. "Without knowing which then, would you do me harm?"

"Bah! You are a pontificating idiot."

"Perhaps. To avoid more of this useless banter, let me make my situation clear. My Father is in heaven," John pointed skyward, "and I serve his Son."

"You are a Christian then?"

"I was one of the twelve disciples, if that means anything to you. Arrest me and leave this poor woman with her grief."

There was a surprise look on the centurion's and the woman's face. However, hers turned into a grin.

"You knew Him?" said Brutus.

"I was there at the foot of the cross when he was crucified. I was there when he rose from the dead and walked among us. Have you not heard about those wonderful events?"

"I...I thought they were only superstitions or the drunken dreams of that rebel's followers."

"Now you know the truth. Let it set you free. Choose Him now as your Savior and you will have eternal life."

"You are not afraid of me, are you?"

"Because you do Rome's evil deeds? In Christ's heavenly mansion there are many rooms, and I will be welcome there. You will not have that chance, Brutus, unless you change your ways and repent." John studied the man who now looked confused. "I see you are perplexed. One among us doubted too, but believe me, dear friend, I was a witness. Those who believe will have their reward in heaven."

The centurion spit on the patio's stone floor, turned, and left.

"Interesting," said the old woman. "I was afraid he was going to run you through with his sword."

John smiled. "A reasonable expectation, given the circumstances. Are you all right?" She nodded. "Let this be a lesson: The first step is to create doubts. He has heard the message now, but he does not yet believe. Give him time. He can become a valuable ally for all of you. Try to convert him. We need all the help we can get, especially among the Romans."

"Come inside and I will give you some bread and water for your journey."

Son of Thunder

Chapter Twelve

Twenty-First Century, Vienna

After Bastiann berated Esther for going alone to Sergio's house, they made up with some late afternoon frolicking and then went to a magnificent dinner in another exquisite restaurant in the inner city. A small sextet played Strauss waltzes. She tried the strudel this time—she liked it almost as much as baklava—and Viennese coffee finished the meal. They ended the evening by going back to the hotel room and going to bed early. He had a long drive back to Lyon awaiting him, and she had an early flight to catch.

Her first stop in London was her gallery. She had forgotten to check-in while away, what with her excitement over the Botticelli painting and the parchment. She was happy to hear there was a customer interested in Ricardo's painting. She didn't understand why, but she would be happy to pad her savings account with her portion of the commission and share it with her employees, who had done all the work in showing it.

Her next stop was Scotland Yard. Even when she wasn't consulting, she popped in every now and then to hear what was going on and say hello to her ex-boss, George Langston.

He took over for her when she wanted out of the Yard's bureaucracy. She valued him and his wife as close friends.

She always thought he had the appearance of the stereotypical erudite professor or publishing editor. His wife dressed him, so he was always presentable, looking better in the morning than at the close of the work day. He was getting up in years too. This mild-mannered man had resisted the trend of leaving the Division and becoming a private investigator for rich clients wishing to recover stolen artwork. He was efficient and dedicated to bringing art thieves to justice like she had been.

"Do you miss me in the Division?" she said.

"You haven't been replaced yet if that's what you mean. But I'm working on it."

"Good luck. I have many qualifications, and you'll be hard put to find them in a single person." She winked at him. "But I'm preaching to the choir, correct?" She was well aware no one was indispensable.

After he took over the Division's administration from her, she made his life miserable, at times. She thought when all positives and negatives were tallied, her contributions made him look good for the most part. *All employees should do that for their bosses, assuming they're decent people who don't make their lives miserable.*

"Let's put it this way: You haven't been gone long enough to preclude your waltzing in here like you own the place. Who knows? Maybe you want to do more consulting? I don't have anything right now." He gave her a sly wink. "How was your time at the castle?"

"Except for being with Bastiann, somewhat boring. And noisy. He rather liked dirtying his hands a bit. I hired a handyman who selected a crew to do some major repairs. Bastiann took it upon himself to join in. Bad scheduling on my part, but the bloke will improve the place. He's trustworthy."

She didn't mention the handyman knew Sylvia Bassett, The Yard was still searching for that thief who had nicked the Bernini bust.

"Not a holiday of peace and quiet, I take it," said Langston. "But I suppose you're more or less on permanent holiday now anyway. Unless you have become obsessed with another painting. Were you running about Scotland all the time since I last saw you?"

She told him about the Botticelli painting and the parchment. "The document is more my obsession. Sergio can have his Botticelli, but that parchment is interesting. Even Anglicans put a lot of stock in St. John. You remember that church near the Oral tube station?"

"St. John the Divine Church in Kennington? Yes, I know it. Many people don't like it?"

"For that awful steeple and the Kelham Rood, that bronze creation that is so out of place. And isn't anything Victorian a monstrosity?"

"Victorian Gothic. I thought you were an art lover?"

She wrinkled her nose. "One's taste in art is subjective."

"But, more to the point, how will finding St. John's burial place affect that particular church?"

"It can upset people who have believed all the legends surrounding the saint. I wonder if his bones will show he was boiled in oil."

"I'm not familiar with the story."

"You didn't know my father." She laughed.

Her father, the vicar, hadn't managed to brainwash her. Esther was agnostic—a doubting Thomasina, she often said—and her last husband, the count, had been an atheist. Not willing to go as far as her husband, she thought most religions—Judaism, Christianity, Islam, and Buddhism to name a few—offered similar guidance for leading a moral life.

Her father hadn't shared her perspective. Unlike him, she thought people could believe what they wanted, but they should respect others rights.

And people full of bigotry and hatred who went after other religious groups—the Turks against the Armenians, the Nazis against the Jews, the Buddhists against the Rohingya—were at the top of her list of criminals because of the resulting ethnic cleansing and genocide, something she abhorred.

She didn't know what her father would think about current events around the world. He could have become less provincial. She didn't know what he thought about the less recent ones either, those that had occurred during his lifetime or before. He had been a man with blinders on, a kind man set in his ways...and maybe just a product of his era.

"I'm here, George, because I need a favor. I'm going on a longer trip. Could you check the gallery once and a while? The girls are good sorts, but they need some adult supervision, you know, and Harry James is too quiet and tolerant to provide it."

"I'll be glad to perform that favor. Either my wife or I will make some surprise visits. Where are you off to?"

"Ephesus. The parchment says that's where John is buried."

"Yes. Under that basilica maybe."

"That might be a crock. The document mentions ruins, not a church."

"Maybe they built the basilica on top of those ruins."

"If I have my dates correct, that doesn't work. The basilica was built in the sixth century. The description of the ruins is from the fifteenth."

He shrugged. "History isn't my forte. A warning, though. Turkey isn't a safe place right now. Hasn't been for a while. Do be careful."

"I'm well aware of the unsettling events in that part of the world. Turkey has become a dictatorship, but there are a lot more dangerous places in the Middle East right now." She stood and gave a little wave. "Don't get into any trouble while I'm gone."

"I should be saying that to you."

*****

Before planning the details for her trip, Esther decided to visit Oxford. While there, she experienced *déjà vu*. She had lived there for a time with one of her husbands, and she had made a trip there to learn about Bernini and his sculptures when she was given the case of the stolen bust. She wasn't a fan of sculptures. She liked Michelangelo's "David" well enough, even though it was also a bit of a monstrosity, but her preference for paintings contributed to her dislike for the Kelham Rood. This time she didn't stop at her old school chum's estate, but instead visited Professor Oscar Willoughby, another friend from her days living there.

After the usual pleasantries, she found her mobile and displayed the pictures of the parchment on its tiny screen to show the professor. "I have here a photographic copy of an old document I want you to examine." She handed him the mobile.

He read it for a few moments. Then he stopped to stare at her with his old man's bushy eyebrows raised. "This is most unusual!"

"Because it's in Latin?" she asked, pretending she didn't understand his comment. "Every educated man back then read and wrote Latin, even if he didn't speak it, correct?"

"Right. There are notable exceptions, like da Vinci, but maybe he was more self-educated. His genius likely couldn't stand the usual plodding pedagogy of the Renaissance intelligentsia. However, it's not the Latin that is unusual in your parchment. It's the meaning of what's written, Esther. They appear to be directions to a burial place."

Oscar looked a little like Prince Alfred, Queen Victoria's son, without all the gratuitous medals. Prince Alfred's right eye drooped; Oscar's left eye drooped. His eyes were blue and peered out over his metal-rimmed reading glasses. His dark hair, now with gray mixed in, matched his eyebrows. He hadn't changed much since she had met him at an Oxford function that her second husband, Alfred, also a professor, had taken her to. They only had phone conversations after meeting. He was a classicist and probably knew more about Greeks and Romans, including their artworks, than most anyone else on the planet.

Esther decided to continue to play dumb. "Whose? Botticelli's?"

"No, he's buried in the *Chiesa de San Salvatore di Ognissanti* in Florence. No one needs directions for that. The church is in most tourist guides. This old document contains directions to St. John the Divine's tomb. Was he in the painting?"

"It depicts the two brothers, James and John." She thought a bit. "I'm guessing they're on the shores of Galilee. Maybe it's when Christ called them to be his disciples. Or maybe it's earlier when they were John the Baptist's disciples. Or maybe it was only a bit after coming in from fishing. In any case, I think Botticelli was his own model for John."

"No sign of the father, Zebedee? The three were all tight with the Baptist, so they say."

"John is between the father and brother," said Esther. "It's an unusual painting. It is what it is. Perhaps someone commissioned the painting to be like that. Now, let's forget about the bloody painting. Do the directions make sense? Could I follow them?"

"I'm not sure. You're the detective. I'll write out the translation for you. Fair warning. To follow them, you'll have to go to Turkey, which is not the safest spot on the planet for foreigners right now. Ephesus, to be precise. If you fly into Ankara, that's a long trip by train."

"I know that. The Turks aren't great friends with the West right now, and they're tight with the Russian oligarchy. You're saying it would be a risk, but that doesn't bother me. I've received other warnings. If I survived East Berlin before the two Germanys unified, what's a little Turkish skullduggery? And they make a dandy *baklava* too."

"I don't want to know what you were doing in East Berlin. Before Scotland Yard, I presume. And Alfred." Esther nodded; Oscar laughed. "Same old Esther. Do be careful."

Esther walked around the university while Oscar made his professional translation of the text found on the parchment. She remembered her time there with Alfred, her Oxford professor husband, with fondness. *Peaceful times after my hectic days as a spy and first marriage. I needed those times to decompress.* She tried to visit another professor she had consulted with after seeing her school chum, but he wasn't there. *I wonder if he knows I was honored for that work on recovering the Bernini bust.* She chastised herself, realizing she was failing to remember to thank those people who helped her. *I'll have to ring him to thank him.*

She had tea with Oscar. He read his translation to her. Except for an introduction about the general area, it was as expected...a word-map to the saint's tomb:

"In Ephesus, not far from the Temple of Artemis and at the ruins of the Heracles Gate, look beyond Mount Koressos and Mary's House. There in the hills, above the river, lies the tomb of St. John. I have seen it, this simple yet holy place hidden from Ottomans so they cannot blaspheme it. Go with me now as I describe my journey there."

The text continued, much like an ancient travel guide.

"What's your opinion, Oscar? Was the author really there?"

"It seems like he was. The document isn't very informative. I'd be hard put to follow his directions. I googled a few items. He considers Mount Koressos and Mary's House as separate places. They're the same place, or at least at the same location. It was also hard to find the area he was describing, but I don't know Ephesus that well. That ancient city is in ruins. A mere ghost compared to its original splendor."

She thanked Oscar profusely, gave him a hug, and left with her complete and excellent translation of the parchment's text. She knew no one could have done it better.

Chapter Thirteen

Twenty-First Century, Oxford

The next morning Esther used her mobile to call Bastiann from the inn in Oxford where she stayed overnight.

"I'm off to visit Turkey. Has it settled down at all?" She knew the situation there, but her question was a test for Bastiann. *Will he try to prevent me from going there? Sometimes he's overbearing that way.*

"You mean since that coup attempt some years ago? You are a bit behind the times. The answer is no. They're still behaving badly, especially with respect to the Kurds. Now the Russian oligarchs are encouraging all those bad feelings. They've also been fomenting unrest almost everywhere else in the world."

"Hmm. Those ISIS devils would still have their caliphate without those Kurds helping the Yanks. I admire their courage as fighters. I have some Armenian friends—they make great *baklava* too—and they've never had much use for Turks either. Makes sense, considering millions of them were killed by the Ottoman Empire. All these ethnic animosities are confusing and so often illogical. Why should I try to follow what's happening with them?"

"The Ottomans have a long history of abuses. They used the Pantheon as a gunpowder magazine, for God's sake!"

"Not any worse than Cromwell stabling his horses in Irish cathedrals," she said. "No wonder they became Anglican churches. But that's all in the past. Any danger I might be in would be in my future, yet tourists still go to Turkey. Why can't I?"

"Because you could be walking onto a mine field? Not literally, of course, but you do have a penchant for finding trouble. I suppose you're going to follow the directions on the parchment?"

"That's the idea. Do you want to come?"

"I'm in Morocco at the moment. Sorry. Kidnapping of a French VIP's daughter."

"I suppose some sheikh wants to augment his harem?"

"Or some terrorist group wants to improve their financial situation by collecting a ransom."

"Good luck with that. Do be careful. I'll be in contact."

"Same advice to you. At least I need to know where to fetch your body."

"Pish-tosh. Always a pessimist."

"No, only a realist. As I said, even if you don't look for trouble, it finds you."

"Goodbye, Bastiann."

She wondered for a moment if he didn't have reason on his side. She had never shied away from trouble in all its many forms. *But I have to return to London and finish packing!*

*****

Esther was a seasoned traveler, but she missed her plane.

That afternoon, when she called the lift to take her last bit of garbage downstairs to the bin in her building's garage, something she always did before a trip, she only took a few steps before a man popped out from behind a support column, grabbed her, and put a handkerchief over her mouth.

What she inhaled took away the force from her kick to his groin...

"You're no more a countess than I am," said the blurred face belonging to a complete stranger when she awoke. "You're just a meddling old hag."

She said nothing. She was waiting for her head to clear before she tried to assess her situation. Her captor patted her on the cheek.

"Your husband wasn't even a count under modern Italian law. Alberto Sartini was only a greedy Swiss banker."

Italian, she thought. *And I'll castrate you for your insults!*

"But to the business at hand. I have talked to someone on Moretti's house staff. That person informed me that two *objets d'art* were found in an old armoire, which used to belong to a priest: a Botticelli painting and a piece of parchment, to be precise." He laughed. "At first I was only interested in the armoire as a family heirloom. When Moretti's slut won that bid, I lost interest until I heard about what was in the armoire." He paced the floor, his hands behind his back. *What an intense man!* "I'm not interested in the painting, whether it's an authentic Botticelli or not. Stolen art is difficult to handle unless you sell it cents on the euro to someone in the black market. But the document intrigues me. Does it prove my ancestor made a long journey with Sandro Botticelli?"

Esther was confused. First, this man was an obvious amateur. Second, had the priest, who owned the armoire, painting, and parchment, dallied in the pastime of many Renaissance priests who sired bastard children? Third, why should anyone care about their ancestor taking a trip with the famous painter?

The conversation was becoming strange. *No, there isn't any conversation. I haven't said anything yet!*

"Sorry. I didn't catch your name."

"You may call me Bruno. My full name is Bruno Toscano."

Her head now clear, Esther studied his features. He had a buzz haircut that gave the impression of baldness compared to the bushy eyebrows that hovered like giant caterpillars above bottle-glass-thick lenses with wire frames. Otherwise, he was a plain man who wore inexpensive and ill-fitting clothes. He was also shorter than she was. *Maybe I aimed my kick too high?*

He continued pacing and muttering to himself as if his ego and id were embroiled in a serious discussion. At times, he seemed to have put himself into a trance. She remembered how the glasses had magnified the malevolence in the cold, blue eyes.

"Very well, Bruno. How about you untie me, and I'll try to answer your questions."

Her adversary grinned. *Some dental work needed.* Everything about him was wrinkled—his shirt, his suit, and his tie, which was too long. She couldn't tilt her head down far enough to see his shoes. She supposed they were also old and worn.

"You'd like that, wouldn't you? You're an old hag, but you're not a fragile old hag. I know about some of your exploits. I don't trust you, you see. Not at all. Not at all, I say!"

"The parchment describes a trip to Ephesus and landmarks in its vicinity. It's almost like a travel log because it's a word-map to St. John's burial place."

"St. John the Divine? Who wrote the document? Does the writer mention a Bishop Leonardo?"

"There was no mention of anyone, of him or Sandro Botticelli. Is this bishop some relative of yours?"

"Not a direct relative. We're descendants of Bishop Leonardo's brother." The man thought for a moment. Esther took the opportunity to test her constraints. *Loose, but not loose enough.* He stopped pacing and leaned over her. "I've now decided a saint's bones would be more valuable than an armoire. If I can't prove my ancestor traveled with Botticelli to search for the bones, finding them and selling them would be a suitable alternative to the armoire and painting."

"Where did you hear this story about your ancestor traveling with Botticelli? The painter rarely left the street where he lived in Florence. He could have been in Pisa for a time, and painted some early frescoes in the new Sistine Chapel, but that's all history knows about any of his travels."

"My ancestor ran the Ognissanti Church, Botticelli's parish church, for your information. That armoire was his and it's where the armoire was stored. Let this Moretti have the armoire and the painting, even though they're rightfully mine. The parchment too. I'm more interested in becoming famous by finding the saint's bones."

"You're crazy! They'd only be bones like any you can find in a grave in an old English churchyard. You might as well dig up some and call them St. John's."

"Maybe there are religious relics with the bones? Maybe even the Holy Grail! What would that be worth? Can you imagine?"

Esther thought of the movie with Harrison Ford and Sean Connery where Indy and his father searched for the Holy Grail. *At least this man doesn't have any superstitions about the Grail's power. He must see it only as a moneymaker if he can find a suitable and discreet buyer*. She digested that thought.

"So your family thinks your relative took a trip with the painter to the Middle East?" she said.

"I have no family anymore, just that family legend. Maybe Bishop Leonardo wanted to find the saint's bones too! The legend probably originated that way."

"And you think he wrapped up the bones he found and took them back to Florence?"

"The legend only talks about the trip. I'm thinking that was a reason for them to make it. It would have been a long one in those days, half the Mediterranean!"

At least he knows a bit of geography! "So are you going to Ephesus or returning to Florence to search for the bones?"

"I hadn't planned that far ahead. What do you suggest?"

Not too bright, this Bruno. She felt a bit sorry for him. "I'm not in a position to offer you advice, so maybe you should read what's on the parchment. I can give you that." *But not the translation! A lie by omission.* "I'm not interested in the saint's bones." *Another little lie, but mostly truth.*

She was more interested in proving the parchment was an elaborate hoax. However, she could also be interested if there were some truth to the man's story. Maybe Botticelli had wanted to go to Ephesus, but she couldn't believe he ever made the trip. *If he did, that would be something new in art history!*

Her captor considered the offer. "Okay I will let you go if you give me the text from the parchment."

I hope you know Latin! "A file of photographs is on my mobile. If you have access to a computer, I can download it to your hard drive."

Chapter Fourteen

Twenty-First Century, London

Bruno didn't anesthetize Esther again, but he left her still bound and with a blindfold and gag in her building's garage. As fate would have it, her irascible neighbor, Reginald Fox, found her. The man she had sued for a dent in her beloved Jaguar did his civic duty. He freed her and waited while she rang Scotland Yard.

When she ended the call, she gave him a smile. *He could have left me lying there!*

Reggie was a swarthy man with oily, black hair and a pompous goatee. His legs were much shorter than his torso, giving the appearance he was top heavy. The bulldog jowls of an elderly man didn't help either. He was refined enough, though.

He dressed like Rex Harrison when he portrayed the character Henry Higgins, except he had never sworn off women and tried to relive his youth by chasing younger ones, many half his age. She didn't know how successful he was at that, but his crisp slacks, checkered shirt, and tweed coat gave him the appearance of a man the American magazine, *Playboy*, could have targeted in its prime. His sculptured hair-do reminded her of America's ex-president's spray-held coiffure.

His BMW had created the dent in her Jaguar. She often considered that car English since many of its parts were made in the U.K. However, she didn't know how that had changed with BREXIT. *Probably not good for the British!* The E.U. had been in a bit of a revenge mode since the U.K.'s departure was finalized. She knew some rural areas were hurting without markets for their agricultural produce. *Fools who voted for BREXIT deserve that.*

"I bet you were happy to see me in that fix!"

"I must say, you do lead an exciting life. Some residents in our building were thinking retirement would settle you a bit. I've now won a few pounds with my wagers to the contrary. The first time occurred with your purchase of the gallery, but that makes sense, I suppose, all things considered."

"Residents here are wagering about my retirement life?"

"There are several wagers. Another is whether that Dutchman will ever marry you. Or should I say that in reverse? Whether you'll ever marry him?"

She blushed. "None of you have any business talking about my personal life!"

He shrugged. "Most are like me, worried that harm will come to you."

"Are you betting on that too?"

"Don't be cheesed off. People now consider you a famous and heroic person. Not exactly a rock star, but they feel they've had a brush with fame, as it were. Before you, no one knew anyone who took down neo-Nazis or stopped a terrorist threat. You're the celebrity among us. Another bet is that someone will want to do a documentary about your escapades."

She thought of Gerald Prince, the obnoxious man from the BBC. *Which side wins the bet? "Offer" is a bit stronger than "want!"* She was about to say something when the Metropolitan Police drove into the garage.

"Are you all right, Inspector Brookstone?" said the driver.

She didn't know him, but he knew she was more than the average victim of a mugging.

"Yes, I'm all right. This kind gentleman freed me from my bonds. Whip out your mobile. I'm going to describe my abductor." She gave an excellent description of Bruno Toscano that the officer recorded.

"You say he might be Italian," said the other officer. "Name sounds Italian. Did he have an accent?"

"Not as much as you do butchering the Queen's English, but yes. He spoke English with an accent. He could be Italian, Romanian, whatever. He's an ugly little cockroach who at least has, or had, relatives in Florence. The name sounding Italian means nothing anymore."

"Can this be connected to that attack in Rome a while ago?"

Esther sighed when she heard yet another reference to the case of the Bernini bust. It seemed the whole world knew the son of the original thief of the bust, not Sylvia Kensington, had nearly killed her when she and Bastiann had been waiting for a taxi after a function. *With the internet, gossip travels at light speed! Warp nine, Mr. Sulu!* That ex-U.S. president had built his whole foreign policy on Twitter tweets and set a precedent many politicians around the world were following. She had tried to make a decision about whether that was good or bad, but she failed. *Brave new world!*

"You can forget about any connection. This is related to something else." She told them a bit about the painting and the parchment without mentioning specifics.

"Almost sounds like a case for MI6," said the first officer while looking at the second.

"MI6 knows nothing about art," she said. "They'd most likely think Florence was some Russian spy-lady's code name. You'd best be checking departures. My attacker might be leaving England at this very moment."

"We will do so. Should we take you home, ma'am?"

"This is my home, gentlemen. My flat's upstairs. Reggie here," the building's resident Lothario bowed, "is my upstairs neighbor."

"And your full name, sir?"

"Reginald Fox, at your service. I found Esther in quite a fix."

"Someone else would have come along." She waved the officers away. "Go do something useful, like finding my assailant. My description was excellent."

"It might be useful for you to go through some Interpol files. He could be known internationally."

"I doubt it. I'm sorry I couldn't take his picture with my mobile. You'll have to work with what you have."

"We'll get right to it. Don't worry. We'll sort this out."

"I won't be holding my breath waiting for progress."

Now I am sounding like an old retiree from the Metropolitan Police. Maybe I should show some patience. Maybe I was like him when I started?

*****

Reggie invited Esther to his flat, which was just above hers. He offered her some sherry. After handing her a glass, he grinned. "Do you want me to check for bruises?"

"There you go, being the lecherous cad as always. There's no place in my life for a misogynist."

"I'm only an incurable romantic, Esther. You hurt my feelings. I did you a favor, you know."

"I suppose so, but don't let it go to your head. All I can say is thank you and leave it at that. My, this is good sherry!"

"Only the best. Lustau Amontillado. I import it."

"Bah! I can buy it three blocks from here, but not often because of the tariffs. How can you afford it on a professor's salary?"

"The same way you can afford your Jaguar. My parents had a bit of money, and I was their only heir. Maybe they weren't as well off as your banker-count, but I really don't have to work."

"And I plan to spend it all before they box me up, Reggie. Besides, I'm too old to have heirs—at least biological ones."

"You're still a good-looking woman, Esther."

"Yes, Bastiann thinks so. Whether it affects your wagers or not, I just might marry the old boy."

"Lucky man. Can I get you anything else?"

"No, I should go downstairs. I now have to change my airline reservations and revise my luggage. That little toad made me miss my flight, but I won't miss another one."

"Going on a trip?"

"To Turkey, if you must know."

"There are much better places to visit. It's not safe there. And what about your gallery?"

"Langston or his wife will be checking-in on the girls." She gave him her last extra key to her flat. Bastiann had the other one. "A first, so don't abuse my trust. If I receive any packages, please put them inside. Also the post."

"I'm honored. I promise not to snoop."

"You better not. I can access my video surveillance on my mobile. Unfortunately, that darling little monster caught me at the lift after the door shut. Otherwise we'd have video of him."

Son of Thunder

Reggie had just left her in her flat when her mobile's ringtone disturbed what calm she had left.

"You better come to the gallery," said Dorothy. "An art thief visited us and wounded Harry."

Can this day get any worse? Esther grabbed her purse and headed for the garage.

Chapter Fifteen

Twenty-First Century, London

At the gallery, Esther met three more officers, two men and one woman. They were a bit more efficient than the ones in the garage. They had already taken the girls' statements. They wanted hers as the owner, as if that mattered. She hadn't been there.

She ignored them for the moment. "Where's Harry?" she asked the girls.

"The ambulance took him," said Dorothy. "He has a knife wound, but the prognosis is good, they said."

"The thief went after Harry with a knife?"

"He went after me with a knife," said Anna. "Harry jumped between us to protect me."

"What a gallant fellow. A true knight in shining armor." *Should I go see him?* She knew he could be in bad shape despite the EMT's prognosis. *I'll give his wife a ring.* "What did the thief steal?"

"Two expensive religious works we had on consignment from that estate collection," said Dorothy.

"They'll be insured if the insurance policy doesn't have some special clause to the contrary. The owner is dead, of course. That's the problem with advertising valuable artwork."

"We only have a newsletter," said Anna.

"Apparently that's enough," said Esther. She turned to the policewoman. "I can't add much more information. I can make suggestions. I know some people in the black market. They should be your first persons of interest. And anyone who receives our newsletter is also a suspect."

The woman looked suspicious. "How do you know those first people, ma'am?"

Esther laughed. "I outranked you in Scotland Yard. Art and Antiques Division."

"You're *that* Esther Brookstone?" said one of her colleagues in a Cockney accent.

Esther rolled her eyes. *A'lo, Mr. Doolittle!* "I take umbrage with your 'that.' But yes, I've had my fifteen minutes of fame, as that crazy American painter described it, and a bit more." She turned to the woman again. "I can make a list. I can't do any more than that, as much as I'd love to do so, but please make sure Langston gives the case to someone who is competent."

The third policeman, who had been consulting his mobile, approached the group. "Inspector Brookstone, do you think this is at all related to your previous kidnapping?"

"I'd be surprised. Let Langston worry about such details." She glanced from one cop to the other. "Are we through here?"

They all nodded. *Just like those little dolls you see on auto dashboards.*

*****

Another irritating event occurred before Esther could leave the gallery. She was tidying up a bit in the rear of the gallery after the Metropolitan Police left when Dorothy interrupted her.

"There's a newspaper fellow who wants to talk to you," she said.

Esther believed in free press, but she had her share of annoying interviews after the Rembrandt painting case. She sighed and handed the broom to Dorothy. "I can't find the bloody dust pan, so I'll tend to him. If you can find it, scoop up that bit of debris, please."

The reporter met her, hand stretched out. "G'day, Mrs. Brookstone. I am Jeremy Faulk. I'm a freelance reporter, and I'd like to have a word with you."

She stared at his hand for a moment and then decided to shake it. "I'm afraid I'm not in the mood. Freelance reporter? Do you write something and then sell it to the highest bidder?"

He smiled. "Sometimes. Other times I'm on a temporary assignment with a contract."

"And which is it now?"

"The latter. *The Guardian* is interested in a follow-up on you. They want to learn more about you as a person, and not only about what you did for the nation."

"And you show up because I was kidnapped, I suppose. Or are you reacting already to this incident where my gallery was robbed? In either case, how does either event relate to studying me as a person?"

"These incidents make the person more interesting. Truth be told, I'd only heard about the kidnapping and thought it was a good time to pay you a visit. However, we can schedule an interview at a more convenient time."

He was reacting to her scowl. "Can you read police reports, Mr. Faulk?"

He fidgeted. "Yes, I can."

"Good. Go read about what happened and report on it. Forget about mentioning me. I've managed to preserve my privacy even with that previous case and everyone on the internet screaming about it electronically. I've always been a private person. All my life I've chosen activities that allow me to achieve that."

"The public has a right to know about its heroes," said the reporter.

Esther bristled. "No, they don't. Have a good day, Mr. Faulk. Toddle off and do your homework. If you're such a good writer, I'm sure you'll find something to write about. Hopefully not about me."

*****

When he rang that evening, Esther debated whether to tell Bastiann about her little escapades, particularly the one with the malevolent Toscano. She eventually developed enough courage to do so. After all, there was some good news among the bad. Harry was going to be fine, although he would be in the hospital a bit longer than expected.

Bastiann ignored the gallery heist and focused on her upcoming trip. "I forbid you to go to Turkey," he said.

"Oh, please. The little incident with Bruno makes me all the more curious. Besides, I want to apprehend that evil little man. I'm sure he'll end up there if he has any brains at all. He said his priestly relative, Leonardo, was a contemporary of Sandro Botticelli. That means: one, the parchment is authentic, if only in the sense that his relative owned it; two, it could predate the fifteenth century; and three, Botticelli could have traveled to ancient Turkey with this Leonardo following the parchment's directions, although I don't think that's likely."

"If they made that trip, why was the parchment found with the painting in the armoire then? Wouldn't they have taken it with them?"

"They could have had a scribe make a copy, or they could have put it back in its original place when they returned. Don't become lost in details, dear Bastiann. You're just trying to discourage me from going!"

"I'm also curious, but I'd prefer to be the one going. And this Bruno is dangerous. I suppose he used chloroform. Administered improperly, that can have adverse effects, even death. I worry about you. Say, I wonder if he was the man tailing me in Trieste?"

"Before your arrival in Vienna?" She remembered Bastiann mentioning a man tailing him. "How would he connect me to you?"

"You said he received information from some servant in Moretti's staff. Perhaps Moretti mentioned to his wife I was going to meet you in Vienna and the servant overheard. By the way, it's likely Bruno was the other bidder for the armoire."

"He admitted as much. The little toad knew more than I gave him credit for. I wonder if he found a good translator yet. The text on the parchment is complicated since the words are written in calligraphy, but Oscar Willoughby did a fine job. Bruno isn't privy to the professor's excellent translation."

"What city are you flying to?"

"Ankara. I'll then take the train to a town near Ephesus."

"Bon voyage, then. I still object to you going, but I'm well acquainted with your stubborn streak. Just be safe."

Part Two

The Investigation

"Howbeit when he, the Spirit of truth is come, he will guide you to all truth: for he shall not speak of himself; but whatsoever he shall hear, that shall he speak: and he will shew you things to come."—John 16:13

Chapter Sixteen

Fifteenth Century, Florence

Sandro Botticelli sipped his wine and studied his old friend. "Leo, among all those people who dwell on Via Borgo Ognissanti, you might be the weirdest. How did you manage to fund this trip?"

The bishop was excited, bouncing up and down on his toes, his fat cheeks marking time with the hops as if they were partners in a *tarantella*. That would be a contagious celebration if Sandro did not know the man so well. *He wants to make his mark in history. That's as good of a motivation as any to go on living in these often unsettling times.*

"Medici was convinced by old Vespucci who owed this old priest a favor. I guess you can say there was a bit of political chicanery on my part. Will you go with me, my friend?"

"I am sure neither old Vespucci nor Medici would approve of that. Vespucci knows we are good friends, and he could suspect I deflowered his little Simonetta as gossipers claim, which I did not—God rest her soul. However, Medici would not approve on general principles. He is in a fit and has not spoken to me since our last encounter." Sandro paused to think. *Why not go? It is a way to have a bit of revenge!* "But bravo! Yes, I will join you. My brother can cover for me. He can tell people who come to see me I am ill-disposed, or busy on an elaborate project. I have not used the last excuse enough. A vacation with all expenses paid by two men who dislike me? I rather favor the concept!"

"It will not be a picnic in the countryside," said the bishop. "It is a long journey and we will be traveling to troubled lands. There they pay no attention to our powerful city-states, with the possible exception being the Vatican. And some heathens are still fighting the Crusades wanting to murder all Christians."

"Are you already making excuses for our failure? Deep down you have to admit that most likely will happen, by the way. We are fools to embark on such a journey."

"You are a pessimist. I am merely saying it is not like an outing to the alpine foothills or the lakes. The rest of the world is mostly uncivilized. For example, I will go incognito on the trip. Priests are often targets in foreign lands."

"It is hard to be an optimist. And I am not being pessimistic, only realistic. The trip will likely be a waste of time as far as finding the saint's tomb goes." Sandro shrugged. "But it will be relaxing for me, and a bit of an adventure. No one need ever know about my participation."

Leo grinned. "I will treat that as a confession. Be assured my lips are sealed about your joining in the endeavor. I will not even mention you in my journal."

"Oh, you can do that. I am sure no one will ever bother to read it."

"I will do so then. And someone might read it if I become famous." He raised his wine glass. "I will need some days to arrange things."

"*Questo vale anche per me,*" Sandro said, acknowledging he would also need some days to prepare, suspecting his arrangements for the trip would be a little bit more complicated than Leo's. He raised his own glass. "To Ephesus and St. John the Divine!"

*****

The journey to Ephesus took Sandro and Leo several months. The priest tried to stay within budget by combining both land and sea travel. He had never been on a boat before, so he spent most of the sea journeys indisposed. The remainder of the time he spent complaining, his good humor left behind with his pampered life at his church in Florence. By the time the pair arrived in Ephesus and stood in front of the ruins of the Basilica of St. John, he had lost about twenty-five pounds, which did not look good on his face with all the loose skin.

Sandro, on the other hand, was enjoying himself, as he had thought he would. He relished seeing new lands and meeting new people. The variety of wines and foods he consumed during the voyage had also been a pleasant adventure. He often left Leo in his misery to party with local women and men while they waited for transportation. Most people he encountered had never heard of him, but drawing a pretty face was often the shortest ticket into a willing partner's bed.

"If the parchment is correct, this Basilica cannot be the burial place," he said to Leo. "I heard it was modeled after the Church of the Holy Apostles in Constantinople."

His friend grabbed his ample stomach and groaned. "Ottomans destroyed that to make a mosque. It almost seems Muslims are bent on destroying Christianity. And Jews never recognized the Messiah."

"Hmm. I do not know about all of that. I have respect for all those groups and their moral teachings, not that I do not waver from time to time. Is it considered blasphemous to say that the Jewish, Christian, and Muslim faiths form a logical chain of development?"

"It is. Christianity is the only true religion. Be careful with what you say."

"I think there are more Muslims around than Christians, so I can offer you the same advice, Bishop Leonardo." Sandro smiled as his friend grabbed his stomach again. He patted him on the back. "Is it the food or the travel by sea?"

"How should I know? Let us continue our business here."

"I suppose we should, but we are probably wasting our time and ruining a good outing. For all we know, your saint became food for worms long ago and is no longer materially here."

"Are you saying men are manure?"

"More like earth, my friend. I am not sure worms touch manure. Mostly grubs and maggots, I would imagine. Not much difference, I suppose, but men are not worm food when they are alive, yet they make a lot of manure. A man with an average lifespan defecates over 18,000 times before he dies. Although, in your case, the count can be much higher."

"You are impossibly gross and morbid."

"Tell that to da Vinci. He liked to draw and paint cadavers who never received a proper burial."

"Again, be careful with what you say. All children of God are blessed. You will need several visits to my confessional when we return."

"Fortunately, all of my sins can be forgiven. You are biased because of your profession, old friend, but let's not argue about theological details. Back to the crux of the matter. The Basilica was built long after John passed on. Ergo, the saint's not here and he never was."

Leo ignored Sandro's logical discourse as he often did. He was already consulting what had been written on the parchment. He had left the original document in his armoire with Sandro's painting. They were working off a copy.

"It is a map in words. It would help if we had a true map." He rolled up the document. "We are not sure the landmarks mentioned on the parchment are still around. The topography can change with the silting of a river or an erosion of a hill. From what I've read, the port was much better in ancient times. And quite busy."

"Indeed. Greeks and Romans of that period depended upon ships. The control of their conquered lands relied on their armadas carrying their armies." Sandro realized what they had just passed. "Instead of trying to figure out what the man who wrote the document was talking about or whether he even knew north from south and east from west, here's a practical suggestion. We passed an establishment that caters to pilgrims of all faiths. Maybe someone will recognize the landmarks mentioned in the document. At the same time, we can have some food and drink."

Leo turned green at the thought of food. "They will not know Latin."

Sandro considered his friend's objection. "But they could know Greek. All of Greece belongs to the Ottomans. The sailors who brought us here were Greek. I know enough to get by, and I have been improving a bit along the way, so I can translate for them. You have to be a polyglot to travel these days."

Friend Leo's language skills are limited. He will have to depend on mine. That's an advantage.

*****

"Yes, there are many ruins in the area," the old man said. "And more in the hills."

They had found him napping with his head on one of the small tables, the only person in a rustic inn that survived on the few pilgrims who visited the area. He was the owner. When they woke him, they offered to pay him for wine, food, and information.

He joined them, sipping on some wine they paid for, and studying the two strangers. Sandro did all the talking, although he spoke Greek with a peculiar accent. The old man focused his attention on him.

"Let me say you are wasting your time, though. Everyone knows the saint is buried beneath the Basilica." He took another sip. "It is a miracle the Ottomans did not finish the job of destroying it."

"Are you Christian?" asked Sandro.

He put an index finger to his lips and peered around as if expecting to see Ottoman spies. "Enough people here are Christians, but we are in the minority. Legend has it, St. John baptized many while he was here. It is said that happened a long time ago when he was here with the Virgin Mary for a while, writing his gospel. It is also said the other Mary helped him."

Sandro assumed the "other Mary" was the Magdalene. He translated a bit for Leo and then interrupted himself. "That's all legend. Is any of it true?"

The man shrugged. "You mean writing the gospel here?" When Sandro answered with a nod, the old man shrugged again. "He had to write it somewhere."

"And Mary Magdalene? Did she team up with John?"

"Who knows if she was even here? I think everyone gets the two Mary's confused, if you ask me."

"And the Church says a lot about them that is questionable. I have heard Christ and the Magdalene were lovers, or possibly married."

Leo understood that, surprising both Sandro and the old man. "Sandro!" Leo said.

Sandro switched to Florentine Italian. "It is true. I mean, that I have heard that. It seems to be a popular belief. Who knows what is true and what is legend? But I have also heard there were many more gospels than four. What were they trying to hide, Leo?"

"I have always questioned your faith," the priest said.

"Oh, please. My faith is solid. Too many details have changed over the centuries, maybe for the convenience of powerful men. You only have to consider some popes we have had. The parchment could be another example of that fakery and deceit."

The old man, who had seemed lost in his thoughts as the two travelers argued, continued his tale when there was a pause. "I have heard many different stories," said the old man, unknowingly agreeing with Sandro and receiving a stern look from Leo. "Let me point out you can only confirm or deny what your parchment says by finding the saint's bones. Not an easy task, for sure."

"If they are truly under the Basilica, it is an impossible one," said Sandro. "They could arrest us for digging around." He again translated for Leo.

"I should hope so," said Leo. "It is all heresy."

"So, you have been wasting my time all along?" said Sandro with a grin.

"No. I do not know. Maybe I want to prove the parchment wrong. If the saint's bones are not in some ruins, they must be beneath the Basilica. End of story."

"That's a specious argument. They can be on Patmos or somewhere else where John traveled. Or in some ancient and ravenous beast's den all gnawed with the marrow sucked out. Maybe the Magdalene was only a traveling companion and here with him. It is all undecided in my mind. And finding the truth is likely irrelevant. We have his gospel."

"And his Book of Revelation," said Leo.

"The prattling of a drugged, psychotic person, to my way of thinking. Four wild horsemen, indeed. It is all symbolism, only smoke and mirrors for the ignorant."

Leo seemed to shrink. "So you think the saint was a psychotic person?"

"It is possible. The saint's gospel and the Book of Revelation are as different as night and day. The first preaches God's love; the second returns to that vengeful God of the Old Testament. Guess which God I prefer."

"You are no expert on theology," said Leo.

It was Sandro's turn to shrug. "I am also not an ignoramus. But come. Let's find those ruins in the hills. They sound more promising and match the parchment's description." He asked the old man for directions.

"Follow the river," he said. "On your journey, you might want to stop at the House of the Virgin Mary. Most pilgrims go there to visit."

Mary's House, thought Sandro, remembering the parchment's text.

"I have heard of that," said Leo after Sandro translated. "That will be our first destination. If we find nothing else, that shrine will make our journey worthwhile."

"Maybe for you," said Sandro. "I have already had some fun. Now I am becoming bored."

Chapter Seventeen

First Century, Rome

John met the Magdalene once again, this time in a villa a bit south of Rome. After pleasant greetings, hugs, and promises to tell each other about their adventures, she introduced him to the group there. *A secret meeting? Is Mary scheming?*

Among that group was the villa's owner, a thin man with sunken eyes who spoke in a deep voice. He was dressed like one of the Roman elites, so John was suspicious. He tried to avoid stereotypes, but it was rare that a patrician worked with Christians. Yet Mary had been rich and made great sacrifices to further spread the good word. John reserved judgement.

"We are putting Claudius in danger by meeting here, but he insisted," said Mary. "The Romans have fear in their bellies now."

"They see us as a threat," said the Roman patrician. "And rightly so. Christ's army is stronger than twenty legions of Roman soldiers."

"That's a bit of exaggeration," said John. "Or thoughts from a wild imagination. The Romans cannot fear us too much because we are disorganized. We must organize and resist. It is the only way."

"That's the purpose of this meeting," said the Magdalene. "We need to organize and prioritize our activities and even decide what those might be."

"There are some tactics I would like to try," said the patrician. "The more we can get the word out to people about how brutal the action of the Roman Empire is toward Christians, the better off we will be. The common citizen of Rome is far more fair-minded than the upper classes are. But they will not pay attention if they do not know what is going on. They must know the truth."

John liked the idea. *Who is this Claudius?* "Will not people consider it idle gossip started by rebel Christians?"

"If enough sources say the same thing, they will begin to understand it as the truth. Assuming no one proves it is false, which they cannot. Christ's message can never be proven false. We all believe that."

"We can also embarrass some of the upper class," said another participant in the meeting. "Servants see their lords and ladies perform all sorts of peccadillos. The common citizen or slave takes note when those situations are happening. When they hear those true stories from multiple sources, it will show what swine Roman elites are, present company excepted."

Mary's silence told John she was thinking. "About the organization," she said. "It should be based on small groups, maybe ten or so, with each member the leader of a group ranked below them. Like a ladder that always leads to a small group like this one. The Romans can only capture, at most, one group at a time."

"I do not understand," said the patrician.

"Each newly created group's leader should have only one vertical contact, no horizontal contacts, and onward up, like a ladder. That provides protection and strength for all groups, yet still facilitates communication."

John thought a bit. "I like it. It is an effective chain of command. It can be secret and strong at the same time. A clever and more intimate extension of the legions and centuries idea. Multiple levels, all working to spread Christ's word."

"And I can imagine other immediate work for those groups," said Claudius.

"What's that?" said John, immediately suspicious.

"The government's weak point is its dependence on soldiers to enforce their will, most of whom are not satisfied with their lot. If their rations and weapons start disappearing, that weak point becomes weaker, and we, my friends, become stronger."

"That's a good start," said John, now becoming emotionally involved yet still feeling uneasy. "We need more ideas like that. Through organization we can resist."

"And convert," said Claudius. "New conversions can form more of Mary's groups. It could take years, but our numbers will grow. We will bring the mighty Roman Empire to its knees and create the Kingdom of God here on Earth."

John was startled by the statement. Claudius talked like ex-military. *Maybe we need someone like him! And Mary to feed him good ideas!*

*****

After his guests were gone, Claudius relaxed and enjoyed the view across the valley to the rolling green hills he loved so much. He sipped his wine and thought, *Success comes so slowly, my Lord.* He had been so enthusiastic when he was converted and baptized. *Did becoming an old man kill my enthusiasm?* Neither Mary nor John were young, but he saw their zeal. *What was it like to have been there?*

He could not remember the details of his baptism. They had all queued up and waded into the water. He remembered being afraid, and the water had washed away that fear. *So long ago.*

Mary told him how she gave up all of her riches to finance His work. He decided not to go to that extreme, figuring he could work from inside the groups of elites and also offer a hospice and meeting place when needed by other Christians. *Is that a sin? Should I give all my riches to the movement and become an ascetic hermit? Go live in the wild and pray all my waking hours? Or should I do what John plans to do? Go and preach the gospel where I can?*

He would have to journey into Rome sometime during the next few days to see what was going on with the emperor. He knew Domitian was not like most Roman emperors. In a way, he admired the man. Their present emperor often rose above the intrigues of the capital to take the bigger view to preserve the Roman hegemony. He was also less of a despot and not a madman like Nero had been. But Domitian still worshipped the pagan gods! Or pretended to do so, at least.

The emperor's rise to power had been haphazard, as it often was. But that was the political world. Claudius did not much care for that anymore. However, he knew there had to be a better way than being governed by emperors with absolute power. Perhaps their movement would lead to the positive result of men being governed by wise, God-fearing philosopher kings like Plato had imagined. Maybe locally a prince who was also the Bishop of Rome, unlike Peter, who had never had any real power beyond his faith.

Claudius was old now, so he knew he would not live long enough to see these worldly changes. His eyes were already focusing on another kingdom, the Kingdom of God in the hereafter. Helping Christian rebels only sharpened that focus.

He liked Mary's ideas. He did not know much about this woman, but she had earned his respect. She and John were a good team and complemented each other. He hoped they would stick around and contribute to the resistance in Rome. Considering their missionary proclivities, he doubted that would happen. *Do they not know Rome is the key? If we can convince one emperor to embrace Christianity, our lives would be much easier.*

*****

Flavius, the ex-slave, put his index finger to his lips to quiet his companions and then peered around the tree trunk, taking stock of the situation. In the dark hour before dawn, there were few guards posted to protect the garrison and its supplies, and most of them were drowsy. That implied an arrogance among soldiers and their leaders. Who would dare attack them? After all, they were in the seat of the empire!

His only weapon was a short sword. He studied his men and grimaced. They were only lightly armed too. Except for their lack of weapons and armor, they could pass for the lowliest Roman soldiers. Even gladiators in the circus were better equipped. The word had come down the command ladder to attack the garrison. Like in their other missions, his group would move fast and attack like a swarm of biting flies. Strike in a flash! Be gone in a flash!

That tactic seemed to be working. His group only had one wounded so far, a portly rebel who had twisted his ankle when he fell trying to keep pace with the others. It had taken Flavius and three others to drag the wounded man away, but Brother Marcus lived to fight another day in the care of his sister.

Flavius motivated his men. “Most soldiers have fallen asleep in a drunken stupor,” he said in a whisper. “We can release the horses and set fire to the grain without their interference.”

“What about the guards?” asked one companion. “Even if they are asleep, some can awake.”

“Kill them!” said another. The Christian next to the man covered his mouth.

Flavius almost throttled him for raising his voice. “No. We can never do that, but we can render them unconscious. Before we torch the grain, we should also sound a warning. I do not want anyone to die in the fire. In the morning, we will start the propaganda campaign. ‘See how Christians can beat you but not kill you. Join with them.’ Or something like that. Even women and children can help spread that message.” He glanced around the little group. “Are we all clear on tactics?”

They all agreed. He knew they were eager to strike. He just hoped they remained focused and did not let their tempers get the best of them.

The group split into two. Flavius and a few others went after the grain. Their enemy had even provided some sconces. They took the torches they contained to set the sheaves of grain ablaze. Soon the fire self-propagated, so they fled.

Flavius heard loud slaps and the snorts and neighs of the horses. Step two was done.

In five minutes, it was all over. Flavius stayed behind a moment to watch the soldiers attempt to put out the flames. Others had run after the horses. He saw one horse running in his direction, probably crazed by the flames and flying sparks he had just passed. Flavius stepped in front of it and waved his arms. It came to a halt and pawed the ground. *Claudius did not say we cannot steal a horse!* Flavius would have to berate those in the organization who had violated that chain of secrecy, but he would have suspected Claudius even without that. He knew the man and admired him.

"Good boy. How would you like to work to spread Christ's word?"

The horse snorted, but it was calmer. Flavius approached it and jumped on its back. He rode off into the night, the horse at a gallop, horse and rider as one.

*****

The next day, two patricians met at a bathhouse.

"There was another attack," one patrician said to another.

The second man agreed. "I heard. A little bit here, a little bit there. These Christians are becoming a major nuisance. We need to make examples of more of them. How dare they go against the might of the empire?"

"They are like the Huns. You kill one and ten take his place."

"Perhaps if we stopped the killing? Their violence seems tame in comparison to ours."

"You better not let Emperor Domitian hear your apologies for these Christian fanatics."

"I thought you said they were Huns." The man laughed and splashed a bit of water at his companion.

"The situation ceases to be comical. This rabble is a threat to the empire."

"So are these bathhouses if we stay too long in the water. I am wrinkling."

When they went to dress, their expensive togas had been replaced by simple servant's clothes with a large cross on the back and the iconic fish symbol placed over the heart. Both dropped the scratchy rags in disgust.

"I will flay someone for this!"

"Easy. This could be the work of one of our own slaves, you know."

"None of mine would be this stupid."

"I would not call any Christian stupid. They appear to be quite organized. And let me rephrase what I said: they caught a patrician's wife praying to this Christ the other day. It is not only the rabble, my friend, who follow this supposed Son of God. Domitian has a major problem."

"It is also our problem."

Chapter Eighteen

Twenty-First Century, London

Bruno wanted to have a head start in case Brookstone followed him, but he had to figure out how to go about that. He wasn't a world traveler. He had hardly ventured outside of Florence his entire life. The trips to London, Trieste, and Vienna were his first outside Italy, and they weren't enjoyable tourist trips.

He did know English, though. The strict nuns who ran the orphanage thought their orphans would have a better chance in the competitive European economy if they force-prepared them with the language of international business. Teaching them English, geography, and business skills, like accounting and planning, were supposed to make them ready to be employees of the new and vibrant commerce among European nations.

He couldn't say any of their oppressive lessons had helped him at all. Knowing how to use Excel didn't seem to have any meaning in his life. His life was the antithesis of success, in spite of the nun's preparation. *Until now! Thank you, Leo!* He imagined the smile of approval from his distant relative, Botticelli's priest.

Maybe I should have killed Brookstone? He had never killed anyone, but he wondered what the experience would be like. He liked the old hag in a way, and felt she could have taught him many more things than all the nuns combined. She seemed knowledgeable about the ways of the world; he knew he was a neophyte.

His first problem was to leave London, for he knew she would have authorities on his trail. *The airline tickets are going to max out my credit cards!* His limits weren't large either. *Florence to Vienna to London to Ankara!* The thought of another airplane ride in the claustrophobic confines of coach made him perspire, but there was no way to escape his predicament.

He had asked around and found public transportation to Heathrow. Once there, he purchased his plane ticket, feeling a bit more at ease when it took off and was soon flying over the Channel. He saw airport police eyeing him with suspicion a few times—nerves had caused him to straighten his rumpled tie—but no one had approached him. *Maybe I should return to Vienna and steal the painting from Moretti. It must have belonged to the priest, so it's rightfully mine.*

He decided he could always do that, but the idea of finding valuable Christian relics motivated him to go to Turkey. *I can be famous!* It was a hard choice: fame or wealth. If he were smart about it, he could have both.

He hated Rome, but he had to change planes there. As his next plane soared into the clouds, he thought the stopover could help him since it would make it harder for authorities to follow him. *Now I'll be an international fugitive!*

He smiled. At least that was some kind of fame.

*****

Walther Beck, another participant from the auction, was in the Rome airport as he waited to change planes. Air Italia workers were on strike, so Walther had flown from Florence to Rome on a small carrier to continue on Lufthansa to Munich. *Perhaps this man I'm following is from southern Italy and stayed in Florence for a bit too?* Such coincidences weren't unusual per se, but he had been reading *The Times* and the story about Brookstone's kidnapping. Upon spying the loser of the bidding for the armoire, it occurred to him that he fit the description of her attacker. *So his name is Bruno Toscano.*

Walther studied the nervous man for ten minutes as he paced in the cafeteria, glancing every once and while at the departures display. Walther's own trip had been a bust, so far. He developed a hunch the Mr. Magoo-like Italian was on to something big. He seemed obsessed. Walther decided to follow him and take the same flight if he could.

They were already within the secure area, so when the flight's departure time and gate were announced, he followed Bruno to his gate. *Ankara? That's unusual. Maybe there are relics to be had there after all. Christian, Jewish, or Muslim, who cares?* At the very least, he could scout around for some relics in that area of the world to find something that would justify his activity. He bought a ticket on standby.

Bruno must have learned something from that woman Brookstone. Walther couldn't make the connection to the armoire. *Maybe there is none?*

He looked at his watch. *Loading time!* He had spent some time in Ankara. He knew the city, and he didn't have to return to Munich for two weeks. *Maybe I'll find something in Turkey that will please the fat members of the museum's board.*

*****

"You're not too chatty today," Denise said to her brother. "*Comme un mime.*" She used the French for "like a mime artist" just to bother him.

Gerald shoved *The Guardian* toward her, an article circled in red. "She does get around, the old girl."

After studying the article, she looked at her brother. "This is the same person, I take it."

"The famous Esther Brookstone, who turned me down cold."

"The article says her attacker was after information contained in an old document. What document?"

"I'd like to find out. As you may recall, our proposed documentary would have been about her obsession with recovering a Rembrandt that led to other trouble. Maybe she's obsessed with something else? I find that interesting."

"Something described on an old parchment? Knowing these kind of people, I bet there's money to be had. She likely wants to recover something and sell it at her bloody gallery."

"What 'kind of people' are you talking about?" Gerald used his index fingers to put her phrase in quotes.

"People with too much money. One-percenters who steal from poor blokes like us. Reverse Robin Hoods."

"You have a twisted view of economics. In the preliminary study for the documentary, I learned Brookstone isn't rich. She's well enough off, I suppose, but not a one-percenter."

"Didn't you visit her at her Scottish castle? Not many people have a castle."

"She inherited it and the place was a rubbish tip." He took a sip of ale and studied her. "Still, you might have a point. I don't have the time, but I can finance travel for you. How would you like to become an investigative reporter? I can't imagine that waitress job pays much, and I doubt your art is selling."

He was expecting a rejoinder, but she must have decided to ignore what he said. "You mean, follow her to see what she's about? What makes you think I have the time?"

"Only what I said, Denise. You're what some people call a free spirit."

"Sure, rub it in. They sent you to school, not me."

"You couldn't pass the exams and flunked out of trade school. You only have yourself to blame."

Again, a frown, and again she appeared to ignore what he had said. "Will I have a per diem?"

"I am surprised you know what that is. I said I would finance travel for you. That doesn't mean you have to travel like a member of the royal family, you know."

"Wouldn't want to do so. They are leeches who haven't done an honest day's work in their lives." She thought a moment before continuing. "All right. What do I do?"

"Tail Brookstone, especially if she leaves London. Keep me informed. Hell, maybe she'll slip up and do something we can blackmail her with, so I can make that bloody documentary. The bosses didn't approve of my failure, damn them!"

"Blackmail is a bit scurrilous, isn't it?"

He put his finger on *The Guardian*. "Better than them stealing my story, I dare say."

Chapter Nineteen

Twenty-First Century, London

Anna French had received permission from Esther to go home early. *She must have sensed I needed some recovery time!* The image of that bearded and bald man coming at her with a knife was still fresh in her mind. *Poor Harry!*

She had never paid much attention to the handyman. He was a pleasant and quiet man who did his job well. *Who knew he had such courage?* She decided she had learned a valuable lesson: bravery can be found anywhere. She shouldn't take anyone for granted.

By the time she entered her flat, she knew what she needed—some Baroque music, a good soak in the tub, and some glasses of a nice wine. Her personal assistant, a luxury she recently purchased, took care of the first two items. It prepared the bath water to the precise temperature and started one of her many music playlists. She took care of the last need, uncorking an Italian red and pouring a glass, saving the remainder of the bottle for dinner.

She slid into the water and sighed. *What would I ever do if I only had a shower?* Her peace was interrupted when she spilled the wine. She stopped breathing and watched it spread through the bathwater, reminiscent of...*Lordy, I have to pay Harry a visit at the hospital!* She gasped for air and jumped from the tub, dripping water but still drowning in the image of what might have been.

*****

Anna went to the hospital early the next morning. They wouldn't let her see Harry; he was still sleeping. She would have to return after work. She headed for the tube station. The sidewalk was chockablock with Londoners going every which way to earn some kind of living. The hour was late, so everyone was in a hurry.

Among the masses she spotted the art thief, Harry's assailant. *What should I do?* Inspiration came to her from her employer. She knew Esther would follow him.

It wasn't that much of a coincidence because he was headed in the opposite direction from hers. *Maybe he was scouting other galleries?* He boarded a train heading away from her destination, Esther's gallery. She boarded the same train in the car behind him. As stops became farther apart, she knew she was in uncharted territory for her. A more residential, but poor section of the city. *I must not let him see me!*

When the thief left the train, she followed him at a distance to what seemed like an inexpensive boarding house or hotel for business travelers. As people were leaving the building in a hurry, late for work, the thief entered it.

She found a small cafeteria a half-block away, bought a cup of coffee, and rang the gallery.

"Mrs. Langston's here," Dorothy said. "Where are you? You're late."

"I've found him!"

"Who?"

Anna explained. Mrs. Langston took the phone, and Anna had to explain again. "You're putting yourself in danger, dear. Do *not,* and I repeat, do *not,* confront that thief. You know how dangerous he is! I'll ring George. Stay right where you are, unless the thief decides to buy coffee too. Do you understand?"

"Yes, ma'am. I'll wait for the police."

*****

George Langston's phone rang. He noticed the "No Video" message and that it wasn't an internal call. There were few people who knew that number. One was his wife; the others would be agents from his division who were in the field. *Or Esther?*

In any case, he needed to answer. He hit the "Accept" button. It was his wife phoning him from her mobile.

"I'm at Esther's gallery. Anna phoned. She spotted the art thief in the tube station and followed him."

He noted how calm his wife was. *Like the Rock of Gibraltar.*

"Where is she now?"

She gave her husband the address along with the nearest principal streets. "She's in a cafeteria down the block. She seemed to be one scared young lady."

"She should be. Bravo for her, but that wasn't a smart thing to do."

"What's done is done on her part. What are you going to do about it?"

"I'll send somebody right there. I'll let you know what we find."

He disconnected and dialed an internal extension. DCI Owen Scott answered. "Do me a favor, old boy." Langston explained the situation.

"I'll grab a few bobbies and head right over."

"Be careful. That thug already put one good man in the hospital. Keep me informed."

After he hung up, George was wondering if Esther had ever expected the Langstons to become so involved in her gallery's business. He'd have to congratulate his wife for remaining so calm.

*****

Three hours later Langston informed his wife Anna was okay, but the art thief had scarpered. Although not all was lost. They now knew who he was, thanks to Anna's quick thinking and good eyes.

Considering the small inn's owners said he had a Russian passport and spoke the language, Langston sent out alerts to all points of departure from Britain. He was afraid they would be too late, like they were with Esther's kidnapper, and the thief had already left the country. Not even a Russian passport would have made authorities suspicious. And MI5 only cared about Russians arriving in the country, not departing.

Langston had never met anyone from MI5 or MI6, unless he counted Esther for the last organization. Some people heard the M and I and laughed, but he knew some military blokes who were quite intelligent, not that the agencies were all military now, he guessed. Politicians were often much worse.

He knew that during the war the British War Office had MI numbers as high as 19. Most were collapsed into MI5 and MI6, but there were conspiracy theorists who believed there still existed an MI7 specializing in extraterrestrials. *What Esther discovered about those neo-Nazis—now there was a real conspiracy!*

He hoped the old girl would have it easier with her current obsession.

Chapter Twenty

Twenty-First Century, Ankara

After an uneventful flight to the Turkish capital, Esther took a taxi downtown and checked into the Ankara Hilton as planned. She then went shopping. *The country has changed since I was last here.* She knew many Turks approved of their dictator and his ostentatious construction projects designed to show how modern his Third World country was, but they still appeared grim as they went about their business. She also saw more police and soldiers. *They don't make me feel any safer!*

She had been in Madrid once after the fall of Franco—*Devil take his soul!*—and was surprised that many Spaniards missed their dictator. A friend there explained the reason: in Franco's time, if a thief was caught, he'd often disappear, never to be seen again. She couldn't sympathize with such an attitude. Democracy was often a dirty business, particularly in Great Britain's current polarized political state, but the alternatives always seemed worse to her.

She was so intent on her observations and window shopping, she didn't pay much attention to the man talking on his mobile not far behind her. As she passed a narrow alleyway, two other men jumped out and dragged her off the narrow street. *Toscano! He's here!*

They bound her hands and feet, blindfolded her, gagged her, and loaded her into the rear seat of a limo. She thought she was in an old movie she'd seen long ago with Bill Murray as the protagonist reliving a portion of his life over and over. With her restraints, she only lacked the chloroform hangover Toscano had given her.

She reconsidered her initial reaction. *Toscano seemed to work alone.* The auto contained three men, two in the front and one in the backseat with her. *Three odiferous men!* One reeked of garlic, another smelled of sweat and liquor, and the third, next to her, had over-indulged with aftershave lotion. The odors blended together in one odiferous trio that now masked the new leather odor that had told her she was in a limo, or an expensive car.

When the limo arrived at its destination, she heard a massive door open and then slide shut. She was now in a place that reeked of dead fish and...?

Cannabis!

They took her from the car and stood her up, removing both blindfold and gag. She found herself in a dim warehouse. The cavernous space was lit well enough that she could take account of her surroundings at once. She recognized the relaxed man sitting in front of her.

*****

Walther had watched the men kidnap Esther. *Either Bruno is more important than I had imagined him to be, or someone else is after her*. He tried to imagine who that could be. *CIA? MI6? SVR? Turkish secret police?* He thought the first three agencies would have used a black SUV, not a limo. The last could employ an old Russian Zil or British Range

Rover. But the limo in question was a black Mercedes like Putin favored. *Maybe it's her neo-Nazi chaps looking for revenge?*

In any case, he became nervous. As a stranger in a strange land, he felt a bit threatened, even if Brookstone was the victim. Turkey had a reputation for assuming all foreigners were suspect, especially since the coup attempt some years ago that had led to a general crackdown by security agents, still standard policy. He didn't want to become involved in anything like that. *I'm not very tolerant of pain!*

It wasn't like Turkey didn't have tourists. Even with that failed coup and its expected reprisals, the government hadn't been foolish enough to halt tourism from the West. And westerners weren't smart enough to stop visiting Turkey, a country that often treated them badly, including fleecing them for dollars and euros.

Brookstone was no tourist, though. He had learned about the ex-Scotland Yard inspector from Kurt Geiszler, an occasional drinking buddy and German federal police inspector. They had met at the museum once where Walther had helped him search for some old Nazi relics. *Life is full of coincidences!* Munich was where the whole Nazi movement had started. The crazy inspector from Berlin had the curious notion that DNA could be found on some old weapons from that period he could compare to in their DNA database. They hit it off and the chance acquaintance turned into a casual friendship.

He inherited a bit of fondness for the Nazis from his family. Many Austrians had been better Nazis than the Germans. His grandparents were members of the party, but their sons and daughters were never in the youth corps. They were now more Austrian nationalists who wanted nothing to do with any foreigners, even if they spoke the same language.

Walther had avoided that too. His motivations in life were more about greed and comfort, a globalist trend.

His thoughts returned to Esther. *No, something else is afoot here.* He decided to stay out of it. *For now.* He would watch the hotel to see if Brookstone returned. He glanced around, only seeing a nun walking along the sidewalk opposite him. He had seen her before. She examined him like a microbe on a slide, but then looked away. *Odd. She seems out of place here.* He couldn't determine her order from her habit, but, by her gait, he knew she wasn't elderly. *Is she from Munich?* He wrote it off as one tourist examining another in a foreign country.

Between women in burqas and women in habits, the Middle East always managed to put women down and keep men from admiring them. *I guess that's the point.* He wondered why European countries were outlawing Muslim garb and not the garb of nuns. *So much for freedom of religion.*

His thoughts then returned to Toscano. *He's likely far ahead of Brookstone and doesn't even know she's following behind. Ergo, I should follow Toscano and forget about Brookstone.*

*****

No, not Toscano, thought Esther. The cartel leader, Ernesto Felipe Lopez Diaz, was dressed in a smart business suit and fashionable tie. He was the good-looking Colombian she had met in the Amazon jungle of Peru. Well-combed black hair with a bit of silver over the ears and flashing black eyes gave him a dashing look. He also had the ego to match. *Is he going to exact his revenge?* The neo-Nazis had been responsible for the destruction of his processing plant, not her.

"*Buenas tardes, señora.* Written any good articles lately? Where's your photographer?" He was referring to their meeting when Esther and Bastiann's covers had been a journalist and accompanying photographer, respectively. She glared at him. "Please. Let's have a chat as if we were friends only meeting by coincidence so far away from home. After all, you two were only doing your jobs." He raised his brandy sniffer to salute her. "You did it well. Your actions hurt me financially, but that's only a bit of unpleasant history. I'm more worried about the present. Why are you here, Esther? How did you know I was in Ankara?"

"My trip to Turkey has nothing to do with you, Ernesto," she said, "but it does have something to do with art."

"Our other encounter began the same way—something to do with art. That aside, your boyfriend and his pal, Hal Leonard, have interfered with my Afghan friends' right to defend themselves. That affects my bottom line once again, you see, because those friends provide raw product for my processing business. Are you working for Interpol now? Is that why you resigned from the Yard?"

He knows too much about me now! "I have no idea what Bastiann and Hal are up to. No need-to-know either." *Are those two in danger?*

He shrugged. "Maybe you don't know, maybe you do. Why don't you tell me what you're doing here then? Make it convincing." She gave him a summary. He laughed. "You expect me to believe that?" He glanced at his employees. All three laughed in unison as if they were filming an American TV comedy and they were providing a laugh-track. "Never mind. I'll just keep you under wraps to make sure you can't make trouble for me again while I figure out what your scheme is."

She was carried to a small room in the warehouse's corner, placed on the board floor, and locked inside for about two hours.

She had company. Two large rats stared at her, their malevolent red eyes filled with hate. She managed to roll toward them to shoo them back into their holes. *Maybe they're dopers becoming high on opium residue?* She figured it was either Ernesto or his men who filled the warehouse with cannabis smoke. They probably weren't heroin users. *He makes money off of addicts but doesn't use his own hideous product.*

When they came for her, they blindfolded and gagged her once again. The limo took her back to her hotel where Ernesto's men released her. One handed her a note: "*Disculpame, señora.* We confirmed your story about this evil man, Bruno Toscano. Please be careful. Turkey isn't a safe place for westerners right now, and this Toscano could have followed you here or even have arrived ahead of you. By the way, tell your boyfriend to watch his back. I won't tolerate more meddling."

Always the gentleman, she thought as she entered the hotel's kitchen from the alley where they had left her, startling the Hilton's cooks and waiters. *How he gets around!*

And Bastiann is in danger!

Chapter Twenty-One

Twenty-First Century, Ankara to Eskisehir

The next morning, Esther took the hotel's shuttle to Havas Terminal and walked to the train station, thankful her luggage had wheels. She bought a ticket to Eskisehir. That ride was a boring hour and a half trip. She spent much of her time on the train reliving her encounters with Ernesto Lopez. She thought he was a bit like the dashing highwaymen of old, but that romantic image conflicted with her knowledge that he was a vicious killer. *And Bastiann is tangling with him yet again!*

Once in Eskisehir, she purchased a ticket for a sleeping berth and rode to Izmir. That leg of the trip reminded her of the Orient Express and Christie's murder mystery that took place on that train. She still found it amusing she and Bastiann might be channeling Christie's two famous detectives, now solving crimes together. Yet Miss Marple hadn't been on Chrisite's train, only Poirot. *Will my trip also help solve a crime?* It could, if only she made Bruno pay for his attack. *I look forward to arresting him. It would serve him right to rot in a Turkish cell!*

She then wondered about her rage toward Bruno. Searching her memory, she figured it out. *He reminds me of a Stasi agent who once made my life miserable while waiting for another train.* That had occurred on her MI6 mission that just preceded her first meeting with Sergio Moretti. She'd been a novice spy back then...

*****

Esther didn't look at the man directly, but she knew he was there on the train platform with her. Obvious agents didn't worry her as much as undercover ones who were more her nemesis but still. *Stasi! Go away, Devil's spawn!*

He approached her. She felt a bit collywobbles but didn't dare show it. When he stopped in front of her casting his shadow upon her book, she glanced up and saw a man who had cold fish eyes and a pocked face. *Maybe a scar or two?* He seemed like any thug one might encounter in the worst slums of London, something she had been insulated from as a child. He was chewing a toothpick. *At least he doesn't smell of cheap beer and bad sausage!*

"Are you waiting for someone?" he asked with a smile. It was more of a leer that could kill any *fraulein*'s desire for male company.

She put her black bookmark with the gold replica of the East German seal inside the book to save her place—it was a cheap pirated novel but one approved by government censors—and pretended to consider his question.

She answered him in German, a lot more educated than his own. "Thank you for your concern, but I'm waiting for my brother. He's always late, although I suppose I'll have to forgive him this time. We can't do anything about train schedules, can we? That's why I always bring something to read."

The situation in West Germany was different. You could set your watch by the departures and arrivals of trains. Cold

War East Germany was nothing but a Third World country run by thugs.

"Mind if I sit beside you?"

"I'm not in a mood for small talk. I'm furious at my brother. He could have taken an earlier train. He can't ring me. The phones hardly ever work." He frowned. She smiled. She patted the bench next to her. "But if you must, go ahead. Everyone deserves to sit and relax from time to time, even when one's on duty. I'll keep on reading, if you don't mind."

"I never make small talk, *Fraulein*...?"

"Anna Hausmann." She offered a white-gloved hand for him to shake. *At least I'll be protected from his filth!* "*Frau* Anna Hausmann. My brother's name is Hans Richter. And what is your name, *mein Herr*?"

But the Stasi agent seemed to lose interest at the mention she was married. *Respects the marriage vows, does he? How interesting!*

"Would you like to discuss that book?"

"Not particularly. It's from some British writer. Terribly written, I'm afraid. I can't fathom why our censors would approve of such trash."

"You see, we've already discussed it."

"All right. I've given you my review. You haven't offered yours and I would like to leave it that way, if you don't mind."

"Even if I agree with you?"

"Then I shall be sad two readers have suffered through it. I might not even finish it."

The Stasi agent stood and glanced around. "You're quite alone here, *Frau* Hausmann. East Berlin can be dangerous."

Nein, unless Stasi are around. "When the train comes in, there will be plenty of passengers, including my brother."

"I wouldn't worry about the delay. My colleagues and I need extra time these days to check papers. It seems every spy from the West is in East Berlin these days." He grinned, but it was one a vulture might make landing to feast on a dying animal. "I will leave you to your family squabble then. Please go easy on your brother. I'll also be busier when the train arrives, so *guten Abend*."

Yes, watching your subordinates check documents and dogs sniffing under train cars for people who want to ride all the way into West Berlin.

"Guten Abend," said Esther.

She watched him slink off along the platform. He disappeared inside the drab station, a perfect example of the rundown condition of buildings in a country that had gone to hell since the Soviets took over at war's end.

She sighed. She put the book down beside her. Hidden inside the back cover was a garrote, her only personal weapon besides her martial arts skills. She took the package wrapped in butcher's paper from her purse and put it into the refuse bin next to the bench.

When the train arrived, she spotted the man she was waiting for, her pretend-brother. She hooked arms with him.

"I was mad at you, Hans, but there's a man inside the station who annoyed me even more." *Code for 'Stasi! Be careful!'* "You can throw the remains of your lunch in that refuse bin." *'Your package is there.'* "Let me visit the powder room and then you can make up for your tardiness by taking me to a late dinner." That wasn't code, but the other British SIS agent had no intention of taking her to dinner. He would collect the package that contained his gun, silencer, and ammunition and leave for his mission, a critical assassination....

Esther frowned at her old memories. Her time with what most people now called MI6 had been filled with excitement and danger. *But now I'm older. Do I need all that excitement? Wasn't pursuing that Rembrandt the Nazis nicked excitement enough for a whole lifetime?* She wasn't after a lost painting this time. She was pursuing something else. She wasn't quite sure what, but Toscano was making it difficult to prove the whole legend about the saint was a bunch of poppycock!

*****

Esther's journey on the train was like a bit of time travel to the early decades of the 20th century on Agatha Christie's Orient Express. Not so much in the accommodations, but the people on the train seemed to have become stuck in that period. She was no polyglot, so she didn't know most of the languages spoken; however, she met two interesting fellow passengers, one of whom spoke French and the other German, proof of the variety found in human nature.

She knew both languages before she lived in Switzerland, and her time with Alberto Sartini had sharpened her ears and tongue to the languages' nuances. There she'd also learned Italian. She had only taken Latin in school, which provided a useful reference for the romance languages and even a lot of German words that had their roots in Latin. Her father had taught her a bit of Greek and Aramaic. He was the polyglot, but maybe she'd inherited a bit of his skill. He always said, "An educated man can never know too many languages." He had her memorize some of the Book of Esther in Latin. She also read sections of the Song of Solomon on her own.

Although the Church no longer used it in its services, except for some in the Vatican, the French woman, a nun, might know some Latin too. She sat beside Esther in the lounge car and opened a guidebook, which was in French. When she glanced at her, all Esther could see was her face because of the strict habit. Her eyes were interesting. *Eye makeup? Why not?* The only part of her anatomy the world could see was her face, and one's attention focused right on her expressive eyes. Eyeliner below well-plucked eyebrows, perhaps light makeup on the cheeks, and no lipstick. *Plain, but with a nod to modern life.* But the habit was awful. *I could never be a nun!*

Esther estimated she was in her early thirties. A young nun, likely not finished with the seven-year process required to become a new bride of Christ. *On a pilgrimage?*

"Are you also going to the ruins?" asked Esther in French.

"*Oui.* A short pilgrimage, *madame,*" the nun said. *Not Parisian. Maybe from southern France?* "Ephesus played an important role in early Christianity. Are you also on a pilgrimage?"

Esther knew many tourists to the area were interested in its religious history. "I wouldn't call it that. I'm a bit of an agnostic, I'm afraid."

"You don't have to worry, *madame.* I won't proselytize. Although you look familiar."

"My name's Esther Brookstone."

"Sister Denise," said the nun, offering a delicate hand. "Your name's also familiar."

Esther sighed and looked at the ceiling. "I can't lie to a nun. I was a hot item in the media a while ago. Ex-Scotland Yard. I helped bring to justice some neo-Nazis in Germany and some terrorists in London."

"But of course! That must be it. I'll curb my curiosity and simply ask, are you here investigating criminal activity of some kind?"

"Not exactly." *Not a lie, Esther. Truth as far as it goes.* "But that's not important at the moment. What does your guidebook suggest we see when we visit Ephesus?"

"There are many attractions to interest tourists of all kinds, including pilgrims. From what I've seen so far of this country, I'm afraid the tourist hyperbole is often an exaggeration. This guidebook is a bit more honest, which is why I purchased it."

A cynical nun. "If I may ask, what makes a young woman decide to be a nun?"

"In my case, a very religious family. Two brothers are priests and two sisters are nuns. My father belongs to Opus Dei, so he's a lay priest of sorts. Are you familiar with that organization?" Esther said yes. "Obviously I couldn't become a priest, although I'm sure my father would have wanted another one in the family."

No, a woman can't be a priest in your church. When will that change? "But it seems like such a major commitment."

"Yes. It's not to be taken lightly. Fundamentally, it's accepting Jesus Christ as our Lord and Savior and choosing a life of austerity, meditation, and service. I've never had any regrets about making that choice."

Esther furrowed her brow. *Not prayer, but meditation. Is there a difference?* She thought of her detective friend in New York whom she had never met beyond phone calls and text messages. *He owes me a curry dinner!* Castilblanco was born Catholic and became a Buddhist. *Maybe it's all about meditation.* She smiled. *Maybe I should try yoga? But not in one of those dreadful hot yoga shops. I could never meditate and sweat at the same time! Why would any cultured woman subject herself to such torture?*

"I think that's wonderful, my dear. I do have regrets, though."

"I'd say you're cheery enough, even for an English woman. I doubt your regrets are at all that significant."

"Oh, they're significant. At least to me. I've lost three husbands."

"*Mon Dieu!* Not violently, I hope."

"No, not violently, but my current boyfriend is an Interpol agent. The only way he'll die before me is if some criminal takes his life. That's a new conundrum, you see, and it could make marriage to him an impossibility."

"I see." She frowned. "I can't help you there. A priest can't either. Nuns are married to Christ, but it's a spiritual marriage and frankly, priests know nothing about marriage. It's almost comical when they participate or lead pre-Cana."

"I appreciate your candor," said Esther.

"Let's keep it our little secret," said the nun with a mischievous grin.

*****

Esther met the German passenger at dinner. He asked to share her table in the dining car. Since it was a table for four and there were no others available, she decided to give up some of her privacy and invite the affable man to accompany her.

"Are you traveling for business or pleasure, *Frau* Brookstone?" he asked after introductions—his name was Walther Beck—and ordering a light meal. He followed her lead and got the soup and appetizers.

She smiled. "If you want to use *Frau*, it would be *Frau* Sartini. I'm a widow. Esther is fine, though, if I can call you Walther." He grinned and agreed. "Do I detect a bit of Austrian accent in your German?"

There were Swiss-German, Austrian-German, and other variations in the language across the unified Germany and in the business world.

"My birthplace was Salzburg. I'm no fan of Mozart, and I rather fancy Anton Bruckner."

"Lush harmonies and complex structure," she said. "Perhaps the last romantic, although Mahler aficionados might argue with me about that."

"I'm at an age when sitting through one of those long Mahler pieces isn't possible without a trip to the loo. An annoying interruption, but I've listened to some of his creations at home. I love the trombone solo in the third symphony."

Trombone? She couldn't remember, but she hadn't heard much Mahler. "You have me at a disadvantage, *Herr* Beck. I don't have your detailed knowledge of orchestral music, although I do play the piano a bit, thanks to parents who paid for lessons, insisting playing piano was the sign of an educated lady. But back to your question: I'm nearer to traveling for business than traveling for pleasure. I'm an art expert, and I'm trying to prove Botticelli was never in Ephesus."

She didn't mention the painting or the parchment and didn't intend to because they no longer interested her. Her work was done there. She only wanted to prove Bruno's family legend was false. The frosting on the cake would be putting him in jail.

"Why would you possibly think he was?"

"That's a long story. I've become obsessed with art and art history, I'm afraid. I built a whole career at Scotland Yard on that obsession."

He snapped his fingers. "I knew I recognized you, but I didn't think it possible. You worked with *Herr* Geiszler to apprehend those nefarious neo-Nazis. Did that involve art?"

What a coincidence! I wonder how he knows Geiszler. She decided not to pry. Instead, she studied the train car's ceiling for a moment. *When will it stop?* "Yes, it did, but I prefer to say no more." *Ghost of Andy Warhol, it's now more than fifteen minutes of fame! Leave me alone!* "What brings you to the Orient, Walther?"

Her reflections on the inimitable Agatha had caused her to use the word "Orient," but she meant Middle East. That area of the world was still troubled. *Maybe it will always be that way.* Her deceased husband, the count, had business dealings there that never required a visit from him; however, she knew he would have refused to go with the current situation. He often railed against European colonialism and British colonialism, but he wouldn't walk into a maelstrom if he had his druthers.

"Archaeology," said Walther, responding to her question. "The area is loaded with ruins going back many centuries, even before Christ. I work for a museum in Munich now. I fancy myself to be an aging Indiana Jones, but I don't want to get into trouble like he did. And I'm not afraid of snakes like Indy. I have two as pets, in fact. My housekeeper takes care of them while I'm gone on my trips for the museum."

"How curious. I trace the origins of that film franchise back to H. Rider Haggard and his Allan Quatermain stories, adventures that might today be called thrillers."

"Please tell me more about your own adventures. I like to live vicariously through others by hearing about more exciting lives than my own."

She told him a few, but nothing sensitive. She avoided her days at SIS, aka MI6, completely. She didn't mention Bruno Toscano or his relative, Bishop Leo, either. They talked for over an hour after dinner until she lost the battle to fatigue.

Chapter Twenty-Two

Twenty-First Century, Eskehir to Selçuk

The next morning there was no sign of the affable Austrian or the Catholic nun. Esther had breakfast and later stepped off the train in Izmir where she bought a ticket on the Izmir-Denizli train to Selçuk. After another hour and a half ride, she left the train station, and noted the bus station was about six soccer fields away, so she went to find a hotel. During the remainder of the day, she wanted to do a little shopping and exploring the bustling town because the next day she would take one of the mini-buses to Ephesus.

The city wasn't large, but it had its share of petty thieves, the scourge of tourists everywhere. She sensed eyes were following her in various places, but there seemed to be police around too. She sported a purse that hung from a sturdy strap and nestled in her left armpit. That had always sufficed in London, so she became a bit complacent. Yet she sensed the tug at her purse before she saw the small boy. She grabbed him just as he was about to slash the strap.

"You little urchin!"

The boy squirmed in her strong grasp and looked at her with wide eyes. He dropped the small knife. "Sorry, nice lady."

His frightened expression and bulging eyes melted her heart, but she held onto him. She tried English, French, and German; however, he spoke more Italian than any of those. "What's your name?"

"Emir," said the boy, still squirming.

"My name is Esther. Say it."

"Ez-der," he said. "Please. No police."

"No police. But why aren't you in school?"

"No school. Mother sick. Needs food."

"A likely story, I'm sure. Take me to her."

"Okay, nice lady. Let me go."

"Not a chance. I want to meet your mother."

Esther kept one arm in her strong grip as he led her through some back streets. On the way, she spotted some establishments that looked like charity kitchens, but the area appeared seedy and rundown. *Is he leading me into a trap?* She thought not; he seemed to be a nice kid—misguided, but nice.

He led her into a one-room hovel where a woman was lying on a cot. She looked up at Esther and said something in Turkish to the boy.

"My mother asks me what have I done. What should I say?"

"Tell her the truth." Esther couldn't decide if he did, but the mother didn't look too happy. "What ails her?"

"Hunger. I can't steal enough to feed us. She only eats what I have left."

"What about the charity kitchens we passed?"

"I still have to pay there, and they often think I'm alone because my mother never comes with me."

"Tell her I'll solve that problem." After he did, Esther took him by the hand. "Take me back the way we came. I'll have a word with that last charity kitchen we passed."

The lady running the kitchen spoke Turkish and English, but the last language not so well. Esther handed her all the change she had. "This boy is stealing to feed his mother and him. Can you arrange to send food to the mother? She's in a bad way."

The woman finally understood. Esther didn't know if she kept her promise, but there didn't seem to be any other solution. *And now I'm feeling too guilty to do any shopping!*

*****

That night she ate dinner in the hotel instead of returning to one of the fine and quaint restaurants she had spotted where it could possibly be less expensive than the hotel. She finished with some *baklava* that was a bit different from what Greeks made, but still quite good, and went up to her room with the idea of going to bed early, so she could have an early start the next day. Upon entering, she noticed the message light flashing on her phone. The message was from Bastiann: "Call me."

She checked her watch. The time difference was in her favor. Bastiann should be awake. She speed-dialed his number with her mobile.

"You must miss me terribly," she said when he answered.

"I do, but I need to tell you something more than that. Bruno Toscano could be in Turkey too." She half expected that. "He took a plane to Rome and then to Ankara. We know he arrived in Rome. We're not sure he made the flight to Turkey, but he had a ticket. Do be careful, Esther."

"That old bastard won't catch me by surprise again, don't you worry. You must have been talking to the Yard."

"I do have some contacts there, you know. As you might suspect, the Metropolitan Police didn't act fast enough to impede his departure. They gave me the flight information, though. He had purchased the tickets in London. His credit is maxed, so I can't imagine what he's doing now for expenses."

"He could nick some purses or wallets and use the cash or credit cards. There are enough tourists around. You know how tourists are. They might as well walk around with a sign on front and back saying, 'Rob me!'" She couldn't help thinking of her little thief and his mother. *Poverty all too often breeds crime.*

"My point is he could be desperate and all the more dangerous."

"And what do you propose I do? He thinks he's about to find St. John's bones. Maybe some relics."

"Just watch your back, Esther. Fanatics are dangerous, as you well know."

"So is crossing a street in London where you can be hit by a lorry. You might be my knight in shining armor, Sir Lancelot, but this Genevieve knows how to take care of herself. You need to trust me."

"You're being catty. And you know what happened to the cat."

"You're referring to my impetuous curiosity, I suppose."

"Good guess. It leads you to obsessive behavior."

"Pish-tosh. Don't worry. I'll be careful. I plan to spend many more years making you bite your nails."

*****

The next morning at breakfast, the police came for her. Her surprise soon turned to smoldering anger. She wasted a full day being interviewed, fingerprinted—no scanners, but with the old-fashioned, horrible black ink that stuck to your fingertips—and locked up in a cell. She had no idea what the reason was, and the nearest British Consulate was back in

Izmir. The Turkish police didn't speak English, or claimed not to, and they wouldn't allow her an interpreter. She couldn't make them understand she wanted to make a phone call. But by evening they had checked her history.

"Mrs. Brookstone, we are so sorry for the mix-up," said the man in charge at the end of the long day.

The adage "if looks could kill" came to her mind as she glared at him. "Now you speak English. All a show at my expense, I suppose. Can you at least explain the reason for the mix-up?"

"Another tourist here visiting our city registered a complaint that you tried to steal from him. We are now trying to locate him as you can't possibly have done what he said you did."

"I suppose you found out that I'm ex-Scotland Yard."

"That, and how you famously stopped German terrorists from attacking London. You have quite a file with Interpol. All good, I might add." *You don't have the story straight, but sure, flatter me, see what it buys you.* "May I ask what brings you to our country?"

"You can, but I won't answer. I don't have to. In England, I would be consulting a barrister when I leave here."

He shrugged and handed her purse to her. She checked to make sure all her documents, tickets, and mobile were inside. They were, but they weren't in their usual places. That implied they had gone through everything. Luckily, they couldn't have accessed her mobile. Its data was protected with encryption and her password wasn't an easy one to crack.

Maybe I'm being too hard on him. I could need help from the Turkish police in the future. "I wish to explore Ephesus. I used to work for the Art and Antiques Division of the Metropolitan Police. I'm retired now, but I'm still very much interested in art. I own a gallery in London, you see."

"If you're going to the ruins, be forewarned. Many of the most valuable relics in Ephesus were stolen by Austrians," said the cop.

She had already heard that story from Sergio. "Can I ask a question?" He said yes. "Is the tourist who framed me named Bruno Toscano by any chance?"

"Do you know him?"

"He kidnapped me back in London." The man seemed confused. *So, you didn't do enough consulting with Interpol.* "I hope you find him. It seems like he wants to play the swan to my Leda."

"I'm sorry?"

"He's a brutal man who wants to rape me." She said, but she immediately regretted the rape metaphor. Rape was serious business.

"Excuse me?"

"Oh, bother, talk to me when you find a sense of humor. By the way, I'd like to return the favor and press charges against him if that can be done. I assume you work with Interpol and use their databases."

"After talking with you and confirming what you said about the kidnapping, we already have enough to arrest him when we find him."

"Then go do it. Am I free to go?"

"Yes, of course. Again, with my apologies. Let the remainder of your vacation be without encumbrances."

Encumbrances? She frowned. *These Turkish police are idiots! I can't wait for the country to leave NATO! Completely uncivilized!*

She then thought of the little thief and his sick mother again. Her time in a cell was nothing compared to their plight. Abject poverty and sickness were all too common in the world, even in the so-called industrialized and prosperous nations. One person can do so little and governments so much, if they were only motivated to do so. She was often too busy with events in her own life to lament the human condition, but that didn't make society's problems go away.

For some reason, those thoughts put the image of her father in her mind. Of his lecturing at the dinner table about how civilization had progressed so much and how the crown had helped that along. She couldn't remember him ever doing any charity work. Now that she was retired, she decided to look into it. The woman running the charity kitchen seemed to be a good soul, a person she could emulate.

I wonder how Harry is doing.

Chapter Twenty-Three

First Century, Rome

Claudius presided at the leadership group's next secret meeting, which took place at his villa. Many other Christians were now more directly involved in the program to embarrass Rome and convert Roman citizens to Christianity, so John sat beside Mary listening to reports about their activities.

"And now we come to a critical concern," said Claudius when all reports were finished. "Because of our successes, we are in more danger, particularly Mary and John." He gestured toward the pair. "I want to design a contingency plan for their escape from Rome. Hopefully we will not be needing it, but it is better to be prepared. I have learned from two of my fellow patricians that the Emperor wants to cut our organization off at its head and make an example of its leaders."

"How can that be?" said Mary. "Few people know we are here. We have been careful to propagate the rumor that John has returned to Judea, and the misogynist patricians and heads of state would never believe a woman is helping to organize the resistance."

"I am the first to say your organizational skills are excellent, Mary," he stated, as if to say he was not one of those patricians. "And I did not say they knew the composition of this group, yet they seem to have a good idea about how we are organized in spite of our group structure that should prevent that." He glanced around the room. "As you have all heard from the reports, some have been captured. If they were tortured before they were put to death, the Romans could develop a rough idea about how we are organized. That makes it all the more imperative no member of this cohort is captured." He looked toward Mary and John again. "For you, it is essential you do not become martyrs for the cause. For the rest of us," he waved a small cloth bag, "I am providing you with poison you must take if the Romans get too close. Carry it with you at all times. I will do so myself."

"We need one of those bags too," said John. Mary agreed. "Any plan for our escape can go awry. Why should we be so coddled?"

"You are the only direct witnesses to the Crucifixion and the Resurrection I personally know," said Claudius. "Your lives must be preserved. I will provide the poison, but you have a tremendous responsibility to Christians everywhere to stay alive. Do you understand that, my friends?"

John shrugged. "I understand it. That does not mean I have to like it. Any suggestions for the plan to spirit us away in case of trouble?"

*****

The meeting paused for refreshments. John approached two men when he heard them discussing future actions. One had suggested assassinating Emperor Domitian.

"I hate to eavesdrop, my brothers, but I would not recommend we Christians pursue that plan. First, it is better to continue as we are, little by little, enjoying our small successes. It could take decades, but bringing the full might of Rome upon us can destroy our movement. We must have patience. Second, Domitian has many enemies among the aristocrats. Given the history of this empire, his days could be numbered. Third, whoever replaces him can worsen our situation. History has seen many people become scapegoats for rulers who want to create distractions from their own evil deeds."

"The Emperor is an autocrat who thinks he is a god," said one man.

"Not true. He believes in false gods like Jupiter and Minerva, but at least he has resisted deification, unlike many emperors. He seems to be an able administrator—for an emperor, that is—and is making many reforms Rome needs and Roman citizens like. We want them behind us, not against us, as time goes on."

"How do you know so much about our situation in Rome?"

"I observe and endeavor to understand my observations. Being a Christian is no excuse for giving up on reason and logic. Quite the contrary. I have also traveled a great deal. Ordinary people everywhere struggle to live their desperate lives and raise their children, but they are also struggling to move from the dark into the light of knowledge."

"Is being a believer in Christ not more faith and emotion than logic and reason?"

"Not when you have witnessed His work. I have done so, but I am still trying to understand. I am sure the Magdalene feels the same way." John shrugged his shoulders. "But heed my words: we are much better off moving slowly. Rome was not built in a day. The Kingdom of God on Earth will not be either. Maybe not until He comes again and destroys the wicked and saves the righteous, raising them into the glory of heaven."

*****

After the meeting, Mary walked with John in the villa's gardens.

"I notice you sre wearing the ring," she said. "I am happy to see that. What does it mean to you?"

"Nothing and everything," said John. "Nothing because I am nothing compared to Him, and I do not deserve even to gaze upon it. Everything because it is a tremendous responsibility. I stare at it every night before retiring. A simple ring, just like the chalice and the sandals I left with Androcles are simple. I am glad someone else is caring for them as I am not worthy to hold His shoes, but their meaning is overwhelming. I can now understand why others want to gaze upon sacred relics. Still, they are just objects, but have world-changing meaning."

"He loved you very much, John. He would have wanted you to wear the ring." She glanced at the cloudy sky and then back at him. "How much longer will you stay in Rome?"

"I am not sure I want to remain here until I have to flee. The provinces beckon me. I feel a calling for Africa and also the northern lands. Each direction from Rome calls me. General Agricola is waging war in Britannia. They must all be fertile ground for sowing more seeds of Christianity."

"You are an adventurer."

"Perhaps missionary is the better word. You have the same vocation, but doing Christ's work is always an adventure. I am not accomplishing much here. Our cohort no longer needs us, thanks to your organization."

"Perhaps you are right, but maybe Roman citizens do. Still, I agree with you. I do not want to remain here until I have to flee either. I will head north and east to where no one has heard the Word of God."

Chapter Twenty-Four

Twenty-First Century, Ephesus

Bruno had always wanted to be rich and famous, with the second his higher priority. Family legends said nothing about his relative bringing bones back to Florence. After thinking it through, Bruno decided Leo and Botticelli must have failed to find the saint's bones. Otherwise that would have become part of the legends.

If he could beat Brookstone in the race to St. John's final resting place, he could be both rich and famous. He had no doubt she would be searching for the saint too, after he'd given her all the information about the priest and Botticelli. *That was stupid on my part!*

He thought fate was finally smiling on him. That old armoire had turned into something grand. Moretti's damn wife had stolen it from him, but Moretti could have it and his Botticelli painting, even if it was authentic. He was now after a bigger treasure—not only the bones of St. John, but religious relics associated with early Christianity. *Even the Holy Grail?*

He had become obsessed with the idea he would find relics and not just bones. He didn't believe in miracles, so neither bones nor relics had much meaning for him. He thought the whole history of the Church was shameful. *Didn't my great-uncle's precursors exclude women by calling the Magdalene a whore? Didn't they select only those gospels convenient for their agendas, including the one written by John? My God, there's even a gospel of Judas that paints a different picture of the man who betrayed Christ!*

He had never read that gospel, though. He only heard people talk about those other gospels after that movie based on that thriller about da Vinci became famous. He struggled through the novel after it was translated into Italian.

He had only heard readings from the standard four gospels as a child at his mother's side and later at the orphanage. He had ceased being devout when his mother passed away. St. Paul had an epiphany on the road to Damascus; Bruno had a reverse one on the road to his mother's burial place. Even at the funeral mass, he was thinking how absurd the sacrament's ritualistic cannibalism was, how absurd the priest was in saying his mother, as a devout Christian, would sit at the right hand of Christ, and how exclusive that same priest was in allowing only true Catholics to receive communion. *Was my great-uncle such a pompous ass? Probably!*

During his great-uncle's time—he figured there were multiple greats to be added there, but he wasn't good at either dates or mathematics—evil men had become popes, even Medici's son. He saw that on television. The papacy was a position tyrants had sought after, no good works nor miracles required. *How many died fighting in wars led by despotic popes?* He didn't know for sure, but he could guess. All three major religions—Jewish, Christian, and Muslim—were servants of violence, where violent despots justified their actions with their religions.

He wasn't a learned man, but he had thought about such things for a long time. He came to the conclusion that life was a travesty. Now he wasn't so sure. Yes, coveting Uncle Leo's armoire had led him to something far grander. He had to take advantage of that surprising opportunity.

*****

When he left the mini-bus and looked around, he knew he was in a fix. *Where to begin? That parchment talks about specific sites. But in the fifteenth century, or in the first, John's time? Now there are just ruins all around.*

That day, though, there weren't many tourists. The sea fog mixed with drizzle soaked into the dry Mediterranean landscape. It kept all but the most dedicated tourists away. There was still a thin film of moisture, but it was being replaced faster than it could be swallowed by the air or absorbed into the ground. It made the ruins treacherous.

He walked along Domitian Street. *Domitian? Wasn't he a Roman emperor?* Bruno wondered if Domitian had also been in Ephesus. *Botticelli. Uncle Leo. St. John. Emperor Domitian.* He mumbled the words again and again as if they were a witch's incantation. *Or a martyred saint's substitute for rosary beads?*

The history of the place was oppressive. He imagined ghosts from all the centuries surrounding him, mocking him, and trying to invade his mind. Several times during his walk he made a one-eighty, expecting some gnarled and ghostly hand to reach out and strangle him.

He realized he wasn't dressed for the weather either. The raw ocean breeze penetrated his light coat and he had no scarf or gloves. *I'm in the Middle East. How can it be this cold?* Tuscany could be cold, but the Alps helped blocked that cold from the north a bit. Here there was a steady breeze from the ocean kilometers away carrying its drizzle and fog up the silted river.

He had stolen a travel guide in the train station and read a little about the area. Ephesus had once been a great Roman port. *Maybe Domitian was here?* That wouldn't help him any. *Was St. John buried here? Did Uncle Leo come here with the painter Botticelli?*

He decided the only thing that mattered was St. John. If he was buried under the Basilica, there was no way he could retrieve his bones. He had translated the old parchment's text the best he could. He thought it talked about some gate. He began his search for it.

*****

Exhausted and hungry, Bruno gave up for the day. He found a cheap B&B back in Selçuk and crashed. The next morning, he had to wait for some fat tourist lady to finish her toilet business in the small WC that served the five rooms on his floor. As a result, he ate breakfast late and arrived at Ephesus midmorning.

The day had improved over the previous one. *It all depends on which way the wind blows,* he guessed. He expected to see Brookstone skulking around. *Would she pursue me?* Instead, there was another man who was exploring the ruins and obstructing his own search. He watched the man for a while. *Not your typical tourist! Can he be following me too?*

Bruno had already found the gate and seen Mt. Koressos, but the man distracted him. There were tourists about, but they were in a hurry to see as much as they could. This man inspected the ruins more sedately, as if he were searching for something.

What is he looking for? Or does he want to make me complacent and think he's only another tourist?

Bruno thought he could handle Brookstone as a competitor; however, he didn't need a second one, a man who seemed to know what he was doing. *An archaeologist?* The man would often kneel, pushing aside rubble. *Searching for a crypt, are you?* He only found a few shards from broken clay pots.

Bruno decided to turn the tables and follow him. *Maybe he'll give me a chance to attack him!*

Chapter Twenty-Five

Twenty-First Century, Ephesus

Walther had followed the bus carrying Esther at a prudent distance. *She's trying to prove Botticelli never was in Ephesus?* He didn't know if he bought that and he didn't care if the artist had visited the old town or not. With a chance she could lead him to some valuable artifacts, keeping her in sight was a high priority. He didn't think the museum had enough money to buy those artifacts, but he knew people who did.

He was also a curious person. He had gone to Florence to curate some Roman relics for his museum—the city had been established by Julius Caesar in 59 BC. However, when most of them turned out to be copies or worthless, he decided to go to the auction where Sergio Moretti's wife outbid that ugly gnome.

He had no interest in the armoire, but the price it fetched had surprised him. She had started with a low bid corresponding to the house minimum. It was lower than he would have made, but the gnome kept increasing his bid. Walther saw the intense expression on the man's face. *I bet he only stopped because he couldn't cover his next bid!*

When two ordinary people, not that connected to the antiquities business, bid so high for a decrepit piece of furniture it became interesting, but the gnome had seemed obsessed while Moretti's wife remained calm. Later, a contact in Vienna had informed him Moretti had called in four art experts for some reason, including Brookstone. All of them were skilled in determining the authenticity of an artwork. That piqued his curiosity all the more.

His conclusion: there had been a valuable painting in the armoire, and, from Brookstone's comment, it was a Botticelli! Interesting in itself, but, if true, Moretti would be guarding it like a hawk, knowing it was priceless.

Walther wasn't interested in a lost Botticelli either—selling a painting on the black market wasn't easy—but Brookstone's comment meant something had spurred her on to prove the painter was never in Ephesus. His conjecture that there could be artifacts there was a wild extrapolation, but Ephesus had been an active area for early Christians. Particularly, John the Divine, who Botticelli and other Renaissance painters often painted since he was the disciple "beloved by Christ." He wasn't about to throw away easy money. *Even if I find only a few items, I can pay for my entire trip by selling them to religious collectors. That would be a nice complement to what I lost with that ornate cross I purchased.*

He knew his logic was weak. He was making mental leaps unsubstantiated by facts, but he had nothing more to do on his trip because of the fiasco in Florence. *And I've never been to Ephesus!* He was still on the museum per diem and they would be happy if he brought back anything of interest from the region. *Especially if I make something up about the provenance!*

He couldn't do that with the cross because the jewels were fake. They would forgive his misuse of funds, not that they ever suspected that before.

His friend, Geiszler, had told him the entire story about Brookstone's obsession with a stolen Rembrandt and how it led her to topple both a neo-Nazi conspiracy and an ISIS terrorist plot. *That old hag is tough!* She appeared focused at the dinner they had together on the train. Walther knew he would have to be careful. He counted on her thinking he was only an erudite museum employee.

His museum job provided him good cover for his black market business in stolen archaeological relics. Collectors around the world inflated their egos by possessing something that no one else could see. It was similar to dealing in stolen paintings, but it could be simpler to pull off because relics were often small—gilded and ornate daggers and other small weapons were popular, for example, as well as small religious items. However, it could become complicated when the artifact was something large—he had once sold a Viking's sword with curious runes on the blade. But at times, it was just as lucrative. He had sold a pair of ancient Chinese vases for nearly three million euros. What he turned over to the museum was worthless junk in comparison.

Halfway through the three-kilometer trip, his hire-car broke down. It wasn't the first time this had occurred in a Third World country—he considered Turkey to be one—but it couldn't have come at a more inopportune time. *I'll have to wait for the next bus!*

*****

Walther wasn't considering the other sites on the tourist guides; however, he had an idea during the short trip on the bus. It had nothing to do with Brookstone; she had already lost him. He decided to go directly to the Temple of Domitian. He knew St. John had lived in the times of that Roman emperor, and the Temple had borne the emperor's name until he had been assassinated. It seemed like a good place to start. Some said it was built to honor Titus. Which one he wasn't sure of, but he also didn't care.

He found nothing at the Temple except for Brookstone. She was at the Gate of Heracles, not far from the Temple. He watched her putter around, peering under and into piles of marble, rocks, and mortar. Every few moments she would stand and look toward the hills. *What's that about?* He thought she might also be searching for relics. *Now she thinks she's an archaeologist?* The woman was most likely a bit touched in the head. She wasn't going to prove anything about Botticelli among the ruins. *Or is there more to her visit?*

He then spotted Bruno Toscano, the man who tried to outbid Moretti's wife. He was hiding behind a column, also watching Brookstone. *Interesting. What is he after?*

Walther soon lost them both. He walked around a bit more, peering here and there, kneeling and peering under stones and rubble until he decided to admit defeat. A stiff breeze was now blowing in from the sea; he was cold and a bit hungry. *To hell with this!*

As he walked past a column, someone attacked him. The last thing he remembered was some scuffed shoes.

*****

Walther awoke in a hospital bed. He stared at the gray sheets and the urban scene outside the small window and shuddered. *Where am I?*

"*Herr* Beck, welcome back to the land of the living."

"Esther? Fancy meeting you here."

"I don't think you know where 'here' is quite yet. We're back in Selçuk. I accompanied you in an ambulance. You're not in good shape. The doctor told me you have a concussion. Can you remember anything about what happened? Did you fall? Or did someone attack you?"

Bruno. He must have attacked me! "No, I don't remember. I saw you at the Heracles Gate. May I ask what that has to do with Botticelli?"

"Probably nothing." She told Walther about Moretti's painting. As he suspected, it was a Botticelli; the subject was John, his brother, James, and their father.

"How can that possibly imply Botticelli was in Ephesus?"

"I'd prefer not to go into that right now, but it's more that St. John was possibly buried in Ephesus."

"There is a legend saying he's buried under that other temple, not the Temple of Domitian."

She shrugged. "Yes, I saw you there. Temples are everywhere. Maybe people become confused. The emperor and John were contemporaries, at least for a time. The emperor was assassinated. Most people say the saint outlived him."

Great minds think alike. "I'm still confused about the Gate's connection to Botticelli."

"Me too. But you should remain quiet. You received a nasty bump on the head."

Bruno! Thinking of the gnome's stature compared to his own, Walther wondered how the little man had hit him on the head. He touched the sore spot at the back of his head. *Of course.* But that could also mean his attacker was Brookstone, but he doubted it. He wondered what Toscano was doing in Ephesus. *Is there a connection between the two? Is he now pursuing her?*

"I must have slipped and fallen. There are a lot of loose stones around still wet from yesterday's bad weather. Did you see me fall?"

"No, but I heard stones tumbling, so I checked. You probably rolled with them. Did our discussion on the train motivate you to go to Ephesus?"

"No, I was on my way here. I don't like returning to my museum empty-handed. It makes it hard to justify my per diem. It seemed like a good place to find some relics."

"There are better places to find relics than in this place, Indy. Relics lying about were likely found and sold to tourists long ago. I'll grant you some could be underground. The port was quite bustling in Roman times, but the river has silted over. I'm afraid you need to be the type of archaeologist who dirties his hands in a dig to find something worthwhile."

"When I was a young student, I had that role working for an old professor. But often items turn up and people don't realize the value of what they've found. There's a museum in Vienna filled with old artifacts from this region, you know."

"Yes, I know. That's not what I'm searching for, though." She glanced at the corridor outside the room's door. "A policeman is waiting outside. He'll be happy to hear you only fell. We can consider it a benefit of an autocratic government that they don't like to learn about locals mugging tourists. Police in Paris don't even seem to care. This is quite the tourist spot and tourism is likely a main source of income here." She patted his hand. "Will you be okay? I have things to do."

"Any idea how long they're keeping me here?"

"You'll have to ask your doctor."

Chapter Twenty-Six

First Century, Syria

"We have good news!" said the woman called Ruth.

John was far north of Rome, in a town called Vindobona, where he was working with the faithful. He thought he might be crossing paths with Mary. *Where is she?*

His visit so far had been a success. He even converted some centurions. Most people in the Christian community were poor, but they were enthusiastic about the Master's message.

"What news do you bring?" asked John.

"The Emperor was assassinated!"

"Domitian?"

"Yes, months ago, but news travels slowly to these provinces."

"I must pray for his soul."

While he did so in the house's small room that served as his hideout, Ruth busied herself preparing their meager lunch. She was the perfect host, even mending some of his clothes. All the poor had reasons to be despondent, but she always seemed to be optimistic. *When one is filled with the Spirit, optimism comes naturally.*

He kneeled beside the cot where he slept and prayed for the emperor's soul. Both friends and foes were often in his prayers. After praying, he kissed the ring Mary had given him, stood, and stared out the small window covered with treated sheepskin.

Did the cohort order Domitian's assassination? He hoped not. That would be wrong. *Christians cannot be violent revolutionaries.* They were supposed to practice love. *Did our Lord and Savior not try to teach us that?* Long ago he sometimes wondered about such violence, when he was younger after he and his brother and father were baptized by John the Baptist.

John remembered the time he spoke to James about the subject before the Crucifixion...

"We are not angry men like He says," John said to James.

"Admit it, my brother; we *are* a bit emotional at times," said James. "Jesus makes us passionate about His work."

"If we could only understand Him. He is a mystic."

"But people follow Him. That's why all the authorities and priests think He is dangerous. The Romans and their sycophants use that to turn people against us. Many people let themselves be manipulated by them because they do not understand. We must increase their understanding."

James studied John, and his brother finally agreed. "There are a lot of vested interests at stake," John said. "He can change our world, brother, but so many people are into greed, power, and hate, not love."

"We will just have to become a force for change, even when He is gone."

John stared at the far horizon. "There are storm clouds brewing, brother."

A puzzled James followed his line of sight. "The sky is clear. Are your eyes playing tricks? Sometimes there are mirages."

"I am talking about the cloudy future. We will suffer through much before we see a new heaven and a new earth; one where hatred is swept away by love..."

John missed his brother. They had been through a lot together. *He is in a better place now, at the right hand of the Lord, like at the Last Supper. My mission still continues. Thank you, Lord, for giving me more time.*

*****

John peered into the street over the rim of his earthen cup. He did not care for the sweet wine of Vindobona, but a meal without wine was akin to blasphemy.

"Is this centurion one of ours?"

Ruth turned and looked, seeing what John saw, a burly man striding with authority toward the small house. "No, teacher. I do not recognize him."

"You must hide, John," said Ruth's husband, Marco. "Please go to your room. You can punch out the window and crawl through it if you need to escape. Others will give you refuge."

"Let us hope it does not come to that," said John, sliding his stool back and rising from the table.

He retired to the room but kept an ear to the door. He kissed the ring, hoping for a good outcome. He did not want his hosts to suffer even verbal abuse at the centurion's hands. *Maybe a false alarm?*

But then he heard angry words exchanged followed by the clash of swords. There was a gasp and then silence. John peeked out and saw Marco standing over the centurion, his sword dripping blood.

"Damn fool!" said Marco. "He threatened Ruth."

Ruth stared at the man on the floor. "Is he dead?"

John stepped into the room and kneeled beside the centurion, feeling for a pulse in the neck. He then made the sign of the cross and shook his head.

"Not quite, but he is dying," John said. "I should give him last rites. He might be evil, but we cannot fight evil with evil no matter how angry we become. My brother was the same way after Christ rose from the dead."

"Forgive me, teacher," said Marco, who went to one knee. "I tried to kill a man."

"You were defending your family." John shook his head sadly, glancing at the couple's children still cowering in their play area in the corner of the room. He had come to love them. Many times he wondered what a normal life would have been like. *Ruth had defended her children; Marco defended Ruth and the children. Roman soldiers are good at threatening innocents.* "And me. I must eschew violence. You have to make your own choices. When my brother died, I wanted revenge. No longer."

"No longer the Son of Thunder," Ruth said in a whisper but with a smile.

"He called us that even before the Crucifixion, but the general stress caused by all this intrigue no longer makes me lose my temper. I have more mental fortitude now. This man would have slain you, good Marco." He grabbed Ruth's hand. "We must warn the others. This man will soon be missed and his thugs will be searching for us. Come. I have no desire to be tortured and become a martyr like my brother just yet."

"I understand. Right now your work in the underground is more valuable."

"As is yours. We must become the many shadows the Romans fear but not because of our weapons."

Marco pointed his sword at his victim. "I will move him somewhere else."

*****

"I will not die here, good Ruth."

The woman had come to visit John in the house of the family now giving him lodging. He had just announced to her and his hosts he must leave.

"With you gone, how will we know when the Savior will come for us?"

"I have no abilities to predict our future, yet my nexus with the Master is a bit more complicated than most people's. My future is shrouded as if lost in the morning mists rising from the Sea of Galilee; however, I do know I will not die here and therefore I cannot stay. There is work to be done. You people can carry on alone now."

"And what if our faith fails?"

"See that it does not. I do not think I can make it any stronger with my presence. Indeed, you might come to depend on me, and that would not be good. You can tell your children and their children you met the last surviving disciple who witnessed all the miracles foretold by the prophets. Many will not have that opportunity, but they will still believe and be strong in their faith."

"Will you die crucified?" asked Ruth with a shudder.

"How I will die is irrelevant because I will be with Him for eternity."

"I prefer to be buried."

Ruth is a simple woman but also devout. She will become a leader in a land that disrespects women; she will become important in many ways. The world will need many more women like her before they are respected and treated equally. How long, Lord?

"I think that will also be my fate. I will probably die of old age." *I am not sure about that, but that little lie can comfort her*. He hugged her. "I must go now."

“They will search for your grave to find the ring.”

The old Son of Thunder laughed a rasping laugh. “Yes. That’s why they must not find my tomb. They could even worship the ring and not the humble Son of God who wore it. The Magdalene’s gift would lose all meaning.” He glanced toward the sky. “If it is His will, I will return to die where I took care of the Virgin Mary.”

She kissed him on both cheeks. “Be careful on your journeys, Son of Thunder.”

Chapter Twenty-Seven

Twenty-First Century, Lyon

Bastiann's trip to Morocco had been preceded by a stopover in Lyon. He postponed reporting to Interpol HQ by visiting his favorite priest, Father Jean Laurent. He had been to the Laurent estate many times before. The Jesuit's sister and her husband lived in the sprawling main house while the Jesuit himself lived in the more modest carriage house in the rear.

The Interpol agent parked his hire-car on the gravel drive in front of what once had been stables. The only horses there now were the few found in the petrol-saving hire-car. Knowing the old man didn't leave his abode except to sit out on the back veranda to watch the sun set, Bastiann walked to the door and knocked hard.

"I'm in the study. I have a gun."

Bastiann laughed, opened the door, and entered a dark hallway. "It's me, professor."

"You must be van Coevorden then. You know where I am. Come join me."

"Only if you put the gun away."

He walked toward the back of the house to where the sister had made the main bedroom into a study for her brother. He slept in a smaller room.

"It's good to see you again, van Coevorden," said Father Jean as Bastiann entered. The priest rolled his wheelchair to a modest bar standing flush against one wall. "I received a fine sherry by delivery yesterday. Right on time, too. I schedule the deliveries for when Marie has gone into the city. She thinks I gave up drinking. I can offer you just about anything, though."

For Bastiann, Jean Laurent was more his ex-professor than a priest. He had struggled through a course in probability and statistics with the old man. Visits to his university office to discuss Bayesian statistics had morphed into chess games and conversations about game theory, philosophy, and religion. All subjects the Jesuit had mastered.

Bastiann looked through the tall windows in the priest's veranda doors to the estate's well-kept gardens and beyond. *So beautiful and peaceful!* The Laurent family was old wealth, but the priest's study didn't show it. Mathematics and other scientific journals were piled high on his work table and modest desk. The room was in its usual chaotic state. He hadn't expected anything less.

He accepted the sherry and took a seat in a worn chair he knew Jean never used. He faced a small, low table, and Jean rolled up to it, opposite Bastiann.

"It's good to see you too, Father Jean." He raised his glass. "A toast to knowledge."

"A most secular toast. Let me add a moral twist to it: and may the Good Lord give us the ability to understand all its ramifications and use it wisely." He studied Bastiann with one eyebrow raised. "Shall I arrange the chessboard, or should we go straight to the true reason for your visit. I'm guessing I'm the only priest who hears your confessions these days."

Bastiann took a sip. *Excellent!* "You know I haven't set foot in a church or chapel since I learned of my mother's death. Yes, perhaps we should play a game to clear our minds."

Jean had Bastiann arrange the board, and they started a game. Bastiann soon found himself in trouble, seeing checkmate awaiting him unless the old man made some serious mistakes to let him win. *But Jean would never do that!*

*****

"You're right, you know," Bastiann said to Father Jean as he studied the board, searching for a move that would end his predicament and save some face. "But there are two reasons, not one, for my visit. The first involves Esther Brookstone."

Father Jean smiled. "You appeared quite smitten with her the last time we met. Has she come to her senses enough to send you packing?"

"On the contrary, our recent adventures brought us closer together. Our relationship seems to be on solid ground, but now I'm afraid she's become obsessed with yet another project." He explained some of Esther's recent history. "So, you understand why a more permanent arrangement might mean I'll be constantly worried about her."

"Do you mean marriage?" Bastiann gave a brief nod, so Jean continued with the all-important question. "That's a big step, *n'est-ce pas*? But consider this: if she's retired, she will be more worried about you, van Coevorden. You're still in Interpol. She's no longer an inspector in Scotland Yard."

"I recognize that, but it doesn't make me feel any better about her obsessions. She can't continue to find trouble, especially if I'm not there to help her."

Father Jean captured a rook. "From what I know about your Esther, she can take care of herself, but you should discuss your worries with her. I know nothing about relationships or marriage; however, when two people love each other, they should not build walls of silence between them. My last word on that. What's your second reason?"

What should I answer? How will this priest react to what I'm going to say?

"I didn't go into details about who is supposed to be in the tomb. It's supposedly St. John the Divine. I'm not sure her quest isn't a dangerous waste of time. I know nothing about the man except maybe he wrote that fourth gospel and the Book of Revelation."

"The books of the Bible have often been a topic of scholarly research. There are more than twenty gospels not included in the Bible, using the term generically. 'Gospel' is simply a contraction of the old English 'god spel,' which means 'good news' or 'glad tidings.' As such, I'll be bold and wager many ancients took their turn at creating their own versions of the greatest story ever told. There are gospels according to Peter, Mary Magdalene, and Judas, among others, but I imagine those people didn't actually write them. There are some indications authors in those times even used famous people's names for pen names. Now that would create many more celebrities' books today, wouldn't it? It seems every week a new one is coming out, so we don't need any more."

Bastiann had listened to his mentor's meandering spiel with patience, but he wondered about its relevance. "You're a scholar. What's your opinion about John being the author of those books I mentioned?"

"Some historical and theological experts say John's buried at Patmos. Others say Ephesus. Scholars have wrangled over the authorship of those two books in the Bible for a long time. His life after the Ascension is a mystery, but to finish those other thoughts, I find the provenance of the other gospels more interesting. Take Peter's. In some sense, it's a counterpoint to Mary's. Mary's is important because it was probably written in the second century and gives a prominent role to a woman. That likely led to its suppression by orthodox Christians." Jean eyed Bastiann. "That's only between you and me, van Coevorden."

"You weren't speaking as a priest, I take it," Bastiann said with a grin.

"Only as a scientist. I'm a mathematician who also happens to be a priest. I don't have the academic credentials to give any weight to my ramblings. Not theological weight at any rate."

"Esther even less so."

"Yes, but perhaps she's also approaching the problem as a historical or archaeological one, not theological. There's little difference between science and art, as da Vinci showed."

"So, should I discourage her or not? What she's doing is dangerous."

"Let's return to your toast. What you said applies. One should never discourage anyone from seeking knowledge. Even work on the atomic bomb uncovered more about the intricacy of God's creation. How we handle that knowledge is more often where the problem lies."

Bastiann gestured toward the chessboard. "I admit defeat, in this match and the philosophical debate. Let's play another one now that I see things more clearly."

"I'll still win. You need more practice."

*****

Father Jean watched Bastiann leave in his hire-car. *The young student has turned into a man.* He waved at the disappearing vehicle.

So much like his mother! The priest had known her. He had been her confessor, as a matter of fact. Once in a confession she let slip that she worked for the Sûreté. Her confessions were never earth-shaking: too much wine here, lusty thoughts for a co-worker there, and often insecurities expressed about whether what she was doing in that spy service was morally correct. One of her first jobs had been to ferret out old Nazi collaborators from the Vichy government who had been in hiding for years. That bothered her to no end. Not because she thought they shouldn't be brought to justice, but because she imagined what could be their fate if she did.

At that time, he was a young priest in Paris. He had fallen in love with the woman and often thought about leaving the priesthood to be with her. He knew other priests who did that. He thought it was easier to avoid carnal thoughts and affections being a Jesuit professor who only dealt with young students, but then Bastiann's mother had appeared in his confessional. He mourned her when she was murdered in 1999. *The Lord tests us in many ways!*

He had lied to Bastiann—a small lie. He did know something about relationships. He understood how a man might be in love and how a man can worry about the woman he loves when she makes it a habit of living dangerously. He had heard enough from Bastiann about Esther Brookstone over the years and liked what he heard, although he had never met her. He was happy for his ex-student. He had learned how to live.

Now if he could only learn how to play chess!

*****

Not long after the meeting with Father Jean, Bastiann walked into Interpol HQ and found a small available desk. He had not been seated five minutes before Karl Schuster called him into his office.

"Any updates on the weapon smugglers?" Bastiann asked after the usual French pleasantries, which came naturally to him since his mother was French.

"Hal and your previous comment about the tip of the iceberg is acknowledged, but at least it's a start. We think a cartel could be involved. DGSE, MI6, and the usual Americans are mucking things up now, throwing their weight around as usual. The case is complex." He opened a file on his desk. "Something else has come up. Likely not connected, but it is important. Get your inner Humphrey Bogart ready. You're going to Casablanca."

"What's in Casablanca?" Bastiann couldn't help thinking of the famous Bogart movie. *Here's looking at you, kid.*

"A kidnap victim. DGSE is involved in that too, but the parents don't trust the French security agency. They want us to keep the *Piscine*'s agents from writing a John Le Carré tragic novel."

"He's British," said Bastiann.

"So are the parents. Mr. and Mrs. Harold Chesterton. He's the VP for Southern Europe from Global Electronics."

"Are the kidnappers demanding a ransom?"

"We don't know yet what their demands are. The family was on vacation in Morocco when thugs abducted their daughter."

"Do we know who they are?"

"The United Front for the Liberation of Africa, so they say."

"Never heard of them."

"Me neither. Near as we can tell, it's a made-up name." Bastiann frowned as Schuster continued. "Okay, Africa is a big continent, so maybe they're starting small by trying to generate some financing."

Bastiann glanced at the folder. "Background on the victim?"

"On the whole family. Between the mother and father, it's difficult to choose who has the biggest ego. Maybe the daughter has one too. She insisted on going shopping on her own. It's a toss-up to which one is more stupid to my way of thinking."

"I'll bet the victim is still scared to death even if she's a spoiled brat."

Chapter Twenty-Eight

Twenty-First Century, Casablanca

DGSE agent Philippa Bernard met Bastiann at the Mohammed V Airport near Casablanca. They discussed the case during the thirty-kilometer ride into the city.

The *Direction Générale de la Securité Extérieure* (DGSE) corresponded to Great Britain's MI6 and America's CIA, while the DGSI corresponded to MI5 and the FBI. Bastiann suspected their involvement was attributable to defense contracts Global Electronics could have with the French Government.

"We have a location," she said. "An abandoned house has some new tenants. Not a good neighborhood by any means, but two different and possibly law-abiding citizens told us about the same place. Those are independent verifications, which are good enough for me."

"Are the kidnappers terrorists?"

"More likely a gang trying to make some quick euros. They've never been on our radar. What about Interpol's?"

Bastiann shook his head. "No known group with that name. How can I help?"

"We're trying to keep the operation low key. You're here because of the parents. I don't think they trust us."

"They could have gone to MI6."

"That would have caused problems," said Philippa. "We don't play well together since BREXIT, although everyone pretends we still do. Interpol is more international. As far as I'm concerned, the Chestertons are residents of France, so it's our problem. They're protected by French law."

But they don't trust the French authorities. Interesting. "Are they here in Casablanca?"

"They're still at the same hotel awaiting news about their daughter. Still no message from the abductors, by the way. No one knows what they want." Her mobile rang. She held up an index finger and said "*Oui*" various times, hung up, and turned to him. "Correction, they want one million euros. The father wants to pay it—probably only a small bit of change for him."

"And the DGSE? What do you want them to do?"

"We're adjusting now and arranging for a drop-off just in case. I hope to hit the hideout and save the girl before any of that occurs."

Instead of taking Bastiann to the hotel he had booked, the driver left the highway and entered a poverty-stricken area that could be the suburbs of any large city in the Middle East. It wasn't in ruins after bomb strikes, but it could have been used as the set for many of the dystopian sci-fi movies he loved. He went through the entire list of titles for distraction.

They joined a small group of DGSE agents who had congregated in a vacant lot. They were forming a SWAT. After introductions, one agent handed Bastiann a gun, vest, and gas mask, and they moved on the hideout two blocks away. Half the agents left the other half at the front door and went toward the back. Bastiann was with the first half at the front, right behind Philippa, gun ready.

He had enough time to wonder about Philippa's story. *If the parents insist on Interpol's presence, why am I not with the parents?* Then he thought, *Maybe they expressed it as wanting someone with the DGSE agents when they stormed the abandoned house. Or do they even know that's going to happen? In any case, here I am!*

"*Un, deux, trois!*" Philippa said into the mike of her two-way.

Two agents hit the door with their heavy ram, turning a good portion of it into kindling. They all entered the old house from the front. The other agents used the same tactics at the rear.

The kidnappers, although caught in a crossfire, fought like men possessed by demons, darting through hallways and rooms in a manner that made Bastiann think they were facing an entire platoon. Bullets zinged around them. The sound of automatic weapons was like having a group of jackhammers start the demolition of the house. Tear gas was thrown by the DGSE agents; their masks went on.

At one point a gang member appeared out of the haze and took aim at Philippa. Bastiann had stayed behind her, focusing his firing elsewhere, but his peripheral vision was good enough. He pushed her aside and took rounds to his chest that were like hammer blows from some ancient blacksmith.

Soon it was all over. The raid was a success for the kidnapping victim. She survived with just a few cuts, bruises, and wounded pride. Five gang members were dead and three more were under arrest. Philippa was the only agent wounded. Her second called for an ambulance and then the local police. It would be Bastiann's chore to work out the diplomatic issues.

Sitting in a lotus position, vest off, and rubbing his chest, he didn't feel very diplomatic.

*****

Bastiann held the glass and straw so Philippa could sip the ice water.

"Your friend was lucky," said the Moroccan cop sitting in the corner of the hospital room, perusing an old copy of *Corriere della Sera*. "The bullet almost hit her carotid artery."

"Bastiann pushed me aside," said Philippa in a raspy voice. "It was just enough." The DGSE agent's weak smile was for Bastiann, not the Moroccan cop.

"I was more an observer," he said. "I observed they were aiming at you. I guess I just didn't push hard enough."

They had salvaged a major operation, turning a disaster into a modest win for the good guys. They rescued the kidnapping victim, so the family was happy, but Bastiann wasn't. Philippa had almost been killed and he had a sore chest.

The French agent's rosy cheeks had turned pale, her blond curls were now lackluster. She led the operation and almost paid the ultimate price. A stay in the hospital wasn't his idea of a good vacation for her. Not for anyone. Recovering from three hours of surgery would never be a vacation, particularly in Morocco.

"Luck, nonetheless, that *signore* was there," said the cop. "Luck too, for the kidnapped woman. I bet you knew our SWAT members tend to enter and kill everyone in sight to ensure we always rid our country of the bad ones."

Bastiann wanted to tell the man they put too little value on human life in his country, but he refrained. "Was the drop made?"

The cop shook his head. "Your action saved the rich people a lot of money, for sure. Much more than I'll make in a lifetime. No wonder bad guys choose that way of life. One *coup* and you can retire."

I'll give you that. Bastiann glanced at Philippa and then back at the cop. He wondered if all the diplomatic mess had blown over. He had done the best he could. DGSE had taken some liberties because their actions hadn't been to rescue a French citizen. *Not my problem anymore.*

"How long will this agent be here in the hospital?" he said.

The cop shrugged and expressed his worry for his own condition first. "I'm only here being bored in case those gang members have some friends who try to exact revenge on this pretty lady. Those are the orders from my superiors who were chastised by your lady friend's country for letting this happen in the first place. Two of my colleagues were at the hotel, safe and sound, but are also taking flak from our superiors as if they should have been at the house to die in the action." He gestured toward the corridor. "You will have to ask her doctors about how long she will be staying."

After a brief text message from Karl Shuster saying "job well done," his boss had told the Interpol agent to take a few days off. Bastiann had informed Philippa, but now he was in a quandary. *Should I stay with her?* He felt he should at least stay until she seemed better.

"Don't worry, Bastiann," said Philippa, as if she were reading his mind. "You should go. Take those few days off."

"You'll be okay?"

"I'm fine, thanks to you. They'll probably release me soon. If Interpol is anything like DGSE, we should take days off when they're offered to us."

How long will I have? Schuster hadn't bothered to be specific, saying only "as long as you need."

He decided not to ask Schuster or anyone else at Interpol HQ for a more definitive answer. He was going to Turkey instead. It was the whole length of the Mediterranean away, but so was Lyon, in a sense. *North, not east, but otherwise no difference, except for Esther.*

He bid farewell to Philippa—he resisted using Bogart's phrase, kissing her on her forehead instead—and then to the cop. He checked in with the doctors once again, who assured him Philippa would be okay, and found a taxi to take him to his hotel where he planned to stand under a shower for quite a while.

However, a message from Hal Leonard was waiting for him: *Meet you in Athens. Shipping container discovered in Piraeus related to our case.*

Bastiann frowned. *So much for the promised R&R and his trip to Turkey!* Piraeus was Athens' port and a major shipping center for the Mediterranean. Instead of buying a ticket for Ankara, he bought one for Athens.

He still took that long shower.

Chapter Twenty-Nine

Twenty-First Century, Piraeus

Hal was at the airport to greet Bastiann upon his arrival. After stashing his suitcase in Leonard's hire-car, he climbed into the passenger seat.

"What's the plan, *mon ami*?" he said as Leonard started to drive.

"First, logistics. I reserved a room for you at the same hotel I'm in, in Athens. This car is in both our names, which will be convenient if we have to part ways afterwards. I have to meet someone in Barcelona, so I'll likely be flying. I don't know what your plans are."

"Depends. How long is this mission going to take?"

"Depends. We're going to Piraeus to meet a customs agent right now."

"To confirm your message: a new container full of weapons and ammo?"

"Not one but three, in fact. They found two more. The arms were hidden in a lot of auto parts destined for Kabul. The bill of lading indicates the containers came in on a Chinese freighter."

"Chinese weapons, then?"

"Mix of Chinese copies of American and Israeli weapons. All better than the Russians'."

"I'm guessing our illegal arms group negotiated the deal. Do we have a name?"

"Henri Manousakis. The Hellenic Police Force has staked out his house in Athens."

"And why are we needed? Can't they handle it?"

"Bureaucracy, I think. You won't be a simple observer on this gig." Bastiann saw Hal's grin reflected in the windscreen. *He knows the last one wasn't simple.* "The Greeks have officially connected this to our previous case. Seems they're correct. I'm guessing Interpol has accepted that determination, at least for now. And the Slovenian connection you discovered makes it appropriate for Interpol to be involved."

"Manousakis doesn't sound Slovenian."

"He owns a mansion in the suburbs of Ljubljana."

"I see. Okay, let me rephrase: why am I needed? Better said, why aren't you sufficient for this gig?" He thought he was using the American term in the same way Leonard did. Sometimes Leonard seemed to speak another language. *And maybe it rubbed off on me?* He found that happened a lot to him with languages other than Dutch and French.

"Just to accompany me? Maybe backup? Because we worked on the original case together? I assume you still have an interest in the case."

Bastiann thought of Esther, sighed, and nodded. "I suppose."

From then on, they rode in silence, until they reached the port.

*****

There were two cops from the Hellenic Police Force and a customs official awaiting them.

"Where are the shipping containers?" Hal said after he and Bastiann identified themselves, even though they had been expected.

The customs agent, Hera Demopoulos, invited them to follow her. The two Hellenic policemen lagged behind the trio as they marched through a maze of containers toward a wharf where they stopped before three gunmetal-gray containers in a row of many similar ones.

"We do only spot checks," said the customs agent. "There are always too many to check, but the Greek intermediary's name caught my attention. We've had him on our radar."

"Good work," said Bastiann. "What ship were these containers being transferred to?"

"They came in on a Chinese freighter and will go out on a Spanish one. The ship's registration means absolutely nothing, particularly for the second ship. Would you like to view the contents?" Bastiann and Hal said yes. "You can all help me with the ladder then."

They found a three-meter ladder and placed it against one container's side. They all climbed to the top. It was partially open. Auto parts had been pushed over to one side under the cover, exposing shiny new automatic weapons, high-capacity magazines, and lots of ammo.

"Between the three containers, assuming the other two are similar, I'd estimate there are enough arms to outfit a small platoon," said Hal.

"Or maybe a large one," said one cop. "We don't even have arms of this quality."

"I'm not sure the Taliban use platoons," said the other policeman.

"Or other terrorists," said Bastiann. "Can we see the bill of lading?"

"Right here." Hera offered some paperwork to Leonard. "They're copies. Interpol can have them. The originals are in my office."

Hal examined them. "Intermediaries are often used and this man's name is Greek. How did you catch it? You said he was on your radar?"

Hera saw Bastiann eyeing her and smiled. She reminded him a bit of his mother—short, vivacious, and appealing, but not the typical Greek beauty of misogynist myths. He wouldn't be surprised if she was a mother of several children and a woman who was devoted to her family.

"Mr. Manousakis is known to us and customs," said one policeman. "He's been suspected of smuggling before and arrested a few times. We haven't been able to put him in jail, though."

"We can only jail his henchmen," said the other cop. "He has some good lawyers."

"Who only work for lowlifes like Manousakis," said the first.

"Understood," said Bastiann. "I'm sure—"

A shot was heard, and a bullet smacked into the one cop's chest. He fell into the container on top of the illegal arms.

*****

Hera, Bastiann, and Hal dove for the container's top. The other cop pulled his gun and fired three times, but then he was hit in the side from another direction.

Bastiann recovered the second cop's gun. "Jump in and load up fast," he told Hal. "We'll need some of that firepower."

He spotted one assailant in the direction where the second cop had been aiming. He was peering around a container to assess the situation. Bastiann fired, heard a grunt, and saw the man fall into the aisle between containers. “One down!” He turned in the opposite direction. No one in sight. *Has the other shooter escaped?*

Hal was soon at his side with a Chinese copy of an Uzi. Bastiann hoped it wouldn’t jam.

“Fifth container over,” Hera said, peering over the lip at the container’s edge. “I see a ladder.”

“Stay down,” Hal told her. “I’ve got this one,” he said to Bastiann.

“There could be more than two,” said the agent.

“I’ve got your back,” Bastiann told Hal.

When the second shooter’s head and trunk became exposed as he ascended the ladder on the distant container, Hal opened fire. Bullets from the Uzi-copy ripped into the smuggler, knocking him off the ladder.

They each did three-sixties to look for more aggressors, but there were none. The silence only lasted a few moments until the three left standing heard other customs agents running along the wharf toward them.

“I want the Hellenic Police to move in on Mr. Manousakis’s house,” Hal said to one agent when they arrived. “And we need an ambulance for a wounded policeman.” He pointed to the agent’s two-way radio. “Can you use that to make it happen?”

The man said yes and transmitted the request.

Later, as they walked away from the docks back to Hal’s car, he slapped Bastiann on the back. “Wasn’t that fun? That broad from customs can feed me *moussaka* any day.”

Bastiann watched EMPs hurry past them, carrying the wounded cop and the body bag containing the dead cop. “Hera is a brave woman. And there goes a brave lad now lost to Greece.”

“I agree. But it was police action, and Hera acted like a seasoned cop. Good show.”

"I'm guessing she has never been in a firefight like that before. I don't like to be in one either. How can you call it 'fun'?"

"Compared to Juarez, my friend, this was a piece of cake."

Bastiann shook his head. *Piece of cake?* He had almost lost Leonard *and* Castilblanco in that battle. *We don't want to become involved, but we do so from time to time. And we seem to suffer casualties when we do.*

Chapter Thirty

Twenty-First Century, Selçuk

Esther left the hospital and returned to her hotel. Finding Walther lying among the ruins had brought to mind another scene from those days in East Berlin leading up to being saved by Sergio Moretti...

"The house is dark," Esther said to her SIS colleague.

"I can see that, *Frau* Hausmann," Stan Miller said to her. "No time like the present, then. We need to find this man and help him escape from this workers' paradise." He patted his sports coat over his heart. "I have tools."

"Let's have a go at it then."

Esther liked Stan. Her spy partner was a consummate professional who was able to take on the role of a downtrodden East Berlin worker at a moment's notice. At one time he had been a struggling Shakespearean actor. In a masterful stroke, SIS had recruited him.

She liked him for more than his professional expertise; she had to control her romantic inclinations. As the team's younger member, she was also his student. He was a good tutor in spy craft. She was sure this nondescript but brilliant man had no such feelings for her, and instead reveled in the excitement and danger. In a sense, that belied his brilliance.

She didn't know yet whether the mostly plodding nature of spy work was worth the occasional adrenalin rushes.

The professor they were trying to help was brilliant in a different way. He had worked on some military projects for both the East Germans and Soviets. One of his old university students, who was also a spy for the British, had mentioned to Stan that Professor Heidrich might want asylum in the West. The British moved fast from that point forward, eager to harvest as many secrets from the old man's brain as possible. In their arrogance, they were sure that anything he had done was surpassed by Western science, but knowing the details, which were bound to be different, would still be to their advantage in defense planning.

They walked across the street, arm in arm, and stopped in front of the entrance to Heidrich's house. Stan climbed the stoop's three steps and examined the locks.

"I might not have the right tools. Not surprising, these are West German locks."

"That's amusing. Let me take a look."

Esther traded places with Stan, turned the knob, and opened the door a bit.

"Never thought to do that," he said with a grin.

Normally she would have made fun of him, but she ignored the comment. "Most unusual," she said. "Either Heidrich's quite forgetful, or there's foul play afoot. Follow me."

She took a pen-sized torch from her purse and went inside the dark house. He followed. "A bit sparse on furnishings, wouldn't you say?" Her beam probed the interior of an empty living room. "What does this man do? Sit on a mat and contemplate his navel?"

"He was expecting to seek asylum in the West. Maybe he sold everything, but that wouldn't be smart. The Stasi could notice."

The lower floor had a combined living and dining room, kitchen, and WC. They found a small table, old chair, and some dirty dishes in the kitchen, a hand towel in the bathroom, and an old grandfather clock with a cracked face in the hall leading to the stairs. The clock no longer functioned.

"You're right," said Stan. "This is so Spartan. The man must be a monk, even if he planned to move."

"We need to check upstairs," she said.

They found three bedrooms. One with a single bed and nightstand, another with a small desk and chair matching the one in the kitchen, and the third empty, except for the body. They stood on either side of Gunther Heidrich and stared at the ornate dagger sticking in the scientist's back.

"Surgical precision," said Stan. "Hardly a drop of blood."

"The murderer went for the main artery. The abdominal cavity must be filled with blood." She kneeled and probed to find the side of the man's neck. "Still warm too. We must have just missed our killer."

"Do you think they discovered his intentions?"

Esther glanced up at her companion. "Yes, I'd venture someone learned about our plans. Either through getting rid of the furniture or a mole—take your pick. Let's see what's in the desk." All they found there were some old pens and a business card stuck in a gap at the back of a drawer. "'Chez Jacques'? Are you familiar with that establishment?"

"I am. Dinner and music. The food's not bad, the music better. And there's usually a game going on in the rear."

She turned the card over. The phone number on the back didn't match the one on the front. "Perhaps a love interest?"

"Who would be male, I'm guessing. Professor Heidrich is gay—was, I should say. The Commies here are more understanding than the Nazis ever were."

"I see. Should we try ringing that number?"

"Not here. Let's find a phone booth. I'll ring the police from there too."

"They'll know we were here."

"Unlikely. The Stasi will know someone was here, but they won't know who. We both have leather gloves on. I'll state on the phone we were passers-by who heard the screams from the street, but we didn't want to become involved. That wouldn't be unusual in East Germany. No one wants to become involved, least of all with the Stasi."

She took a small camera from her purse and shot some pictures. "The person at this number might want to know how he died if they were close."

"You're jumping to conclusions about that number."

"You're right. It could also be someone from a card game who owes Professor Heidrich money, or vice versa. Whatever. The exchange is local, though."

"Let's leave. This place gives me the creeps. *Après vous, madame*. You have the penlight."

They found their way down the dark stairs...

Esther sighed. Finding Walther made the same impression on her as Professor Heidrich did so long ago. She had thought Walther was dead like that professor. It was fortunate that wasn't the case.

*****

Esther would have to leave her next visit to Ephesus for the following day, so she went shopping. She ignored all the tourist trinkets, many of them cheaply manufactured and overpriced—they weren't "authentic Christian relics"—but she enjoyed strolling through the streets, seeing other tourists, and hearing a mix of languages in conversations. There were several dialects from Great Britain and America's Boston, New York, and the South too. The American tourists looked more the part; they were informally dressed and gaped a lot. Almost all snapped too many pictures with their smart phones.

She wondered what people did with all the photos they took. Not many people made photo albums anymore.

In one store, she was examining a nice fake leather purse —she would never own real leather—when she spotted the image of someone across the narrow street reflected in the store's wavy mirror. *Bruno?*

She turned, but the man had disappeared. She put down the bag and dashed out, running full tilt into another man. He grabbed her arm.

"I've been tailing him," he said.

"Excuse me? I mean, tailing whom? And who are you?"

The man produced credentials. "We're searching for the man who falsely accused you."

She glanced at his credentials. "I'm sorry, Inspector Erkan. I don't know you. Do you mean Bruno Toscano? I just saw him!"

"Yes, but now we have lost him. Too many people." He put his credentials away after she returned them and took out his smart phone, showing her a picture of Bruno. "This matches what we have on record. Is he the man who attacked you in London?"

"Yes, that's him. Good luck in catching him. I'm not happy he's here...and, perhaps, pursuing me!"

"You shouldn't be, but I didn't know he was following you. I'll have to pick up his trail later. I'll inform my assistant to watch for him." He took out his phone and made a short call. He then glanced at her one package. "Are you enjoying your shopping excursion today? I hope so. Perhaps I can indicate some stores to visit?"

"More enjoyment found in watching people and the bustle. It differs from London, but there are similarities. London also has far too many tourists."

"Many of ours are as afflicted as Thomas was, ma'am."

"Pardon?"

"They are doubters, so they want proof Christ existed. Or at least St. John the Divine, which is nearly the same thing." He looked up and down the street. "Considering I've temporarily lost this Bruno, may I invite you to coffee?"

"Not your coffee. It's too strong and seems unfiltered. But I'll accept a cup of tea."

He laughed. "Our tea can also seem a bit strong to foreigners, but follow me."

She decided "follow" was the wrong verb. He offered his arm like a true gentleman, and off they went.

*****

Esther found the Inspector's choice of coffee houses a bit Spartan, but charming. The Kallinger 2 Coffee House was buried on a narrow side street with a discreet sign in Turkish she couldn't read. Parkland with palm trees began on the street's other side. The coffee house must have been in some tour guides because it was crowded with both takeout and in-house clients. They waited for a table and then sat down.

"I hope you're enjoying your stay here, Esther," Inspector Erkan said over the din. "My country is poor, but its history is not. As you've seen, we are at the crossroads of three great religions here: Judaism, Christianity, and Islam. We can't compare with Jerusalem, but we have many pilgrims visit here who are from the other two faiths."

"Catholic nuns in habits, Muslim women in burqas. I haven't seen any Orthodox Jewish men, though."

"Oh, we have Jews, the grandfathers of all three religions. They maintain a low profile in the Muslim world. There is justification for that on their part, but I personally find anti-Semitism repugnant. I have a more global perspective. As for Muslims, all sects venerate the Virgin Mary. There's an entire book in the Quran dedicated to her, and there are many legends about her historical presence in the area. But at least our government pretends to be tolerant to all religions here. As a member of NATO, that would seem to be prudent."

She decided Erkan believed—or wanted to believe—what he was saying. *How that differs from some western countries.* The ban on "political Islam" in Austria was a case in point, and anti-Semitism was still rampant in many European countries, including Britain. She decided the neo-Nazis she had fought would have had a better chance in Austria than in Germany now, but Hungary was the worst in its turn to the right.

In spite of the peaceful location, tourists and locals created a white noise background. It didn't interfere with the pleasant piano music coming from the speakers, which was just loud enough to rise above the din. That took her back to yet another Berlin episode as she and Stan followed up on the professor's murder...

No one had answered Stan's call, but their handler was able to verify that the number on the back of the card corresponded to *Herr* Otto Schneider, who also happened to be the pianist at the night spot Chez Jacques. After visiting the nightclub and watching the flamboyant Schneider for a bit, they wondered if Otto was Heidrich's lover, which would exclude him from the list of suspects.

He was much younger than the professor. Esther and Stan had searched his flat while he was at work at the night spot and, at first, thought finding nothing confirmed he had nothing to do with the professor's death. He didn't appear to have any contact with anyone British either, but they still wanted to know the origin of the leak that had led to the professor's death.

In a small café, Stan sipped his coffee, deep in thought. "You know, Anna, before we give up on finding the leak, consider this: maybe there are three people involved."

She understood. "The leaker, an intermediary, and the leak's recipient. That would explain why we don't have much on Otto, assuming he's the end of the chain."

"Precisely." Stan pulled out his notebook. "Since I still can't absolutely exonerate Otto, let's review his contacts."

The handler had provided a list. There were many people on it, and it didn't even count the frequent visitors to the pianist's workplace. As Stan went down the list, Esther stopped him.

"The cigar and cigarette girl," said Esther. "She spoke good English to me when we were at the club until she changed to German when I answered in that language. And she seems to be friendly with Otto."

"We'll follow that cigarette girl then."

The cigarette girl led them to a man from the British consulate. The leak-chain might now be complete. That supposition also made them think Otto was a Stasi agent. Their handler told them to prove it. He would take care of the person at the consulate and the cigarette girl. They decided they could only find proof at the club, so they visited it again that same evening.

She smiled at the pianist. There was some comfort in knowing his returned smile would likely go no farther if he was truly gay. *And you can't pretend about something like that!* She thought the alleged Stasi agent had possibly been assigned to maintain surveillance on the professor after receiving the tip. Or seeing him sell off furniture. Still, he couldn't know what they knew, so after he finished the set, she curled a finger at him. He rose from his piano bench and walked over to her.

"I would like to buy you a drink," she said. *And some more time so Stan can inspect your dressing room.* "What strikes your fancy?"

"You have me at a disadvantage, *Fraulein*. You've been here before, so you know my name from the marquee, but I don't know yours." She told him her alias. "Then I will have scotch, no ice."

"They might not offer any," she said. "They've put a terrible tariff on it, you know." She flagged a waitress. "Do you serve scotch here?" The waitress said yes. "More than one brand?" Again, the positive response. "Do you have a preference?" she said to her companion. When he replied, she said, "Make it two, *bitte*."

She managed to maintain a conversation about American jazz and its popularity in Europe until Miller returned to the bar. When he shook his head in the negative from across the room, she decided to be creative and try something else.

"We have a mutual friend if I'm not mistaken. *Herr* Gunther Heidrich."

At the mention of the name, Otto jumped to his feet and shoved the table hard, sending Brookstone, her chair, and drink flying backwards.

Should I assume he feels guilty about something? She grinned as she watched Miller pursue the pianist. *Temperamental musicians…*

Sometimes recorded music is better than live.

*****

"You speak excellent English," Esther told Inspector Erkan, smiling at him over the brim of her tea cup. *He's a handsome man. Would Bastiann be jealous?*

"My English improved considerably during my time spent with the RAF."

"You were in London?"

"No, I was at the RAF Station Lakenheath in Suffolk. NATO training. Fortunately, I'm no longer a Turkish pilot."

She didn't know if NATO was less popular with the Turkish government or the American one. *The world order is changing. Are we all just huddling into our tribes?*

"Because of all the problems, I presume," she said. "You weren't involved in that dreadful uprising, were you?"

"If I had been, I'd most likely be executed by now, or serving a life sentence. No, I was already a policeman." He frowned. "Just between you and me, I feel we've gone a bit astray and have become a little too cozy with Russia. However, I'll deny ever saying that."

"And I shan't repeat it, Inspector. World politics have become strange of late. They're still trying to prove Russian operatives used social media to encourage people to vote for BREXIT. I expect MI5 is heavily involved in that, but they don't seem to be accomplishing anything."

"Yes, it's a strange world. If you're retired, why worry about any of it?"

"Because politicians are such fools. You never know what foolishness they'll think of next that will make too many people suffer. Maybe even me. Governments tend to go after old people these days. Everybody does."

"What was your work like at Scotland Yard?"

"You would most likely find it boring. I was in the Art and Antiques Division. It dealt with crime associated with art thievery and selling stolen artwork on the black market. I worked with the American FBI a few times. That's about as exciting as it got, I'm afraid."

"Except for your pursuit of the stolen Rembrandt."

"There's that." *Not limited to the Andy Warhol moment*, she thought. The inspector had likely read about the case in preparation for his assignment to find Bruno. "What about your work?"

"More computers and databases these days, I'm afraid. I'm actually enjoying this new task to find Bruno Toscano. More like old-fashioned police work. We now have an Interpol warrant for his arrest, by the way, for your kidnapping in London."

Did that originate with Bastiann? "Does that include extradition?"

"Yes. We still deal with Americans and Europeans, although we like them less than the Russians. Officially."

"But you still like the money from our tourists, I presume."

"There's that."

*****

Esther hadn't counted on the pleasant time spent with Inspector Erkan. They had quite a bit in common if one stepped back and considered the big picture. She had wished him well in his pursuit of Toscano and returned to her hotel.

"Message for you, ma'am," said the desk clerk when she asked for her key.

It was from Bastiann: *Gunfight in Morocco; gunfight in Greece. I'm tired of being a target. Want some company?*

How was she supposed to answer that? He'd been terse, but maybe Interpol had given him some time off. *He knows where I am. He'll probably just show up as he often does.*

But the message made her think that she would have to pressure her Dutchman to leave Interpol. She didn't want someone she dearly loved to be killed in a gunfight. His job had always been more dangerous than hers—the pursuit of the Rembrandt had been an exception where they shared the danger. Interpol agents weren't in the line of fire as much as local law enforcement, but trouble seemed to find Bastiann all too often.

That was also his complaint about her, and he didn't know much about her days in East Berlin—long before she had met him. Life does have its twists and turns.

She groaned. She hated ultimatums. *Is now the time for one?*

Part Three

Journey to Discovery

"Neither pray I for these alone, but for them also which shall believe in me through their word."—John 17:20

Chapter Thirty-One

Fifteenth Century, House of the Virgin Mary

Sandro Botticelli and Bishop Leo walked around the ruins with their guide.

"I think the Virgin would have been better served by returning to that legendary manger in Bethlehem," Sandro said.

"Blasphemy! And it is only a legend."

"Whatever you say, friend Leo. Is this house *not* legend?"

"It is a shrine for both Christians and Muslims," said the guide. He looked around the area at the other pilgrims. "And your friend is correct. You have to be careful with what you say here. Thieves are the least of our worries. The Ottoman Empire has little patience with pilgrims from abroad, especially Christians."

"From what they tell me," said Sandro, "they are as ruthless as the Romans once were, which is saying a lot. I guess they feel beheading someone is more civilized than crucifying them. However, do they understand our Florentine dialect?"

"I would not put it past them. The Empire reaches far into Eastern Europe now. As far as the Turkish soldiers go, all foreigners are guilty until proven innocent, and few locals will have the courage to swear you are innocent if they arrest you."

"Nice fellows," said Leo. "Good thing your mother was from Padua. My ancestors are also from there."

The guide smiled. "And good thing for our tourist trade that Christians from foreign lands are bold enough to come here on a pilgrimage to see the site where St. John took care of the ailing Holy Mother."

"About that," said Sandro. "I do not see any evidence for any of that happening here."

"He is a doubting Thomas," said Leo.

"I understand," said the guide. "My mother was a Christian; my father was a Muslim. Both were believers. They needed no evidence to believe. Their faith was strong. But I can understand why some people have doubts. Everything happened so long ago."

"So, is there some evidence?"

"Only in the winds of time," said the guide, "yet revered by the many locals who carry on the great traditions. Are you trying to disprove the legends?"

"No," said Leo.

"Yes," said Sandro, "but more in a specific sense. We discovered a claim the saint is buried around here. I do not believe a word of it. I say it is Patmos. You have a curious meeting of legends here, by the way."

"I have seen you sketching and your friend crossing himself. Are you an artist?" Sandro said yes. "And you a holy man?" the guide asked Leo.

"A priest," said Leo. "In fact, a bishop, but please do not advertise that."

"I do not know what to say about your quest except we need to return to Ephesus before dark. I will rest in the shade of those trees with the horses while you look around some more. When the sun falls to its last quarter, we must leave. Even then, we can encounter bandits on our return journey."

"Great," said Sandro. He turned to Leo. "You are going to get us killed."

*****

Sandro leaned against a gnarled tree and waved at the ruins they called the House of the Virgin Mary. "Have you heard of this place before?" he asked Leo, eyeing the guide who shared the better shade tree with the horses.

"No," said Leo. "I am inclined to agree with you: these ruins are not a likely abode for the Holy Mother. Then again a manger was an unlikely birthplace for the King of Kings."

Sandro decided to go easy on his friend. "Maybe before, this house was what they say it is, but the centuries have not been kind to it. If what the locals say is true, the Assumption took place here over fifteen hundred years ago." He now gestured toward the fountain. "Amazing it still has running water. Quite a miracle, considering how arid it is. Maybe a spring feeds it?"

"We know so little about this place, Sandro. Most everyone asked us for money to give us information. Why would we consider any information they gave to be reliable in that case?"

Yet you believe the parchment, thought Sandro. "At least our guide is honest, or seems to be."

"Because he has some relation to Padua? Bah! I have no use for them." He waved his hand to indicate their general surroundings. "We are here because this place approximately matches the area's description in the parchment. Given the house's condition, any other ruins could also serve in that regard, and I do not think anyone would allow us to dig up the floor of the house." Leo shrugged. "Pardon me. I am a bit depressed. You are not helping."

"Remember, for me, it is only a vacation—too long and tiring, to be sure. But let's take another walk around. We should not admit defeat so easily. It is possible we will never return here again. We might as well take it all in. If what natives say is true, this is holy land." He framed the house with his hands. "I can spruce it up a bit if I put it into a painting."

Their final survey included circling the house's outside wall one more time. Sandro stopped at one point where a stone block at the bottom of a wall appeared to be loose. His eyes started there and followed a dark line of earth and sand straight to the fountain.

"What's caught your attention?" asked Leo.

"The spring feeding the fountain could be under the house. Let's go inside again."

The house's interior was also in shambles with some parts of the roof gone. On the floor of a small room attached to the main one, he found something interesting. To the right of where the spring would be were a few raised tiles. "The floor's tile stones are a bit raised right here." He used the toe of his sandal to indicate the edge.

Leo inspected the area where Sandro was pointing. "An artist's eye for detail. Do you think there's something under them?"

Sandro rummaged around in his shirt and pulled out a dagger still in its scabbard. "Always be prepared, I say. I should start a youth group with that motto someday."

"That dagger would not do much good against a scimitar."

"I brought it along in case you annoyed me so much I had to kill you." Enjoying Leo's shocked expression, he continued, "But we can also pry up some tile stones with it."

*****

Under the thick tile stones so heavy that it took both of them to raise them, they found an animal skin wrapped around old papyrus. It made the whole trip worthwhile for Leo.

"We need a place to examine this," said Sandro. "I am loath to do it anywhere around here. It appears as old as..."

"...Mary and John," said Leo, finishing his friend's sentence. "Let's examine it on the dry sand outside."

"*Va bene*, but let me see what our guide is doing." Sandro peeked out the doorway. Their guide was still napping. "All right, my friend. Let's be quick about it."

They spent several minutes studying the old document written in Latin by a masterful hand.

"We have to tell the Vatican about this find," said Leo in a whisper.

"Why not take it back with us?" Sandro said. "We can drop the papyrus off to his holiness on the way to Florence. It might be worth a few blessings."

"They need to organize an official expedition to carry it safely to the Holy City. We cannot protect it from thieves. Certainly not with your little dagger."

Sandro was astonished by what Leo had just said. "And the saint's tomb? We have yet to find it. St. John must have thought he was going to die soon if he planned his burial place at the same time as the Virgin's."

"We neither have time nor money to continue the search," said Leo. "And I want this papyrus kept safe. I repeat, Lord knows what could happen to us on the return trip if we take it with us. This area does not have a monopoly on bandits."

"What? So, forget about both the tomb and the papyrus? We have come all this way, finally find something important, and you want to put it back?"

"A bit more protected maybe. Let's see if we can find a better hiding place for it. Anyone can discover these loose stones and, if they ever make this a proper shrine, workers might redo the entire floor."

"I saw a loose block on the outside wall when we were going around the house. We can hide our find under that, if that's what you want to do. I think you are crazy, but it is your decision, not mine."

Unfortunately, the loose stone covered a conduit for the small trickle of water feeding the fountain. It ran in a miniature aqueduct from under the house and went into a clay pipe.

"I like the original hideaway better. Who knows what will happen if there's a major storm?"

Leo was on his hands and knees peering into the channel. "The water marks are low in there. This is still a good hiding place, but we need to find something to protect the document better. Even a little bit of nearby moisture could damage it. We also need to push the stone in more tightly."

"The groundskeeper's shed is out back. Let me see what I can find there. For now, rewrap it in the skin. That's watertight."

Leo pulled his diary out of his knapsack. "I am also going to include some pages I have written about our journey. We also need a map describing what we have already seen that matches the few words St. John says about his burial site and what is in the original parchment. Do you remember that we went past those hills yesterday?"

Sandro said he did. "Do not worry, Leo. I will make the map when I return if you have a blank parchment. I know something about maps. You do not. I even drew some illustrated ones for Amerigo."

"Then do not dawdle. Our guide can awake at any moment."

Sandro glanced again at the sleeping man and grinned. "Our poor guide does not know what he is missing. Now you are making history, Leo."

"So are you."

Chapter Thirty-Two

Second Century, Dacia

"We are going to war with the Romans, John." The Dacian king, Decebalus, raised his wine glass in a toast to his guest. "I will miss your company and counsel, but perhaps it is better that you leave our kingdom before the battle begins."

John frowned. The king spoke in Latin, but it was not his language nor the language of his people. He appeared to be stressed and tired. John should have also been weary, but his success in Dacia had given him energy.

He considered the king's warning and then made an observation. "The Romans view Dacia as a threat."

"No, they view us as a buffer between them and the hordes from the north who are also furious warriors, even their women. To the far west, Boudiccia proved that when she led the Britons to temporary victories and sacked Londinium. I also fear them."

John inclined his head in a bow. "Perhaps we are both right. Nerva making his adopted son, Trajan, his successor did nothing to diminish the ex-general and consul's ambitions. Do you think they will attack first?"

"Does it matter? Can you see the future? Will I have to bow to Emperor Trajan?"

"Sometimes it is better to lose a war and receive help from the enemy in order to become even stronger. Little by little, Christianity is spreading throughout the known world by often using that tactic. Reeds along the river bend to the gale only to grow stronger afterwards."

"You speak in parables, but wisely, John. Will your religion provide me any strength to vanquish my enemies?"

"Belief in the Son of God is not a weapon you can wield in battle. He will give you peace whether you win or lose. Events occurring on Earth can only matter if we are to bring His message of peace to all people, but they are also irrelevant in the afterlife if you have lived a moral life. You must believe that."

King Decebalus grinned. "And what if I consider you a doddering old wizard who is trying to hoodwink my people?"

Wizard? John found humor in the pagan's choice of words. *Everyone has a different view of Christianity. To the king, Christ did not create miracles; he created magic.* "If you truly thought that, you would not have permitted me to go about my missionary work here."

"No, I did so because your prattle is harmless dogma and it could make my soldiers all the more willing to die for me. The promise of everlasting life." He finished with a smile.

John did not like that logic, so he chose to ignore it. "If I stay, will you let me do the Lord's work until you go into battle? I need a distraction. Unless you are absolutely sure you are going to win."

"You will have your warning. And, if it means anything, you can pray for me. I know the Roman gods will not be on my side, and they claim to have all-powerful gods."

*****

"For once, I agree with the king," said John's host after the disciple told him about his session with Dacia's ruler. "You should leave. We can accompany you to the border, and you can slip through the Roman lines while the soldiers are asleep."

"The question is when," said John. "Sometimes I wish I did have powers to read the future."

"Trajan will not wait too long," said the man's wife. "It costs money to keep legions on the border, and he hates to spend money unnecessarily. That is his major motivation for invading Dacia. He is jealous of our economic successes."

"He is also feeling pressure in Rome from the patricians. Given all his failings, old Domitian was the better emperor." The husband winked at his wife. "Not that I like any of them. They are all tyrants."

"I like your plan," said John, "but I have more work to do. Decebalus promised to give me warning, after all."

"The warning will not come if the Romans mount a surprise attack," said the woman.

"Even in that case, our plan is sound." He glanced out the window at the fading sunlight. "I have a sick sister to visit, my friends. Do not delay dinner on my account. I will return late."

"Be careful. The king has protected you here, but there are still those who work against us, including many Roman sympathizers."

"I will be careful." John jerked a thumb toward the low ceiling. "He watches over me as I do His work."

*****

Sara had been his first convert in that kingdom so far from the Roman capital. That occurred sometime before Decebalus's soldiers had captured him. The king had decided

John was not a Roman spy and was harmless. He even expressed some curiosity about Christianity, but not enough to convert.

The king's attitude was common. Many were fence-sitters with respect to the new religion—interested but not committed. Most of those were powerful elites like the king, people who had money and power and were afraid John's bold message would make the rabble rise up against them. Even though she was well off, Sara was not one of those.

Her fervor made John uncomfortable. However, at that moment, she had neither fervor nor fever, so he could explain her temporary lucidity. She gripped his hand so hard it hurt.

"I will see Him soon, John. Do not fear. I will die in peace now that I have heard your message and found His grace."

The hand tightened. "The Virgin Mary once gripped that hand," said John. "She will be waiting for you too. I envy you."

"I am old. It is my time, but why should you envy me? When your work is finished, you will join me and all the heavenly hosts above."

"My work will never be finished, but my body will fail me too, as yours is failing you now." He watched her eyes close. "Can I do anything for you to ease the pain?"

"Only some water."

John left the room to find water. When he returned, she had passed on. He wept for her.

Chapter Thirty-Three

Twenty-First Century, Ankara

Bastiann was repeating Esther's route, but he stayed in a different hotel in Ankara. He stayed in the Bera Ankara since he had lodged there before. He had a quick dinner, bought a copy of *The Times*, and returned to his room.

He saw the small piece of thread he had placed on the hall rug wasn't where he had left it in front of the door. Considering the hour, he didn't think it would have been disturbed by maid service, although he couldn't remember if they turned down the bed and left candy on the pillow at this hotel.

He opened the door and peeked inside the room, dimly lit by outside light coming in from the curtained window. He sighed. *False alarm.* He turned on the entry light and stepped inside. As he passed the entrance to the bathroom, a gun barrel was put to his head. He froze.

"Interpol Agent van Coevorden, I presume?"

He stared straight ahead, not daring to make a move. "At your service. What can I do for you?" *Slight accent but educated English. A mix of American and British. Steady hand. I'm in trouble.*

The barrel went to his ribs and someone pushed him farther into the room.

"Sit in the chair." Bastiann did so. The gunman turned on the desk light. Bastiann blinked twice but recognized him immediately. "Let's hope this meeting is better than our last one," Ernesto Felipe Lopez Diaz said with a grin. "Can you give me a good reason why I shouldn't kill you?"

Bastiann shrugged. "I suppose you're somehow involved in my weapons smuggling case." Ernesto grinned again. "Your presence here means we were too successful, then." The grin turned to a scowl. "So you want revenge?"

"Perhaps I do now," Ernesto said. "I should have taken your actions in Northern Italy as a warning. But, you see, I'm a businessman with several pots on the fire to stir and other businessmen to meet to make deals with."

A murderer dressed in a three-piece suit of an international businessman, thought Bastiann.

Ernesto had menace in his eyes for a moment, but the evil grin returned. "I am willing to admit I don't like Europe or Europeans very much. During the colonial period, you made a mess of everything, especially in South America. But let me make my own Spanish Inquisition. Let's discuss your role in this latest fiasco."

*****

Bastiann thought his end was near, but Ernesto only seemed to want information at the moment.

"We weren't responsible for the destruction of your camp, you know."

"I'm well aware of that. I can still argue your actions led to that, but if you and the old lady hadn't killed those neo-Nazis, we would have. All that's past history."

"Maybe, but I have a question. Did you provide ISIS with non-lethal material?"

Ernesto smiled. "I'm the one doing the interrogating here. Let me add, even though I do business with many people, terrorists are no one's friends. They blasphemed an interesting religion to promote a medieval agenda that would return the whole world to the Dark Ages. I prefer to scam them by taking their money and then screwing them over. They're so blinded by their stupid debunked ideology they can't see it coming."

"A bit of no honor among terrorists, because selling drugs to addicts and creating new ones is also a type of terrorism, and that's your main business."

"I don't force drug addicts to want their highs. If someone wants to commit suicide, let them do it. We have too many people on the planet anyway."

"So addiction is a mental disease, and you only offer some relief for it?"

"One way to put it. Many people have pain, both physical and mental. Liberals call addiction an illness; conservatives call it a crime. I call it a business opportunity. But I digress. Let's hear about the roles you and the American recently played."

Bastiann shrugged. *What the hell?* He gave Ernesto a summary, leaving out many details about how Interpol aided local authorities. The cartel leader probably knew most of the tale.

"So, my take-away lesson here is I have to be more careful about whom I hire," said Ernesto. "I thought as much. It's a shame one can't find decent help these days."

"You implied you hate terrorists. Aren't those arms and ammunitions destined for them?"

"You don't understand, and consequently you are wrong. The people who need the guns are protecting opium poppy fields. They're protecting innocent farmers, in fact, who can't make a decent living otherwise. None of them are terrorists, only people trying to make a living, like me."

"I see." Bastiann couldn't accept the man's flawed logic, but he believed what he was saying. "So, you make money in two ways, from their opium and by selling them guns."

"The weapons I sell them are less expensive than any others they can purchase. It's a successful business model. I learned from the failures of a competitor in Juarez. If I'm not mistaken, Leonard was also involved in that operation. He does get around."

"He was nearly killed."

"Our work can be dangerous." Ernesto stood. He put his gun in his shoulder holster. "In any case, I learn from my mistakes and the mistakes of others. You, sir, on the other hand, are only doing your job." He pointed a finger at Bastiann. "You have some affection for the old woman, don't you?"

Has he talked to her? Bastiann thought. "Have you done something to her?" The thought had just occurred to him. *And here I am worried about myself!*

"The two of us also had a pleasant little chat. I warned her about your activities. Now I'll warn you and you can remind her: stay out of my way. I respect you both, but my patience wears thin as I age. They tell me it's characteristic of the elderly, so your Esther could know more what I'm talking about. In any case, next time there won't be any more chats." He drew a finger across his throat. "I don't care how much I admire you two, I'll have to make the required business decision."

Bastiann held his breath as he watched Ernesto leave the room.

The man's a sociopathic lunatic!

*****

Bastiann rose from his chair and took one of the little bottles from the stocked cabinet and poured it into a water glass. He sat in the chair for another hour, sipping whiskey. He didn't like the brand, but he considered it medicine to calm his nerves.

Our work can be dangerous? Now he knew another of Esther's obsessions had put her in jeopardy. *Will she hide her encounter with Ernesto from me?*

He assumed he would have heard about it if something had happened to her, although in these parts he had no right to assume that. Turkey has more dangers than just having an unstable, oppressive government.

He found his mobile and dialed her number. It went to voicemail. "Call me," he said.

He would wait until morning. If she hadn't returned his call by then, he would have to take some kind of action.

Damn it to hell, woman! Why do you do this to me?

He found another little bottle to help remove the frustration of the failed call.

Chapter Thirty-Four

Twenty-First Century, Selçuk

Bruno considered himself lucky because he hadn't been caught. He knew the Turkish police were after him. His plan to move ahead of Brookstone had failed. He eliminated the German who was in his way, but now Brookstone was in the way, again, and a Turkish cop was after him.

Life isn't fair! He had been a loner all his life. Now that he was pursuing something that could change that boring life, people stood in his way. He cleaned his thick glasses and thought about a different plan of action. *I have to eliminate more of them!*

After scheming a bit, he called the police with an anonymous tip, saying he knew the whereabouts of the man who had framed Brookstone. A risky tactic, because the police might be suspicious that someone knew about that incident, but he thought it was worth the risk. *God helps those who help themselves!* He smiled and wondered if St. John ever said that. He couldn't remember. He had often daydreamed when the nuns led the orphans in bible study.

He had already checked out of one hotel and into another, his third hotel in Selçuk. He told the police their suspect could be found at the second. Its entrance was at the end of a narrow alleyway. There were all sorts of crates, pieces of lumber, and broken furniture piled against the wall at the side of the entrance. He hid behind the refuse and waited.

After two hours, he was about ready to give up his vigil. *Molto estupido. Cops in Turkey must be even less efficient than Italian ones.* He took out a flattened sandwich from his coat pocket, deciding to work on that until the detective he had spotted showed up. If the inspector didn't make an appearance, Bruno would be off to Ephesus, where he'd likely have to eliminate Brookstone. *She's a stubborn woman! What's her motivation?* The ex-Scotland Yard inspector hadn't yet found anything. *Does she understand what she is searching for? That parchment said the tomb was somewhere in the hills. 'In Ephesus not far from the Temple of Artemis and at the ruins of the Heracles Gate, look beyond Mount Koressos'... Maybe she was trying to line up that damned Gate with the mountain? Why doesn't she toddle home to London and leave me alone?*

He was two-thirds of the way through the sandwich when the Turkish detective arrived.

*****

Denise had been tailing Bruno. She saw the little toad take out the German bloke. *What's he up to now?* She was intelligent and could guess the answer to her question. Brookstone, the Italian, and the German were all after the same thing. *So, I suppose I am too, if this Brookstone is about to make headlines again. If I obtain that story for Gerry, he'll have to respect me.*

She had tried all her life to please her stepbrother. She knew he only tolerated her because of some obligation to their common mother. He thought her only motivation in life was conspiracy theories. *No wonder he doesn't have any documentaries about those!*

Unknown to her stepbrother, she had enough courses under her for a doctorate if they were lumped together into one discipline. She was a bit knowledgeable about many subjects, but a specialist in none. She had a hard time holding jobs as a consequence because she knew her bosses were stupid, so she would walk out on them when she had enough. Gerry considered that a major failure.

And here I am playing a nun in the middle of Turkey! In a way, that was amusing. It was just a disguise, but she hated nuns. She thought they were an anachronism from a church modern times had left behind. *Are their faithful any different from those people in Guyana?* Communities of nuns were cults too, with their initiation rites and so forth.

But then guilt accompanied that thought. She didn't know any nuns. She also knew it was easy for people to be judgmental about other people they didn't know. *Like my friend, Rachel.*

They had mocked the girl in school, that skinny Jewish waif with acne who spoke peculiarly. The other girls stole her coat one dismal day and the poor girl had to walk home in the cold rain. She became sick, so Denise visited her in the hospital. She was in an oxygen tent, but they could still talk.

Denise didn't tease Rachel after that. When she returned to school, they became best friends. Much later, Denise went to her wedding where Rachel's rabbi made a pass at her. *Nuns. Rabbis. Priests. Other bad people pretending to be good.* The world was full of hypocrites and she couldn't stand them, but she was smart enough to know most people were good. They weren't perfect, but they were trying.

She could tell the policeman following Bruno was a good chap. She didn't like cops, but she liked him. She saw Bruno was waiting for him. *The cop is walking into a trap!*

She watched Erkan knock on the inn's door and wait. Before anyone came to the door, he must have heard steps behind him. He turned and saw Bruno, a long meter away, wielding a wooden four-by-four.

The inn door opened, and a woman cried "Stop!" It was enough warning for the cop to raise an arm in defense.

*****

"This is becoming a terrible habit," said Esther. Inspector Erkan couldn't raise his right arm, so he touched his head with his left hand and found bandages. "Broken arm and a concussion. Fortunately, your arm took most of the blow's force."

"You possibly noticed I'm left-handed. It could be worse. 'Always look for the positive,' I say. By the way, my attacker was Bruno Toscano."

"I figured as much. He also put another man in the hospital. That incident occurred in Ephesus. He must have wanted you out of the way too. I hope I didn't cause this. He won't catch me unawares again, that's for sure."

"He must be stopped."

"One of your colleagues is outside. You can tell him all about it. Even though I'm not frightened by that pest Bruno, I'll need some backup before I go back to Ephesus. An old friend will help me out. You're in no shape for that task."

"He set a trap for me. Diabolical." He told her about being sent to the inn in response to an anonymous tip.

"The two women at the inn saved your life. One said Bruno was ready to cave in your skull when she opened the door. Her scream frightened him off." Esther paused a moment. "A nun also helped you."

The inspector considered Esther's words. *Nuns weren't common tourists, but they were seen often enough. The area attracted many devout people on pilgrimages.* "You said there was another victim?"

"Yes, earlier in Ephesus. His name is Walther Beck. He's an archaeologist who works for a Munich museum. He purchases relics for them. He fancies himself an Indiana Jones-type, it seems."

"Did he make a police report? That should go into Bruno's dossier."

"I don't know, but if the police didn't think Bruno was dangerous before, they will now after what happened to you. That was attempted murder. On second thought, *Herr* Beck's attack probably was too." She squeezed his good shoulder. "I do hate to see you like this, Inspector, but it's better than seeing you on a slab in the morgue. Rest and recover. I'll send in your colleague when I leave."

"When you go to Ephesus, accompanied or not, please let the police know. We can keep an eye on you."

"Thank you, Inspector Erkan. My friend should be here this evening. By the way, he's an Interpol agent and my boyfriend."

"Agent van Coevorden? I read the files. I'd like to meet him. Scotland Yard and Interpol, that's quite a combination."

"Ex-Scotland Yard, but I still do some consulting. I'll be going now. Take care."

*****

Inspector Erkan watched his new friend leave. *A kindred spirit in many ways!* He didn't know much about Esther Brookstone other than what he had read online, mainly in Interpol records, but every detective is an amateur psychologist. He made a quick analysis and deduced they would have been good friends if fate hadn't separated them by geography. He had never doubted all good human beings could get along at a personal level, no matter what accidental differences there were between them. The current us-against-them mentality so common at the governmental and international levels amounted to human beings remaining immersed in ancient tribalism, often expressed as denials of an increasing economic globalism. Denials that seemed to warp everything.

He had never vocalized his thoughts about his own central government to anyone except to Esther since, in certain circles, they would be considered treasonous, but he knew his government had gone astray. They were still blaming a cleric who had sought asylum in the U.S. for the coup attempt as far as he knew. The inspector had become a basketball fan when he was in the U.K. He thought the ongoing feud years back between the government and a Turkish NBA player, to the point of cancelling his passport and arresting his relatives in Turkey, had been over the top. If he had still been in the air force, he might have participated in that coup attempt!

Corruption ruled in the provinces as much as in the capital. What was visible was only the tip of the iceberg. He smiled at the unlikely metaphor he used when he'd never seen an iceberg...or even snow!

His country didn't have a good historical track record either. The Ottoman Empire was almost as bad as the Roman one and the genocide laid upon Armenians was an atrocity that shamed him since his great-grandfather had participated in it. Some colleagues would envy him for that with their Turks-against-everyone-else worldview, but he had never mentioned it to anyone.

Unlike his country's leaders and those elsewhere, he never thought of policing as a tool for oppression. He saw it as a means to ensure ordinary and innocent people could have a safe and orderly life unfettered by crime, hate attacks, and oppression. Making that happen was more difficult as time went on, both in Turkey and the rest of the world.

What drives the world into madness? He didn't have an answer. He thought it could be an intrinsic flaw in the human psyche producing quirks that all too often made some human beings act like rabid dogs.

Drowsiness attacked his mind, but he struggled to stay awake. He had to tell his temporary replacement something important.

*****

Walther Beck. Walther Beck. Erkan kept on repeating the name to himself until his colleague entered the room. "Do me a favor and write two names down for me before I forget them: Bruno Toscano and Walther Beck. The first is the man who attacked me. The second is a man who was also attacked by Bruno. You need to interview Beck and see what he knows."

His colleague jotted down the names. "We're a bit shorthanded now, Inspector, but I'll give the person inheriting your case the names. Who knows? It could be me, even if I am swamped. Can you describe what happened?"

"Yes, of course." When Erkan finished, his colleague put away his notebook and relaxed. *Too relaxed!* "We need to catch this man, Bruno, before he kills someone."

"The old lady who was in here before, she looks familiar. Who is she?"

"You might have seen her at the station. She was falsely accused of trying to mug Bruno. He's a shifty and violent person. He lured me into a trap...but I already said that, didn't I?" The colleague nodded. "Be careful about calling her old, by the way. She showed some neo-Nazis a thing or two not so long ago." Erkan took a sip of water and cleared his throat. “Most of what I told you is in the case file, so you can check my memory. I’ll be adding some data when I recover, which I hope is soon.”

“How urgent is this case?”

“I’d call it high priority. Brookstone’s friend will have his hands full protecting her, so we can’t expect them to apprehend Bruno. Given their history, I won’t fear much for her safety once he’s here, so we can concentrate on bringing Bruno to justice.”

“‘We’ is too many, sir. You’re not going anywhere anytime soon. I now have your statement. I promise to get Beck’s.”

“Thank you,” said Erkan. Now sleep was losing the battle against hunger. *What does it take to get some food in this place?* He frowned. He expected his hospital food to be bland and boring. It always was.

Chapter Thirty-Five

Twenty-First Century, Selçuk

Esther had ignored Bastiann's previous call, assuming she would see him soon enough. She saw him step off the train three cars from where she was standing on the platform. He was dressed in a light tropical suit under a light raincoat, recalling again that wait for the train in East Berlin. *Agatha Christie or John Le Carré? Take your pick!* She waved at him. He put his suitcase down and waved back.

"Good to see you, love," she said, kissing him full on the lips after she closed the distance between them. "I'm happy you could get away."

"They owed me some quality holiday time. Being shot at twice in so short a period is a bit extraordinary for an Interpol agent. What would our friend Castilblanco think?"

"You do remember your colleague, Hal Leonard, was shot to pieces when they went after that Mexican cartel? He was lucky to survive."

Esther knew Bastiann well enough to read a bit into his frown. *What's his problem? He seems to be upset.*

"That's precisely the point," he said. "He was with Castilblanco. We're not usually in the line of fire." He shrugged and hugged her. “I seem to have too many friends who are.”

“Oh, pish-tosh. And we’re not friends, we’re lovers.” She eyed him. “Aren’t we?”

“Friend or lover, I’m here to rescue my damsel in distress.”

“Let’s go talk over tea. A lot has happened during these few days. We’ll first drop your luggage off at the hotel. You also look like a tourist. We should minimize that.”

“No more so than you.”

*****

Esther and Bastiann had tea in the Efes Konaklari, the hotel’s restaurant. She brought him up to date on her adventures since they had parted.

“Now you know why I called,” he said. “You’re in danger. Two others have almost been murdered by this Bruno. He could have killed you with chloroform back in London. Maybe we should focus on helping local police arrest him?”

“He wants to find St. John’s tomb. I don’t think it’s here, unless it’s under the temple’s floor. I conjectured that perhaps the legend partly exists because he’s buried somewhere in the Temple of Domitian, but that doesn’t appear to be the case either. If he’s here, he must be in the hills, just like the parchment said.”

“There are ruins all over. The Ephesus area was a hotbed for ancient Christians fleeing the Roman Empire’s wrath. Maybe there are catacombs like in Rome. In spite of Turks wanting to destroy any vestiges of Christianity from the ancient world, they tend to focus more on Ankara, Istanbul, and their surroundings. If it weren’t for tourists, this place would be as poor as any other place in this awful country.”

"You don't like Turks much, do you? One of Bruno's victims was a charming Turkish inspector, remember."

"I had Armenian friends when I grew up in Paris. They didn't like Turks, so some of their dislike was bound to rub off on me. We are all biased somewhat by our upbringing. Prejudices aside, I can maintain an unbiased viewpoint at the professional level."

"Good, because I will eventually present you to Inspector Erkan. He's nice and a true gentleman, just like you."

"Besides that, what's the plan if we're not going to help authorities arrest Bruno? Interpol has international warrants out for his arrest, by the way."

"Hmm. We both know how much good those will do." She thought a moment. "Let's continue the search for the divine bones. We'll have to be careful. I have a hunch Bruno will be shadowing us and reappear if we find anything."

"Specifics, my lady? I haven't been on a dig since my college days. I'm not sure I'd have the patience anymore."

"Likewise. If that parchment had been an actual map, we'd be better off. I'm inclined to think nothing is here, but if we knew where it was supposed to be and can't find it, that would be the end of it."

"I wonder if Botticelli found anything?" said Bastiann.

"I don't think he made the trip."

"Doesn't matter what you think. It only matters whether he did or not. Can we prove it either way?"

"That doesn't make sense," she said. "So, what if he did? It would have been fourteen hundred years after St. John was laid to rest. The saint could have been buried in some city long gone by now."

"Not if Botticelli found his bones here."

"Hmm. I'm thinking I should have hired another bodyguard. You're not helping."

"Because you won't listen. I think Botticelli is the answer."

She laughed. "Okay, he's the answer. Now what?"

"And he came here with Bruno's ancestor. Where would they go?"

Her brow furrowed, but then she broke into a smile. "The priest would want to see the House of the Virgin Mary, especially because it's mentioned in the parchment."

"Where is this house?"

"Seven kilometers from here, near Ephesus. It's a Catholic and Muslim shrine located on Mt. Koressos, which is not much of a mountain, by the way. The parchment's writer seemed to think the two places were distinct—at least, that's my impression—but they're not." She took a sip of the strong tea. "Legend has it, St. John took the Virgin Mary there sometime after the Crucifixion. Leo would have wanted to see it."

He glanced at his watch. "Sounds like a bit of a trip outside of town. Do you have a hire-car?"

"We can hire one tomorrow morning. A Range Rover will do the trick. Or we can take a taxi."

"Taxis can leave one stranded, you know. Some drivers don't like to sit around and wait, which makes sense if you think about it because they could be out and about rounding up other fares." She shook her head. "There can always be a language problem too. If we're going to spend any time there, I'd opt for the Range Rover, or any other SUV, depending on what's available. But what will we do until tomorrow morning?"

"There's a Greek restaurant that serves an excellent rack of lamb and has an ensemble complete with a young Zorba as a singer. Or so they tell me."

"Have you been there?"

"Walked by it. Tourists who are hoping to save their souls tend to avoid it. It's a bit risqué. Nothing lewd, mind you. Only Greeks enjoying life."

"My experience is that all Christians around the Mediterranean also do that and many others. The topless beaches in France come to mind. You might be surprised."

"All the better."

*****

"That man at the far table behind you is watching us," Bastiann said at the Greek restaurant.

Esther found a mirror in her purse and pretended to check her lipstick. An old spy trick that didn't work if the person you were observing was paying attention and had good eyesight. "He's Turkish police. I saw him at the hospital. Perhaps Inspector Erkan told him to keep an eye on us."

"Are we under suspicion for a crime?"

"No. The dear inspector wants to protect me and he wants to arrest Bruno. I can tell the bloke to go away, that you're all the protection I need."

"No, it's fine. I didn't know who he was." They had already finished their aperitifs and were waiting for the main course. "Tell me more about this House of the Virgin Mary."

She took a sip of her red wine and blotted her lips discreetly. "First, some scholars doubt the Virgin was ever there. They think she stayed in Jerusalem. Others, including pilgrims who frequent the shrine, believe Mary was taken there by John and lived there until her Assumption. Whatever the truth, the legend was solidified somewhat in the nineteenth century when a bedridden German nun, Anne Catherine Emmerich, reported a series of visions about the last days of Jesus and details about the Holy Mother. An author, Clemens Brentano, wrote a book about the visions. One vision contained a description of the house. People say the house we'll see matches that description. In 1881, a French abbé rediscovered the house and the pilgrimages began, including visits from several popes, the last being from Pope Benedict XVI in 2006."

"You're knowledgeable about the place's history, but it all appears to be quite recent compared to John and Mary, or even to Botticelli and his friend, Leo."

"Those who believe the Virgin Mary lived there base that belief on the presence of the Church of Mary built in the fifth century. It's the first Basilica in the world dedicated to the Virgin, which is found in Ephesus. It's a stretch, I'll admit. You never know what's true and what's legend, although legends can be true."

"Yes, but if the house wasn't discovered until 1881, how could Botticelli and Leo know about it?"

"Whether the author was Paul or not, there's an Epistle to the Ephesians written in the first century. It's possible the shrine was already venerated that long ago. With all the history between then and 1881, maybe people forgot the house existed at various times. Yet Botticelli and Leo could have known all about it or learned about it from the locals. Again, it was mentioned in the parchment." She put a finger to her brow. "Pope John XXIII in 1961 removed plenary indulgences from the Church of the Dormition in Jerusalem and then bestowed them for all time on Mary's House in Ephesus. A bit of Christian politics there, Bastiann, because Roman Catholic doctrine about the Assumption differs from the Eastern Orthodox doctrine about the Dormition, one occurring in Ephesus and the other in Jerusalem. Interesting, right?"

"For the daughter of an Anglican vicar, you seem to be well versed in Catholic history."

"The English church would still be Catholic if Henry the Eighth hadn't wanted a divorce."

"There's that. Here's our dinner. And the band to boot. Is that mustache real?"

"As real as yours, love. He's a young Zorba. The original Zorba was Kazantzakis's friend."

"I wonder if this one can dance as well as the original."

Chapter Thirty-Six

Second Century, Dacia

John put his finger to his lips to ensure silence. He then peeked around the building's corner to survey the area.

"The street is clear," he said in a whisper to his host, "but in the distance I hear screams and see fires. Is there another route to the Danube?"

"We will leave the city by the east and circle around," said another man who was accompanying them. "We have to cross the lines before morning when both sides will be fighting again."

Even with that route, they met trouble. *Is this the night I die, Lord?*

Again, he had to fight, jumping into the fray with his bare hands. He throttled one soldier and struck another as he remembered the skills his brother, James, and he had practiced when they were children.

A sword thrust nicked his ribs, but one of his companions had parried the thrust enough to make it miss its lethal mark.

The sound of clashing swords and combatants' grunts turned his blood cold. *So much violence!*

The battle turned in favor of the Romans, so the Christians had to run for their lives with Roman soldiers chasing them. The soldiers' pace was slowed by their heavy armor, so much so that John was in no danger even though he lagged behind the others.

He was lost in the strange capital city of Dacia. He could only follow his friends between houses and along narrow streets. Ahead, an old woman gestured to them to come inside her house. He recognized her.

They hid in the house's patio. Most soldiers passed by, but three broke down the door. John heard the woman's protests and crossed himself.

"Over the wall," said one of his companions. They were younger, so they helped him scale it, something he could not have done alone.

And so it went for most of the night until John parted ways with his friends at the new border created by the attacking Roman army. To his right and left he could see fires where other soldiers had bivouacked; the flames from their campfires turned the clouds the color of his drying blood.

John melted into the forest. He only stopped once at a creek to wash his wound, which started the bleeding again.

*****

At the Danube, John sensed he was trapped yet again—not by the city but by the dark waters. He looked along the shore to his right and left. *Which way to go?* He kneeled and put his palms together, asking for divine intervention. He then saw the ring, which he managed to remove to read the inscription as he had done so many times. His fingers thinned over the years.

"Please give me strength, my Lord," he said in a weary voice. "I am exhausted, my legs are old and feeble, but my heart is still strong even though I have lost my way."

He stared across the waters, his pulse slowing to a more restful rhythm. A light that outshone the sun then appeared upon the waters, blinding him for a moment. The Mother of God appeared within the light and walked toward him. Once on the shore, she grasped his hand once again.

"John, you must go to the land where you prepared your tomb. It is time."

"There's so much left to do," he said. "My missionary work calls me elsewhere now that I have finished in Dacia."

"Let others continue that work. We are waiting for you."

"But Holy Mother, I have lost my way."

She pointed along the shore in one direction. "There lies your route."

He watched as she and the light faded from view. He pounded his head, hoping the awful residual headache from the vision would go away. *A blessed headache, to be sure,* he thought, smiling in spite of the pain.

He then stood with new resolve. By following the Danube's shore in the direction she had indicated, he found a ferry. He used most of the money he had left to book a passage.

"Looks like you were in quite a fight," said the ferry's owner as he took John's coins.

"I come from Dacia. There's a war on."

"Yes, I heard. None of my business. Romans are always fighting someone. The world would be better off without them."

"You speak boldly, but you are a citizen of the Roman Empire."

He shrugged. "Who is not? They own most of the known world. They will soon own Dacia. That does not mean all the people in conquered lands are loyal to their invaders." He said the last in a whisper and continued in that mode. "Many people want them gone, you see. Myself included."

John drew a symbol in the ferry deck's muck. "Do you know what that means?"

The ferry's owner covered the symbol with his foot, using his sandal to erase it. "Never show that to any Romans. They do not like Christians. We have to be careful."

We? The Word is spreading. "But maybe you can help me, brother. I have a long way to go."

"I can only take you across the river. You are on your own after that."

"I am just asking for advice. What's the best way to Ephesus?"

The ferry's owner helped John with more than directions once he found out who he was. He provided some food and money as well as suggestions about how to meet with other groups of Christians, including some groups other disciples and apostles had created long ago. Most John had not heard of, but they were helpful along the route to Ephesus.

The last was a group there—one of many—because the city had a strong Christian tradition dating from the Apostle Paul's days in Ephesus. John had not been there in years, so they were suspicious of their visitor.

*****

"Even here we must be careful," Paul, the group's leader, said. "What proof do you offer that you are the disciple John?"

I am suspicious of this foreigner. Paul studied the older man. He had curly white hair, wide eyes, and pronounced cheekbones. He only lacked a laurel wreath to appear like an old Roman emperor. A haughtiness in his expression added to that effect. *How can he be the disciple?*

"I carry no proof but my belief in my Lord and Savior Jesus Christ. I escaped the troubles in Dacia and made my way here. As you can see, I am an old man." He lifted his blouse, showing the scar from the Roman soldier's blade. "I was almost killed, but some brothers in Christ helped me escape."

"I grant you are an old man," Paul said. "But the disciple Jesus called beloved was last seen around here more than fifty years ago, long before my birth. How can you be that old?"

John laughed. "You are of Jewish blood, so you know of Methuselah, but I am not claiming to be him." He glanced around at the faces of the young, strong men. "Shall I quote words from my gospel to you?"

"That would prove nothing," said one of the other men. "I can quote words from the gospel of John. Many know Greek here. We prefer to speak it over Latin."

"I stayed with the Holy Virgin until her Son took her," John said in Aramaic.

Only Paul understood. "The ancient language of Christ! Still, that's no proof."

John shrugged. "You all would compete well with Thomas."

Paul saw John's hesitation. He then took off the ring. Paul had noticed it before because it was loose on the man's finger. *He is old and emaciated. His fingers are the slim and knobby fingers of an arthritic old man.*

He handed the ring to Paul. "Can you also read the ancient language?"

Paul read the inscription, handed the ring back to John, and fell to his knees. "*Rabbouni*, please forgive us for doubting, but you are so old now and you have been gone for so long."

"Stand, Paul, and the rest of you. We have all been busy teaching the good word. However, I need your help now. Years ago, I prepared my final resting place here when I cared for the Virgin." He glanced around the sea of faces again, all now enthralled. "I need all your help to carry me there after I have passed on."

Chapter Thirty-Seven

Twenty-First Century, House of the Virgin Mary

They found no tourists or pilgrims at the house. Esther pointed out the "Wishing Wall" where pilgrims hid their prayers written on paper or fabric in a stone wall. "They say that the water fountain uses water from a well or spring underneath the Virgin's bedroom. Some pilgrims think it has powers of healing or fertility."

"Superstitions, no doubt," said Bastiann. "Considering what you said, should we call the posted prayers wishes instead? And with all the visitors, how can we possibly find anything Botticelli left here?"

"It's probably like the Wailing Wall in Jerusalem. Caretakers likely clean all the prayers away every so often and burn them. I'm only guessing about both sites, but they're both limited spaces used by innumerable visitors. I must confess I've never been to Jerusalem, though. I'd like to go someday." She peered into the house. "Let's go inside, Bastiann."

The house wasn't large. The structure's restored sections were distinguished from the original remains by a line painted in red. They had entered a room with a central altar along with a large statue of the Virgin Mary. On their right was a doorway into a smaller room. Bastiann followed Esther inside it.

“They say the Virgin slept here.”

“It’s not obvious Botticelli could hide anything here. I’m still worried about that 1881 discovery date.”

“Discovery or rediscovery? We can only decide one way or the other by searching for some evidence Botticelli was here. Like you, I can’t imagine what he would leave behind for us, though.”

“An artistic ‘Botticelli was here’ in place of Kilroy? Something leading us to John’s tomb, possibly? Maybe a real map?”

“We have a word-map, but I haven’t spotted anything like what’s described. I’ve tried to line up that Heracles Gate with this mountain and look beyond. Only rough hills. I had a hunch about the Temple of Domitian, but it didn’t hold water. It’s been frustrating.”

“Here’s a thought: even if Sandro and Leo did come here, they didn’t find the tomb. Isn’t that a possibility?”

“To parrot a famous popular quote from a famous TV series, ‘You know nothing, John Snow.’ You’re the one who suggested Botticelli would offer us a clue.”

Bastiann shrugged. “I’m regretting it, but let’s not waste the trip. We’ll explore the shrine completely. Consider it religious tourism. My mother was quite faithful, you know.”

“In honor of your mother, then. She must have had great patience to raise you.”

*****

“Not much to see here,” said Bastiann. “Too many tourists and too many years have homogenized this site until it’s nothing more than a way for tour guides and buses to make a lot of money.”

"I wonder if Leo and Sandro wanted anything to be found," said Esther. "And, if they had an idea where the saint's tomb was located, why not go there?"

"Maybe they had to return to Florence. Maybe they ran low on funds. Maybe locals were after them. The Ottoman Empire existed even then and they didn't like foreigners. Who knows?"

Esther paused to think. He waited patiently. "Any of those circumstances, or similar ones, could mean they were planning to return one day. In that case, they'd take all their clues and notes with them."

"Ha! You're thinking Sandro Botticelli kept notebooks like Leonardo da Vinci. That's a big assumption, my dear, and there's no evidence for it. Botticelli had no inclinations toward scientific endeavors, for example, where such notetaking was a must. For all we know, he was lazy because he had so many young painters copying and selling what he managed to paint originally."

"Sod it! That's nitpicking, old boy, and unsubstantiated. Plus, the poor man's not here to defend himself." She rubbed her hands together. "My, it's dry around here. My skin's starting to crack."

"Using your hands like those brushes used in archaeological digs won't help."

"Genius! That's it! It's always been dry here, right?"

Where is she going with this? "I don't know. I suppose so. But we're near the Mediterranean. Breezes blowing in from the shore must carry some moisture inland—fog and such. Nature's version of the foggers in the patio at my hotel in Casablanca."

"But none of that is enough to alleviate the dryness for long, especially up here. The eastern and southern Mediterranean area is dry. Suppose they thought anything they found would be safer left here instead of making the journey with them back to Florence."

"I guess that could have occurred. Or they were afraid anything they found would be stolen on the return trip. Police didn't go out of their way to protect tourists and adventurers back then. You're agreeing with me then that something or someone forced them to leave?"

"And maybe they were planning to return."

"I would still take any clues with me, if I were them."

"We're working with a word-map that's a copy. They could have also made a copy."

"I will not be reading it, that's for sure. I'm only taking the word of your professor friend's fine translation. And, by the way, anything John left might be in Aramaic."

"And for Leo and Sandro, possibly in Latin or Florentine Italian. John certainly spoke and wrote Aramaic, but he also could have just written something in Greek or Latin."

"We're jumping around through the centuries like we were in H. G. Wells' time machine." *And arriving nowhere with nary an Eloi around to help us!*

"Hmm." She put her hands on her hips. "That may be the first dystopian novel, but it's irrelevant to our discussion."

"Okay then, let's assume all we've discussed are possibilities. So what?"

"They didn't want anyone to find the clues, that's what! They wanted to return and find them where they hid them."

"If they had any. That puts us in a bind, doesn't it? Maybe we shouldn't waste any more time here. This place has been turned into a tourist trap. Workers probably had the whole area dug up in order to make the place presentable. If they didn't find anything, there's nothing here."

He put his hands on his hips too. *That did it.*

She started pacing. As she paced, she muttered. "Where could they have hidden something?"

She stopped, grinned at him, and dashed out the door. Bastiann followed her to the Wishing Wall. She pointed to the water fountain. "Maybe this water here is holy in the sense it comes from under the house, just like they say. Even pagans consider water to be a source of life. The baptismal ceremony recognizes it as giving the baptized eternal life. Early Christians were immersed when they were baptized. The source of that water can be the essential clue."

Bastiann still wasn't clear on where Esther's thoughts were leading her. She often had good hunches, but, like all hunches, many of them were sometimes wrong. He decided to humor her, wherever her thoughts led her, until she admitted defeat. He would encourage her to give up, from time to time. *Someone has to be practical.*

Chapter Thirty-Eight

Twenty-First Century, House of the Virgin Mary

Esther and Bastiann weren't used to crawling on their hands and knees, but that was the only way they could trace the underground path the water followed to feed the drinking fountain. It wasn't easy, because cobblestones and sandy soil over that pathway were only a bit darker than their surroundings. There were stretches where they had to brush the sand away.

When they arrived to the house, Bastiann started patting the wall. "Possibly a loose block here, Esther. Should we try to remove it?"

Ha! Maybe he's remembering the escape from that house in Norway. Esther had tried to outbid the representative of some Middle Eastern prince for the Rembrandt painting. *Seems so long ago!* She heard the doubt in his voice, so she pointed to the intense blue sky. "Do you think Jehovah will strike us down with a lightning bolt if we fiddle with this block?"

"No, but isn't it a bit of sacrilege if the Virgin Mary did once live here because it was her house and all?"

"Oh, please. If that were the case, most archaeologists would no longer be in business. They break into tombs and ruins all the time. Science facts are better than untrue legends."

"Help me then."

He used the pen he had taken from the hotel to remove what remained of the loose mortar. It was recent and of poor quality, so he didn't have high hopes. Some sloppy workman had likely layered the mortar in to fill the cracks. Or his foreman provided inferior materials.

They removed the stone block, which uncovered a tiny aqueduct where a trickle of water flowed. It was enough to feed the fountain through a clay pipe that had been sawed in half and then rejoined, but it was hard to see farther in under the house's wall.

"Retrieve my backpack from the hire-car," said Esther.

When he returned with it, she took out her penlight torch and used it to see underneath the wall.

"There's pottery in there, some kind of plain vase. It's watermarked, but the highest watermark is just about two-thirds of the way up." She moved away and handed the torch to him. "You have longer arms. Maybe you can reach it."

He managed to pull out the vase without breaking it. Inside they found a thick cloth bag with a leather drawstring.

"Seems promising," said Esther. She tried to open the bag. The drawstring disintegrated. She probed around inside. "There's something rolled up in animal skin. Someone went to a lot of trouble to waterproof the bag's contents."

He glanced around. "Let's put the stone block back and return to the hotel where we can examine the contents at our leisure. Will you agree that if anything appears to be genuine, it goes to a museum?"

"Or the Vatican."

She didn't want to say how long that might take.

*****

Back at the hotel, Esther and Bastiann examined the bag's contents by spreading them out on the room's general-purpose table pushed against one wall. They made a list of what they found rolled up in the animal skin: four brittle pages torn from a journal or travel diary of some sort, a real but old map of the area on parchment, and an older document written on papyrus.

"I'm feeling like Indiana Jones," he said.

"You still look like Hercule Poirot, so get over it. Let's see if we can find any mention of Botticelli or Bruno's relative."

The first thing she did was take overlapping pictures of all their finds with different zoom settings on her mobile. They were then going to split up the work, but the four journal pages were written in an Italian dialect. Esther declared it must be Florentine Italian, so she helped him with his translation. From her days in Switzerland and trips to Italy, she knew variants of Italian, but the writing was a bit hard to decipher and the interpretation wasn't helped by having an incomplete journal entry.

"'...arrived at the house'—there might be a 'we' missing here, among other things—'where they claim the Virgin spent her last days. I am in awe.'" Then there was a switch to different ink. "'Sandro, being the heathen he is, did not seem too impressed. When we found the papyrus, he became more excited.'"

The journal entries went on to describe how the artist Sandro Botticelli and Bishop Leonardo da Padua translated and copied what they had found. They then made the map to St. John's tomb after reading what was on the papyrus and comparing it with the original parchment's text. Then they hid the originals so no one could find them.

"So, we only need the map," said Bastiann.

"Shush. Let me continue to examine the papyrus. It's the most delicate relic we have here—brittle, but well preserved. Let me try to unroll it."

"Shouldn't we be doing this in a controlled environment? Maybe a clean room under a museum curator's supervision?"

"It's not from a computer chip production, Bastiann, but your caution is justified. The Dead Sea Scrolls were handled badly, for example, and who knows how Botticelli and Leo handled this papyrus. But whoever put it in the bag and put the bag in the vase was being careful."

"Sandro Botticelli? He was the artist."

"But Leo would have treated everything with reverence. That was then. Now we have to treat both the map and the papyrus carefully. Both are delicate, but the papyrus even more so. They could have carried the original parchment with them, but this find seems to surpass that one, which dates from the time of Botticelli. Historically, it's not as useful for directions. I think this papyrus is much older."

"Is it signed?"

"Patience. We're dealing with an ancient artifact here." It took her over fifteen minutes to unroll and unfold the ancient document. "To answer your question, it's not signed. The black ink is likely obtained from olive oil, whether it's from John's time or Botticelli's. No matter. Let's try to translate it. My Latin's a wee bit rusty, though."

They both had learned Latin in school. Together they managed a translation, writing it all down on hotel stationery.

*****

Esther's voice wavered a bit as she read their tentative translation of the old document, ignoring the possible optional translations they had indicated.

"I am worried for Mother Mary. I cannot determine what is wrong with her. Neither can the physicians who the faithful secretly bring to the house to attend to her. I suspect our Savior is coming to gather the Holy Mother into His arms very soon, and I feel helpless, for I can do nothing.

While I care for her, I am trying to finish my version of the life and times of our Lord and Savior, Jesus Christ, so all the faithful may have something to remember Him by. Perhaps they will remember me for my own small role in history too, for I have endeavored and will continue to endeavor to tell the world about His wonderful teachings and messages of hope. If it is His will, I will live a long life and preach.

I have already lived longer than my brother, that other Son of Thunder, so I count my blessings, but I believe Our Savior planned it this way. There will be many who tell the tale of how God's Son came to Earth to save us all, so my account will only be one of many. Most likely it is not needed, but something drives me to finish my writing. After it is done, I will be able to meet with congregations face-to-face, allowing them to see a witness who was there, and they can prepare for my visits by reading my text.

I have found burial places in the hills south of the city for Mother Mary and me, but I am not sure she will need one if she is lifted up to accompany her Son and share in His heavenly glory. I know she expects that, and, after bearing witness after the Crucifixion, a mystery no mere mortal can hope to understand but I must believe because I saw it, I must confess she is probably right. She has also said she will sometimes appear to the faithful in centuries to come, a reminder that God and his Son are still watching over us. Nevertheless, she will have her place of rest out of an abundance of caution on my part, for she is holy and should be revered forever, undisturbed until the end of time.

My own burial place will also be in the hills overlooking the river, not far from where the Virgin might lie. Sometime in the future, I will return to this place to join the Holy Mother and also pass on into His grace. I hope my earthly remains will also lie undisturbed for all time, but one can never tell with the Romans and the unrest in this area of the world. Also I expect men and women will stray from the path of righteousness for many centuries to come.

I also expect there will be righteous men who will carry His story of salvation to the ends of the Earth. To believe otherwise would be giving in to Satan and all his minions, something that would imply a horrible future for all people and God's creatures. Perhaps Christ will come again and send the unfaithful and the unrighteous down to Hell and raise everyone else up to be at His side, basking in the glory of the one true God.

I showed this text to the Magdalene before she left. She said it was a good plan. She says she might return here too, and that we should meet in Rome if at all possible. Let her travel in the Lord's grace."

Chapter Thirty-Nine

Twenty-First Century, Selçuk

Esther was nearly dancing with excitement.when she finished. *What a find!*

She looked at Bastiann and he was smiling, enjoying the moment too. When her adrenalin level subsided a bit, she had second thoughts.

"He didn't seem too certain about his future. What do you think was his writing project?"

"I'd say it sounds like his gospel. A bit too early for the Book of Revelation, even though no one's sure he wrote that."

"Okay. We know he lived much longer than the Virgin Mary. Doesn't the legend say her Assumption occurred about a decade after Christ's Ascension? If I remember my father's words correctly, it was about fifteen years."

"John wasn't sure that would happen. Another doubting Thomas."

"On the contrary," said Esther, "Thomas doubted Christ; John didn't. The disciple is speaking for Mary and himself. He has no reason to know what their fates might be. He can only hope."

"We're wallowing in non-productive theological musings here," Bastiann said. "Let's get focused. How could Leo and Sandro draw a map from this?"

"If John wrote this," Esther said, "then legends about the house were true, and he was there taking care of Mary. However, his whole life after the Ascension is a mystery. We do know one important fact: unlike the Shroud of Turin, which was proven not to be Christ's burial cloth since it dated from just before the Renaissance era, we could have proof for the occurrence of true events here and not mere myths. Perhaps the House of the Virgin Mary is more than a tourist trap."

Bastiann returned to the initial piece of Esther's spiel where she mentioned the Shroud. "Didn't John himself describe that burial cloth in his Gospel?"

"Bravo, Bastiann! You have read the Bible. But there's no mention in the other three books, as far as I can remember. I don't know about the non-canonical gospels. My father wouldn't have read any of those, nor allowed us to do so. He even considered the three synoptic gospels as duplicates, calling John's the more original. He also swallowed the old interpretation from the Middle Ages that the Magdalene was a prostitute. That's been debunked."

"The other Mary," said Bastiann. "But if John mentioned the Shroud?"

"Well yes, he described a linen used to cover Christ's face. That linen isn't the Shroud of Turin, if you accept the scientific facts. In the same way, I have to test this piece of papyrus. Anyone could have written these words, even Bishop Leonardo da Padua. To prove they're John's will never be definite but dating the papyrus will help." She paused to think. "Do you know where there's a scientific lab nearby?"

"Maybe at a university?"

Esther searched her memory. "There's one in Konya, although I'm not sure they would have the equipment I need. We might need to go to Ankara or Istanbul, but I've never visited any university in Turkey, and I don't have any erudite friends in this country. I prefer to take all the artifacts back to England."

"Would that be legal?"

She smiled. "Temporarily, but maybe not. I'm not certain giving any of them to the Vatican would strictly be legal either. I can imagine the Turks taking it right to the Hague. The House of Mary is a Muslim shrine too." She pondered a bit more. "But the artifacts are like any work of art, aren't they? The public should know about them and, if possible, be able to observe them. Or biblical scholars, at least. After all, you do have to give the antiquity experts something to do." She now flashed a sly grin. "Whoever we think is deserving to receive them, there's nothing that says there can't be a bit of a delay."

"So we're smuggling them out of the country?"

"No. For now, I'll put everything back in the vase as they were and put the vase in a secure place. I'm not sure there exists such a place in this country right now with Turkey continuing to cozy up with China and Russia and retreating from the E.U. and NATO, but I can open a bank account and rent a safety deposit box. That will have to do for now while we follow the map."

"So one little sentence in all that John wrote led the dynamic duo of Leo and Sandro to make a believable map?"

She pointed to the map. "The river is far different now. But in John's time...no, even in Botticelli's time, there were hills. We just have to compare Leo and Sandro's map to a current one. Rivers change, but hills don't."

"Doesn't that assume they found the tomb? Otherwise, we don't know if they confirmed what's stated in the original parchment."

"One can only give it a try."

"I see. I thought you just wanted to prove Botticelli was never here."

"Apparently, he was. The next logical step is to find the saint's bones."

"What if Leo and Sandro took them?"

"That would be a problem."

*****

"See. I told you!" Esther pointed at the topographical map she found in the hotel's concierge center, comparing it to the map from Mary's House.

"I hate to dampen your enthusiasm," said Bastiann, "but all I see is that the river is situated a bit differently with respect to Ephesus and the hills. That can just mean Leo and Sandro were terrible cartographers."

"Perhaps. Botticelli wasn't as good with perspective as da Vinci, who was a genius at it, but that might be irrelevant. Look at the hills sketched on their map. The river moved, but the hills couldn't have."

He seemed doubtful. "Next you're going to tell me we're off to explore those hills."

"If I'm reading this modern map correctly, none of them are higher than five-hundred meters and John would have wanted to be above any floods. I think I read somewhere there was one course change in the river that occurred quite a while ago and it silted over, making it unnavigable. Maybe that happened many times since John's days." She jumped to a new idea. "Good thing we still have the Range Rover. Come on, we have a bank account to open and some bones to find."

Finding a bank with safe deposit boxes wasn't easy, but she spotted the central bank in Selçuk corresponding to a common national bank and guessed correctly. It had safe deposit boxes. She entered, the bright street sun changing to cool fluorescent lighting with whispering overhead fans. The wood and old plaster was a comforting bit of Europe. The clerks were helpful too.

By the time the vase was stashed away as safely as possible, the afternoon was gone. She smiled at the nun who was exchanging euros at one of the bank windows as she left. She couldn't see her face, but she thought of Sister Denise. *Can it be her? She did say she was on a pilgrimage.* She tried to remember details about her train companion's habit, but she couldn't. *I paid too much attention to her young, innocent face.* Esther had also seen other nuns visiting the Christian sites. They appeared to mingle well among the other devout tourists. *Maybe a bit of escape from the solitude of the cloisters!*

They had decided to wait until the next morning to follow the map into the hills. They opted to visit Inspector Erkan instead. Although he seemed more chipper and greeted Esther with a broad smile, after introducing Bastiann, Esther asked him how he was feeling.

"I'll be discharged later today," he said. He was sitting on the edge of his hospital bed. "Any luck finding that weasel, Bruno?"

"We weren't exactly trying," she said. "Although, I may have looked over my shoulder once or twice."

"We saw your colleague at dinner last night," Bastiann said. "Thanks for keeping tabs on Esther. She always manages to find trouble, or vice versa."

"I'm afraid Toscano is more than trouble. He tried to kill me, after all. And from what I heard, that German victim was also lucky."

Esther glanced at Bastiann and then back at Erkan. "That's why Bastiann's here, but we appreciate your colleague's watchfulness. I hope he can find and arrest Bruno."

"That's part of the plan. I doubt my colleague was following you two, by the way. He's pursuing Bruno. I'm sorry if we're using you as bait, as it were."

Bastiann grinned. "I would have done the same thing." He gestured at the hospital bed, thinking of Philippa. "Perhaps we can see each other tomorrow evening in a much better setting."

"I'd like that. I will look forward to our meeting. Hopefully we can make it a dinner. The food here is terrible."

Chapter Forty

Second Century, Ephesus

"We are wearing you out," said Paul, who was dining with John several weeks after his arrival in Ephesus. "But all of us want to hear your stories about your times with Him and your adventures afterwards. Even your more general sermons leave us spellbound. You bring life to the parables you wrote down, for example. You do not realize what this means to the community here."

"I can only guess, and I am honored," said John. "And yes, I am becoming a bit tired. I have been weary these last years, you know. We have had four Bishops of Rome since Peter, and our movement is still persecuted by the Romans. I have to confess my patience wears thin."

Paul shrugged. "I will probably die before the first emperor accepts Christianity. What of it? His Kingdom is not here on Earth." He broke off another piece of bread and bit into a fig. "What was she like?"

"I only knew her in her later years. Her Son was busy elsewhere and we were His followers."

"I do not mean the Virgin Mother. I mean the Magdalene. I presume she gave Him the ring."

"From your first reaction when you read the inscription, you must know that." He raised his chalice and stared into the dark wine. "I am afraid we lost track of each other. I regret to say I have not heard from her in years. I did hear she was working on her own gospel. I wonder if she has read mine, the finished version."

"But when you knew her, what was she like?"

"Why are you so curious?"

Paul seemed embarrassed. "There are those who speak ill of her."

"Most likely some of those same people who would exclude women from doing the Lord's work. Let me tell you this, Paul. Mary is a smart, strong woman who is a planner and organizer. She believed in Him and His movement, and she did everything she could to support His work before He was crucified, and to continue it long afterwards. Do not belittle women or how they can help spread the good news. Men and women must work together in that, complementing each other."

Paul smiled. "Almost another sermon. You should expand on it for our next service. It might make some of our men better husbands." He fidgeted. "You would not put stock in what rumormongers say then?"

"Take it from someone who knew her well. If she is now in Heaven with Him, I will see her soon. If she is still walking among the living, I wish her a long life." He thought a bit before continuing. "Beware of those who would bend His message for their own purposes. They are no better than the old Temple scholars our Christ debated with. Too many succumb to lust for power and exploit their fellow men. That is not the way of Christ."

"Can I preach those words myself, John?"

"You may use them. I would be honored."

*****

That night John dreamed. In his vision he saw Heaven. All His disciples were there save two, standing in a circle around a figure all dressed in white. The two Marys were in the circle too. The central figure turned, but the face was so radiant John could not tell if it was Him. He knew the voice, though.

"The day is coming when I will gather you up to join us, John. Be not afraid. My Mother and the Magdalene are also here and will welcome you."

"I have tried so hard to spread your Word," said John. "I believe I have failed you."

"Many who follow you through the centuries will feel like that sometimes. It is not always easy for men and women to accept the Way of my Father or His love. I can ask no more of you, John. Be at peace until your time comes."

John awoke, drenched in sweat. He left his bed and threw open the window curtains, but there was no breeze coming from the river to cool him.

He chided himself. He had not inquired about the Magdalene. *I just had that discussion with Paul! Apparently she has passed on if my vision is a true one.*

He became sad at that thought. He had lasted far longer than he had expected.

As dawn broke, he was still standing there, but then he collapsed.

*****

"Seems like a lonely place for him," said Paul's friend.

They were standing over a huge slab covering the disciple's body in the crypt below. Some of their group waited outside, ready to have the simple ceremony the disciple had requested.

Yes. Lonely and maybe not appropriate for such a great man. Paul had known him for a short time, but the teacher had left them all motivated. He knew the Jewish traditions and respected them, but he had also implored them not to forget about all other men and women who needed to hear His words. He said He was the Messiah for all of them, not only the Jews. He may have been repetitive at times, but he was old. And the repetition reinforced those great ideas.

He said other holy men would follow him and spread the Good Word near and far. They would call the Word by different names and speak differently about God, but their motivations would always be the same: prepare all men and women to be at peace and enjoy God's grace in the hereafter.

Paul thought some of those words might be only an old man's ramblings, a man who had lived too long and seen too much, but he had to respect him. One day he too would be old and ramble on to his grandchildren about his days with the great disciple. *And burying him!*

"He will be safe here. The cave is well hidden."

"So simple, yet a clever design."

"He designed it himself," said Paul, "but some of your ancestors also built it and the Virgin's resting place."

"I wonder where that is?"

"It is better that no one knows. You realize she is not likely there, right?"

"And will he...you know."

Paul thought a moment and then smiled. "Does it matter? His work will be known in all the centuries to come. He was Christ's beloved disciple and wrote about his time with Him. For that he will be known at least. The Church might forget John's missionary work, but his gospel will live on."

"I will miss the old man."

"We all will."

They made the trip back to Ephesus in silence as slowly as they had come, a humble funeral procession fit for a humble man.

Chapter Forty-One

Twenty-First Century, Selçuk

"Where are those two going?" Erkan asked his colleague, Mustafa, as they watched the Range Rover disappear down the street.

Mustafa checked his mobile. "It's a local rental, so they're not going far. A lot of these crazy Christians go out to visit holy sites. They were at the House of the Virgin Mary, for example. They all go there. Even Muslims go there if they're not from around here."

Erkan shook his head. "But they're not your typical tourists. In a sense, they're not even..." He grabbed his colleague's arm, pointing to a man who was walking fast. "That's Bruno! I'll never forget that weasel's face!"

"And where's he off to?" asked the colleague. "Should we follow him or the other two?"

"Let's follow Bruno. We need to arrest him. He belongs in jail. Esther and Bastiann will be fine if he's no longer in the picture." He stared once again along the street where the Range Rover had disappeared. "I'd love to know where they're going, but Bruno is our priority right now."

They followed Bruno for two blocks. Their quarry then turned down a side street. They followed him and stopped to watch as he climbed into an SUV and took off.

"We'll lose him!" said Mustafa. "I'll go get the car."

The deputy dashed off, leaving Erkan in the narrow backstreet. He wasn't in good shape still, so he leaned against a wall to wait for his ride. *At least there's shade here.* He didn't have to wait long.

Bruno returned in his SUV and headed directly for Erkan. *He's trying to kill me!* Erkan squeezed flat into an inset in the building's wall. The edge of the inset clipped off the side-view mirror of the SUV as it passed within centimeters of Erkan's belt buckle.

The inspector watched the SUV speed along the narrow street in time to confront their small patrol car turning the corner. There was a horrible crash and the sound of ripping metal as the heavy SUV turned their small police vehicle into scrap metal. *The petrol will explode!*

Erkan ran and pulled Mustafa out just in time. He dialed dispatch. "Inspector Erkan here! Mustafa is down! We need an ambulance!"

*****

Bruno had seen Brookstone and van Coevorden put something away in the bank, so he knew the two were onto something. He had planted a tracking device in their hire-car. *That pesky inspector and his colleague are now eliminated and I can follow Esther and her friend without them knowing it.*

As he headed away from town, Bruno grinned as he watched Esther's blip on his laptop's screen. *Isn't modern technology wonderful? Even in Turkey you can find GPS tracker units.* Most likely not in Selçuk, but he had purchased some things in Ankara using a stolen credit card. He had a hunch he might need it when he saw the German buy a GPS unit. He also purchased the cheap laptop; Google Maps was a great help. He hated to waste the money but figured all his investments would soon pay off. Now he was living off of stolen credit cards, but figured the local cops would take forever to do anything about it since they belonged to tourists.

By then he was obsessed with finding the saint's bones. That would make everything worthwhile: losing the armoire, losing the Botticelli painting, attacking the German and the Turkish inspector, and now killing him and the other cop. People would pay good money to see St. John's bones. Or he could sell them to the Vatican. *Yes! Leo would like that! And I will be famous!* His smile turned into a frown. *But I'll have to kill Esther and her companion, or I'll be infamous. And maybe I'll return to Vienna and take back the Botticelli. It's mine, after all! Moretti's slut deserves to die too.*

He saw when the blip stopped. He slowed and proceeded with caution. *They can't know I'm pursuing them.* He soon spotted their Range Rover, parked the SUV off road in a small copse of scraggly trees, and walked toward their hire-car, gun in hand. No one was in it.

He looked up at the ridge. *They have to be up there. But where?*

He soon spotted Esther's corpulent friend a good two kilometers away and two hundred meters up. *Should I wait here and let them bring down the treasures we're all seeking?*

He wasn't athletic, but he decided not to wait. It would be just like the two do-gooders to leave the bones where they found them and report their location to the Turkish government or the Vatican.

*****

Bruno no longer had the aid of his GPS unit, but it would have done him no good. He pulled the tracker from under the car and pocketed it. *Thank God I spied the boyfriend. He reminds me of someone.* Bruno sighed as he approached the hill and looked up. He had to climb the steep slope and then make his way along the ridgeline toward where he saw the Interpol agent. He cursed in a low voice every time he nearly slipped on the loose dirt and rocks. He hoped all this effort was worth his while. *For causing me all this trouble, they deserve to die!*

He passed by various caves and counted himself lucky he didn't have to follow the two into them. His claustrophobia reared its ugly head even at the thought, but he had to steel himself just in case they did find anything.

Yes, they were onto something. Or, at least, they thought they were. The caves' existence didn't mean bones were inside. They might not find anything at all. He figured he would kill them anyway, if only for giving him false hope. At least their murders would give him time to make his getaway. *The police probably aren't too happy I killed two of theirs!*

He wondered if his ancestor had come this way. *Maybe with Botticelli? Now there was a pair!* Sandro Botticelli was a man of the world and an enemy of Leonardo da Vinci while his ancestral relative, another Leonardo, was intent on finding Christian relics for fame and fortune. *Was my old uncle Leo even pious? Or was he like all those worldly princes from city-states who became popes?* Bruno wondered how Leo viewed the Medici. He had read some of Machiavelli. *That's one way to be remembered, write a book on how to be a despot!* He preferred to avoid both reading and writing, if he could.

Perspiration was pouring from his brow now. It almost blinded him, forcing him to stop from time to time to clean his glasses with a dirty handkerchief that left them smeared even more. He nearly missed the two disappearing into the hillside.

They found something!

Part Four

Discovery

"Greater love hath no man than this, that a man lay down his life for his friends."—John 15:13

Chapter Forty-Two

Fifteenth Century, House of the Virgin Mary

After they hid a vase containing the old papyrus, some pages from Leo's diary, and Sandro's hastily prepared map, the artist woke the guide. "It is time to return," he said.

The guide squinted while looking at the position of the sun. "Good man. Yes, we need to return. It is not safe to stay here any longer."

They were soon on the road back to Ephesus. After half an hour, they were attacked by midges, not bandits.

"They rise from the river as the sun crawls toward the horizon," said the guide. "We need to ride a bit faster. We can leave them behind when we turn away from the river and it becomes deeper and runs faster."

The midges were gone after another fifteen minutes, but Leo needed to stop to relieve himself. Sandro and the guide also dismounted to stretch their sore muscles.

Sandro looked up the road ahead and saw a cloud of dust approaching them. "I see lots of riders," he said to the guide.

The guide stared at where he was pointing. "Bandits or soldiers coming on the road from Ephesus. No matter which, we will soon have trouble."

"What should we do?"

"Try to outrun them to the sea."

"You jest. That is a long ride and in the wrong direction."

"There are fishing villages on the coast. If the riders are bandits, we will be safe and can return to Ephesus another day."

"And if they are soldiers?"

"They probably will catch us. They have stronger steeds."

"We have nothing for them to steal. The innkeeper has all our papers and valuables, remember?"

"My cousin is a responsible man. Your property is safe until we return, as I guaranteed. The question is: can we return? If these are bandits, they will steal our clothes and horses and then kill us."

"Damn it to hell! Leo, finish your business! We have a race to run!"

*****

The horsemen were Ottoman soldiers, not bandits. They caught up with the trio and surrounded them. Their leader ordered them to dismount from their lathered horses. Other soldiers took the reins and led the horses off to the side.

"These men are guests in our country," the guide told the leader. He translated what he said for his clients.

The leader's uniform was old and tattered, but he had a few medals compared to the others. They all wore turbans, long coats, and puffy pants stuffed into boots. Each was armed with a long rifle and scimitar. The leader brandished his sabre as if he were going to chop off their heads, but his long mustache twitched in amusement as he studied Leo and Sandro.

"We have no use for foreigners," he said.

"They are pilgrims," said the guide, after translating. "We thought you were bandits, not fine soldiers from the empire. We were returning from the House of the Virgin Mary, the Holy Mother of the Prophet Jesus. They are searching for the tomb of St. John the Divine." He translated that too.

The leader paused to think about that and then spat onto the dusty road. "Christians? We have no use for them either."

"Tell him we are faithful to Allah in our own way," said Leo after the translation.

The guide gave a curt nod and passed on Leo's message.

"I'm hot and tired and in no mood for a philosophical discussion," said the soldiers' leader. "We will keep your horses. Consider that a tax levied by the Ottoman Empire. Count yourselves lucky we were not bandits. We are after them."

"Does he expect us to walk back to Ephesus?" said Sandro after the translation.

"You can find the river and swim upstream for all I care," was the answer passed on to them. He waved to his men.

They watched the soldiers as they rode off back the way they had come.

*****

"Great way to end our trip," said Sandro as they walked into Ephesus past the Temple of Domitian. Leo looked exhausted. "And it is not over yet. We have the whole return journey to Florence still ahead of us. Some vacation. Leo, you are responsible for this fiasco."

"The soldiers' leader spoke correctly," said the guide. "If they had been bandits, our bones would soon be bleaching in the morning sun, if vultures were not still picking at them after their nighttime feast."

"A miracle then," said Sandro. "You will have to walk with us to the inn so we can settle our accounts."

"I am sorry you found nothing," said the guide.

"Say, how did you know we were searching for St. John's burial place?" asked Leo.

"The gossip was all around town. Plus, many foreigners come here to try to prove the saint was buried here or never was here. The number of gossipers does not compare with the one of foreigners, but it is a large number."

"I do not need any saint's bones right now," said Sandro, "only a pitcher of cool water before my own bones turn to dust."

Leo nodded but said nothing.

"I would like to stay and search for the burial place," he said later at the inn after their meager dinner of a questionable stew and stale bread that evening. "We have come so far and we are most likely near it. It must be in those hills somewhere. The papyrus confirmed what the parchment said."

"Assuming the old man returned here to die," said Sandro. "Near as I can make out the timeline, the legends say he was here to take care of the Virgin. He then took off for parts unknown and only returned here to die. That's all at least more or less consistent, but the last is suspect. When death comes, it often is a surprise unless you believe he could read the future. They say some prophets and saints had special powers. Visions and all that."

Leo shrugged. "I have never questioned the powers prophets or saints had, including foretelling their own fates. And we all have visions."

"Hmm. So, they say. I call mine dreams or nightmares. But what would you do if you stay? Mope about until our Lord and Savior decides to take pity on you and put you out of your misery?"

"I would hire some cheap labor to help me dig for the saint's bones," said Leo.

"Not a bad idea, but you would have to know where to dig, my friend. Old John's 'burial places in the hills' is a bit obscure and the parchment's writer seems to have confused Mt. Koressos and Mary's House. Nothing he says allows me to put a mark on the map. We have no clue where the saint's bones are. Not specifically, at any rate."

Leo tapped his head. "We have directions and your map stored in our heads. You see the wine bottle half empty. I see it half full. We have clues, Sandro. Albeit imprecise ones. Will you not help me find the burial place? Help us dig after we find it?"

"I will not have the patience, and I do not share your religious enthusiasm." Sandro laughed at Leo's expression. "And what will you pay laborers with? We only have enough money to return to Italy, old friend. Of course, if I just have to pay for one traveler..."

"All right. We will leave all our clues where they are at the house as planned in case we die on the journey. If not us at a later time, maybe someone else can use them to find the tomb."

"You are a morbid sort. What a great traveling companion."

"The feeling is mutual. Are we still stopping in Rome?"

"Likely useless," said Sandro. "Who will believe us? The Vatican probably receives many accounts of legends and myths from travelers. They most likely discount them as the dreams of religious fanatics or fools, although I never will be included in either group. Besides, expeditions cost money. Ours did, and they are astute businessmen, those princes of the Church."

"We can give a detailed description of our search and what we found. If they have any sense, they will try to confirm our story."

"It would have been a lot easier if you had not left those diary pages in the vase. That's evidence we could use. Now your journal is incomplete."

"I will write everything down again on our return journey."

Sandro shrugged. "I understand. You want the Vatican to mount an expedition, make it all official, and give you a pat on the back, or have the Medici or the Vespucci family pay you for it. Neither will occur, but we can hope. Be forewarned, they will take all the credit. You will receive none, and it is credit you want, my friend." He glanced through the dirty window at the dusty street. "I wonder if I will have any clients left who want to commission paintings when I return. I have to make a living, you know."

Leo grinned at Sandro. "You can always become a priest."

Chapter Forty-Three

Twenty-First Century, Ephesus

"Stop here!" Esther said sometime before Bruno had discovered their hire-car.

Bastiann parked the Range Rover, exited, and walked around to open the door for Esther. They studied the hills, sharing the binoculars.

"I'm not the mountaineering type," he said. "And we don't have climbing equipment."

"Those aren't mountains, Superman. We'll be okay. Do you see that broken line about two-thirds the way up?"

"I do, and I fear you're going to tell me we will be climbing up there."

"That's the plan. I think it's some kind of ledge or trail." She turned and faced back toward Ephesus, using her compass to orient herself. "Line of sight to the Heracles Gate could hit about in the middle of the ridge. I'm no surveyor, so we should start at the far end where it drops down a bit and the access to that ledge will be easier."

"And what do we do if we follow the path and it truly is broken—that is, it disappears from time to time, and it's only our eyes telling us it's continuous?"

"We either work around the gaps or admit defeat. I'm sure the old boy didn't want to make it easy for anyone to find his tomb."

"Erosion could have made the path to it an impossible one now. Two thousand years of erosion, to be precise." He shook his head.

"Nineteen hundred and fifty is a better approximation. Hitch your pants up, love. We're off to find a tomb."

"My pants are on just fine. I'll leave my jacket in the car, though."

*****

Their climb to the path was difficult. Esther took the lead. In some spots, she would start to slide down, going on all fours to stop her fall. Bastiann had a slightly lower center of gravity, so he helped her continue by pushing on her butt. Their way was far from a straight line as they moved up, sideways, and backtracked, but eventually they both stood on an outcropping that was a part of the path they'd spotted from below.

"Don't look down," said Esther.

He had already glanced down the slope to spot the distant Range Rover. It seemed like centuries separated them from the hire-car. He smiled at her. "Now you tell me." He found his handkerchief and mopped his brow. "I believe it's warmer but less humid here. The breeze has disappeared too."

"Or the climb has taken too long. The sun's much higher now. Stiff upper lip, love. We're nearly there."

"Where is there? You have no idea if we'll find anything, I wager."

"We can't know if we don't look."

"What exactly are we searching for? More ruins? There are enough in Ephesus."

"If there are ruins up here, they aren't in plain sight below. Probably more like a crypt tucked into a cave somewhere, or maybe just a cave *au naturel*. Hard to imagine anyone constructing anything major up here."

"We don't have any idea how many Christians were around here in John's time. If he died long after Mary, they possibly had time to work on his burial spot."

"Only guesses until we find the tomb."

They continued to search.

"There!" Bastiann pointed. They both saw a meter-by-meter opening in solid rock that would be hidden by boulders to anyone on the road below. They worked their way toward it.

"Lots of loose rock. This better be it. I'm knackered. Becoming old is no fun." She paced on the ledge in front of the cave's entrance. "It's possible the opening was larger initially, but there was a bit of a landslide and your erosion. Find me that torch." He searched her backpack and handed it to her. She went to her knees and shined the light into the opening. "It goes down. The landslide wasn't enough to bury everything. I think it becomes bigger inside."

"Can we enter?"

Esther's torso was already through the opening, but she backed out. "Empty." She stood. "But where there's one cave, there's likely another. Let's keep searching."

*****

As they continued on, Esther slipped. Bastiann grabbed her hand before she tumbled down the steep cliff. They embraced for a brief moment and then kept on going. There were more caves. The fifth one they found was more promising, but it was like the first and had an even smaller opening.

This time her initial inspection was followed by "Eureka!" when she backed out and stood. "Some stone masonry has been done in there. Let's clear away some rubble to make it easier to enter."

An hour later they were standing inside the cave. The air was cool and dry.

He walked around the huge stone slab. It was not raised more than a meter above the floor of the cavern. "It looks like a tomb's cover, but how will we move it?"

She sat on the slab and glanced around. "Good question? Here's a logical antecedent: how did they move it? It looks like it could take all the disciples to do so, and then some."

"Maybe we should just leave well enough alone," he said, taking a seat on the slab beside Esther. "I'm thinking of the Book of Revelation."

"What do you mean? By viewing the saint's bones, we'll cause Armageddon?"

"I'm for the most part agnostic, but maybe there's something to all the miracles and avenging angels."

"And maybe Ezekiel's wheel was a flying saucer? How can you battle a bunch of cartel members and still be afraid of myths?" *That reminds me, I never told him about my meeting with Ernesto. No sense worrying him now.*

"Parents still give their children a religious education. Your parents in particular."

Bastiann, ever the critic. Education at all levels was important to her, but she didn't know if it ever inculcated moral principles in students. Most professors at all levels were bored and boring, even in public schools, the mainstay for all parents to ensure the rise in class stature for their offspring.

Am I an elitist? Maybe. Education was one place where she differed with Labour leaders and fell more in line with her father's educational preferences.

"Let's consider the good side of that. Morality has taken a beating throughout world history; it's not in style today. A truly religious education does wonders to create individual morality, but schools don't provide it. Christianity moved beyond a punishing God, for the most part. Except for the Book of Revelation, the New Testament features a loving God, not the vengeful one from the Old Testament. You will find the Jews hoped for that in Isaiah. At any rate, I see all that as an evolution toward a better sense of morality."

"So you're ready to greet the Four Horsemen?" Bastiann said with a smile.

"I go to the racetrack occasionally. I like horses. I would be at that extravaganza in Kentucky every year if I had the money to trot off to the States."

He scowled. "Okay. This is taking us nowhere. Our discussion is irrelevant because there's no way to remove this slab to find the sarcophagus, if there is one. It might only be an old well or something."

"No, I suspect the slab and what it covers is the sarcophagus because St. John would want to keep it simple. But, as you say, for all we know, there's nothing inside. We'll never know until we take a peek." She thought a bit. "I wonder if Leo and Sandro managed to enter." She glanced around. "By the same token, that same simplicity would imply it should be easy to move the slab. No obvious levers around anywhere, unless they were wood, which means they would have rotted away by now."

"Maybe the top has hinges."

"Now that's thinking outside the box, if you pardon the clichéd metaphor, but maybe not hinges. Move your bum."

He stood and watched her walk around the edge of the slab. At the far side there was a rumble and the edge opposite Esther tilted up a little more than a meter.

"You see, simplicity. Or not, depending on your point of view. It's balanced. No hinges, just pivots. But I'm not heavy enough. Jump up here with me."

The huge slab tilted upwards some more, leaving an opening of almost a meter and a half in height and revealing crude stone steps covered by rubble.

"I'll bet it closes by walking up the slab," he said.

"Forget your analysis of ancient engineering techniques for now. I'm going down."

He followed her.

*****

The two were soon standing in a vault that had been crudely fashioned from the simple cave by some ancient stone masons. There was a lot of rubble—a section of the ceiling had collapsed—and skeletal remains rested upon a smaller, thinner slab atop a stone pedestal.

"Do you think it's the saint's bones?" whispered Esther, walking around the remains, snapping pictures with her mobile.

"Maybe just some old VIP," said Bastiann, walking behind her. "No resurrection here that I can see." He spotted the ring on one bony finger. "Not a great place for grave thieves, either. Only one simple ring to be had."

She bent toward the skeleton, gazing into the eye sockets. She imagined the saint's eyes there, angry they had disturbed his peace. She jerked when the skull moved as if he were awakening from the sleep they had disturbed. She saw his arms reaching for her.

"Mary, you have arrived to be with me at last. You are old and I am dead. How are we still here?"

Oh, Lordy! "I'm not the Virgin or your Magdalene. They're gone, John. Long gone. Their souls now at peace."

"No, you are Mary the Magdalene, the organizer of our movement. Do you know...?"

"Esther! Are you okay? What's that you're mumbling?"

"A bit of Aramaic? And I hardly know the language!" She shook her head to clear it and then turned to stare at him. "Just overpowered by the moment, that's all. And the air is a bit stale in here." She removed the ring and looked inside the band at the inscription. "Something is etched here. Speaking of Aramaic, that's what this is, I think. I'd say that dates it a bit. How many Aramaic speakers do you know?"

"One simple ring doesn't make a saint."

"Doubting Thomas. I'll have to convince you by carbon-dating the bones." She pulled a pencil and paper from her pocket. "I need your good eyes."

In spite of himself, he glanced at the skeleton's eye sockets. "Why don't you take the ring?"

"Seems a bit sacrilegious."

"Aha. Now it's your turn. Do only a rubbing then and put it back, if you're against robbing gravesites."

"Good idea. But I also want to write it down the best I can."

He took the ring and studied it. "Looks like Hebrew."

"The Aramaic alphabet came from the Phoenicians and was a predecessor to the Hebrew alphabet. Shine my torch here so I can see better. The rubbing will allow us to correct any errors later, assuming I don't lose the paper."

*****

After Esther finished the rubbing, which hadn't been easy to do, she put the ring back on the finger. "Go up. I'll join you in a bit." Bastiann saw her bow her head and then went back up the stairs. She soon followed. They walked across the slab to close it.

"I guess that ends this adventure, Bastiann. We only have circumstantial evidence we found St. John's burial place."

"If the carbon dating proves everything is from more recent times, it will be a clear negative."

"But if it doesn't, it's still only circumstantial evidence. That would be even more depressing."

She plopped onto the slab's edge and let out a sigh. He joined her and put his arm around her.

"Our pal, Castilblanco, would call this a real cold case," he said with a chuckle.

She grinned. "I didn't see any evidence of a homicide."

"Or any other crime for that matter. Maybe just some old man whose bones we've disturbed." He paused before going on to another thought. "If John truly lived to a ripe old age, I'm betting he saw a lot in his life that's not in his gospel."

"If he truly wrote it. Many events in antiquity are difficult to prove. They're lost in the fog of myths and legends. We're free to believe or disbelieve, depending on our predilections. That's sad."

"Don't become all maudlin on me, old girl. Let's leave this morbid place."

"I want to return the entrance to its original condition, or cover it completely."

"Not easy to do." He gestured at the rough stonework around them. "And maybe not appropriate. In a sense, Esther, this is art, albeit ancient. It's better not to disturb it."

"I suppose. Historians and scientists would love to play around here. But that's the point. Should we allow them to do that?"

"I'll agree with whatever you decide." He smacked his knees and stood. "But if I miss lunch, you might need to bury me with the saint."

She stood and gestured toward the stone stairway leading to the cave's entrance. "Carry on, then."

Before they took the first step, Bruno stepped from the shadows at one side of the cavern, waving his gun at them.

"Is he under that slab?" he said.

Chapter Forty-Four

Twenty-First Century, Ephesus

Bruno had hesitated at the entrance to the cave. He tried to clean his glasses better as he thought, *Perhaps I should wait and see what they bring out?* He didn't even like the confined space in lifts, let alone close quarters underground.

His internal debate continued for nearly five minutes until he gathered enough courage to face his phobia and follow Esther and Bastiann inside. *At most, there's some old bones and them, and I have a gun!*

He walked in a crouch through the opening and found the cave became bigger, not smaller. *Thank God! That makes it a bit easier.*

He didn't see torches. *Where are they?* He was able to find his own in the feeble light from the entrance and flicked it on. An expression of awe flooded his face. *Definitely appears to be an ancient tomb!* He then noticed the slab tilted upwards. His torch lit up the eroded stairway. *There's more to it.*

He could make out scattered light from their torches and heard their voices, but he couldn't understand what they were saying. He turned his torch off, counting on the dim light from the cave's entrance and the light from them to see.

And if I go down the stairs, they will surely see me. Once again he hesitated. *I'll wait until they come up. Then I'll kill them!*

He backed away from the stairway and nearly broke an ankle when he tripped over a large stone that had fallen from the ceiling. *My glasses!* He had to crawl and search for them and was relieved to find them unbroken. He sat and rubbed his ankle for a bit, found the gun, and slunk into the shadows to wait.

Many minutes passed as he waited for them to climb the stairs. It sounded like there was some philosophical debate going on, but he understood less now because of the increased distance to the crypt's entrance. When they came up, he watched how they closed the slab over the stairway. He figured he only had to reverse the process to open the tomb again once they were out of the way.

He stepped out to confront them.

*****

Inspector Erkan had collected his new and temporary partner at the station after delivering Mustafa to the hospital. Aslan Remzi helped him along the last bit needed to reach the cave's entrance where Bruno had disappeared.

"You're not healthy, sir," said the colleague.

Aslan had met Erkan at the station as he was signing out another patrol car and announced he was Mustafa's replacement. It was a bit strange since Erkan hardly knew the man, but he confirmed it was okay with his superiors.

Aslan's curly salt-and-pepper hair and squinting dark eyes belied his age of thirty years. He had just finished his training. Erkan knew this training would probably continue with him, so Aslan was most likely only eager to acquire some experience with a seasoned policeman. But the inspector also knew he had three children and was the sole provider for his family. Volunteering for a potentially dangerous mission was a bit reckless considering the situation.

Like Mustafa, he wasn't much of a conversationalist. That suited Erkan just fine, and he didn't bother to pursue Aslan's motivations further.

"But it is my obligation to enter," said Erkan. "I consider them friends. You'll be my backup. Don't let that thug escape. If Esther and Bastiann are in there, they're probably dead."

"Do you mean you think he's killed them?"

Erkan wondered if Remzi had ever witnessed a homicide. There weren't that many in their jurisdiction. Most of their cases were robberies or less serious misdemeanors. "He tried to kill that German tourist, me twice, and Mustafa. I wouldn't put it past him. He's a violent, evil man."

"Maybe we should both go in then?"

"He can pick us off one at a time coming through the entrance. On the other hand, he has to come out eventually. You'll have a clear shot out here. Just wound him so we can execute him. With two or three murders and the attacks to his name, our courts will show no leniency."

"I suppose. I'll hide behind that boulder. Be careful, sir."

"I will. Remember, there's two of us and only one of him. We have the upper hand this time." *And no SUVs up here to use as a weapon!*

Erkan took a deep breath and entered the cave. He spotted Esther and Bastiann. *Where's Bruno?*

As if to answer his question, Bruno stepped from the shadows, waving his gun at his friends.

*****

"Is he under that slab?"

"Hard to tell," said Bastiann, "if you're asking about St. John, that is. We found a small, compact skeleton, likely a male, but I'm no forensic anthropologist. Go take a look."

"Are there any religious relics in there besides old bones?"

Throwing a warning glance at Bastiann, Esther said, "Like he said, go take a look." She had seen Erkan's silhouette against the light from the cave's entrance. She also received a whiff of his aftershave as more identification. *Does Bastiann see him?*

"Maybe I will do just that. You can have this tomb all to yourselves after I remove the bones and whatever relics I find. You'll be like Romeo and Juliet. Truly romantic. In fact, I'll toss you down those stairs and give you both a proper burial." Bruno took aim at Bastiann, likely figuring Esther was less an adversary.

"Drop the gun, Toscano!"

Bruno spun and fired in the direction of the voice. Erkan fell, a wounded silhouette in the light from the entrance as he slowly collapsed onto the cave's floor.

Esther sprang into action. She reached Bruno first and tackled him below the knees, an illegal hit in both rugby and American football. He crashed to the ground, leaving him blind as his glasses went flying. The little ogre was surprisingly strong. She struggled to keep his gun pointed away from her as he tried to aim it at her. *Hello, St. John! I need some help! Rembrandt had his angel, his son! I need a vengeful one now with sword and shield!*

In the dim light, Bruno's bloodshot eyes appeared to be those of a satanic demon who had crossed over the river Styx, bent on mayhem. They stared at her without blinking. "This is my family's heritage!" The scream reverberated throughout the cave, its echo drowned out by the sound of the gun as it fired right when Bastiann's fist crashed into the man's larynx.

She rolled off Bruno and glanced up at Bastiann. "I'm all right. Check Erkan. I think he's wounded."

Bastiann retrieved the gun just in case there was still life in Bruno and went to Erkan. Esther examined Bruno; he appeared to be dead. He had shot himself by blindly trying to aim at her.

"Beginner's luck," muttered the inspector. Bastiann had propped him up. "I figured the fool had never fired a weapon before."

At that moment Erkan's partner crawled into the cave and knelt opposite Bastiann at his superior's side. "I'll call for a medical copter, sir."

"Don't bother," said Erkan.

"Femoral artery," said Esther, standing over the trio. She noticed the wound and all the blood. She knelt and took Erkan's hand. "I consider you a dear friend, Inspector Erkan."

"Same here," he said. "I only have one regret."

"What's that?" said Bastiann.

"Not knowing who's in that tomb."

"We think it's St. John's skeleton," Bastiann said.

Erkan smiled.

Esther watched the light leave his dark, beautiful eyes. Everything blurred because of her tears.

Chapter Forty-Five

Twenty-First Century, Ephesus

The three of them—Esther, Bastiann, and Erkan's young partner, Aslan Remzi—stood on the ledge at the cave's entrance and watched the helicopter rise and head toward Selçuk, carrying the two bodies. They had pulled them from the cave and sealed the cave as best as they could. The police from the helicopter rappelled down and snaked the bodies down the steep slope in body bags.

She hadn't had much time to get to know Inspector Erkan, but from what she knew, he must have been a leader who balanced kindness and toughness, confidence and humility. That much was certain, but she wished Bruno hadn't interrupted their budding friendship. She didn't lie to the dying man. He already had become a dear friend to her and their friendship would have most likely aged like a fine wine.

As she watched the copter disappear, she brushed away some more tears for her friend. *I get into some fixes and I tend to lose more friends that way...*

She saw Stan Miller's mutilated body on the gurney and nearly lost her lunch. She then stared at Otto. "How could a man produce such beautiful music and be such a monster?"

She had feared that Otto was responsible for Stan's disappearance. She managed to follow him to that dim warehouse filled with machine parts only to find him next to the gurney holding a bloody knife.

"How can such a lovely woman be a spy?" he said. He pointed the knife at Stan's body. "He was another traitor to my country, like the professor. I'll have to kill you too, you know. All of you—Heidrich, this man, and you—are enemies of the state."

"So, you want me to suffer the same fate as them, is that it?"

His assassin's sneer produced a chill. "Worse. He couldn't stand up to the torture. Your betrayal is greater. I'll hack you into small pieces but also try to keep you alive as long as possible. Heidrich was only a scientist we had under surveillance, an old man with too many secrets we didn't want him to divulge. You are the enemy intent on destroying my country."

While she agreed about his assessment of her general goal to work against Soviet communism in all its evil forms, her frown slowly turned into a thin Mona Lisa smile. When he approached her, she took her gun from her purse. She shot him right between his hate-filled eyes at close range as the blade started its deadly downward arc.

She watched him fall, tears still in her eyes. "Maybe we didn't succeed in helping *Herr* Heidrich flee East Germany, but you won't be able to kill any more good people like Stan and the professor."

She turned and left the building.

Yes, I have a bad history in that regard. She then thought of Bastiann. *I couldn't bear to lose him too!*

*****

The young policeman, Aslan Remzi, turned to them. "I share the inspector's curiosity," he said.

"You should have asked earlier when we were inside," Esther said. "If it's any consolation, we don't know whose bones are in that tomb. Let's keep it that way for a while, shall we?"

"You're trusting me not to tell anyone about this cave?" said the young man.

"That's correct," said Bastiann. "To honor Inspector Erkan, please keep our secret. We need some time to decide what should be done. He would want to do what's right, you know. Trust us to do what's right too. Let's not turn this into a media circus, please. There will be time enough for that later when we know more."

"You'll be running some tests then? Are you stealing my country's legacy?"

"Whatever legacy there is, it must be shared with the world," said Esther. "I'll insist on that. Be assured that we don't have any intention of profiting from this find."

The cop smiled. "I'll try to do what the inspector would have wished. Will you be leaving Turkey? If so, please keep me informed."

"We'll be returning to London," said Esther.

"And Esther will keep you informed," said Bastiann, looking at her.

"Let me help you both down," said Aslan. "Step carefully. Sometimes the descent is worse than the ascent."

After another long trek, they all entered their respective vehicles and headed back to Selçuk. The trip in the Range Rover was made in silence.

Part Five

Aftermath

"And ye shall know the truth, and the truth shall make you free."–John 8:32

Chapter Forty-Six

Twenty-First Century, London

Esther carried the samples with her on the flight back to London with Bastiann. He stayed with her for several days in her flat until Schuster called him back to Lyon.

She decided the ring's message would have to wait until later. When the tests on the other samples were finished by the private lab she contracted to do them, she decided a face-to-face with the technician was appropriate. He had done some work for her gallery.

Bob Andrews used to be a lab technician in MI5. He had left to take a post that paid better.

"Esther, so good to see you, again. When you first rang, I thought you had another painting you wanted me to examine. What a surprise this was. Thank you for letting me be a part of it."

"I'm dying to hear what that part is," she said taking a seat in the wingchair in front of Bob's desk and trying not to wince at the old springs. "What are the probable dates for the pieces of parchment, papyrus, and bone splinter, and the error bars for your estimates?"

"Right to the point." Bob sorted some papers. "Carbon dating is a bit inconclusive, so I also did some tests of molecular composition," he said. She leaned back in her chair. *Will this be a long story?* Bob tended to ramble at times. "That one small piece of papyrus is from the late first or early second century, no doubt about it. Fifty-year error bar, more or less. So is the bone fragment, with a thirty-year error bar. What little marrow there is was a godsend. I might have been able to recover some DNA, but that's irrelevant; there's nothing to compare it to. The bit of parchment is from the Renaissance era, a thirty-year error bar bracketing the turn of the century again. Can I ask what's going on?"

"First, a comment. All those services who tell us our ancestry, I wonder what they would do with a DNA sampling? We might find some interesting relatives." She composed herself a bit in the chair, trying to find a more comfortable position so a spring didn't skew her. "Probably wouldn't prove anything. As you know, I'm not into archaeology and historical relics, but here's the scoop on the later piece of parchment: it was taken from a map most likely made by Botticelli."

"The painter?"

"None other. If authentic, it would mean he was in Ephesus, Turkey."

"Is that significant?"

"There's a shrine there called The House of the Virgin Mary. We found a map at that site; the piece of parchment was taken from that. Apparently, it was drawn by using information from a document contemporary to the map and comparing it to information on the papyrus we also found there, the last corresponding to the other piece you tested. We used those documents to find a tomb that could be the last resting place of St. John the Divine."

"Remarkable! Who then wrote that second document, the papyrus? The saint? Was the bone fragment from his skeleton?"

Esther held up her hand as if to stop traffic. "The story is a bit convoluted. The map took us to that tomb, more or less, although the Renaissance parchment was more useful. It was described in the words of the Renaissance parchment."

"Maybe detectives should be archaeologists. I must say there's a most unusual spread in dates. From the first century to the late 1400s or early 1500s, and on to the 21st century. How certain are you the tomb is St. John's?"

"All circumstantial evidence. Can you be more precise about that bone fragment?"

"Maybe a slightly later date than the bit of papyrus, if that's what you're asking. It's not conclusive, I'm sad to say."

"Everything's consistent, so far. We have one more test to complete."

"You only brought me three samples."

"For the other test, I needed an expert in Aramaic."

"Ah." Bob's face lit up. "Are we talking about some religious artifacts?"

"If the last test is positive, then it's more likely that bone fragment you tested is from St. John's skeleton—the tip of his finger, to be precise. Some rocks that fell from the ceiling had snapped it off. A ring was farther up on the bone. I think the inscription is in Aramaic. He also could have written the papyrus; fortunately, that was in Latin."

"St. John the Divine! Imagine! It sounds like your circumstantial evidence is strong."

"Considering where we found the relics, yes. That shrine's name goes hand-in-hand with the legend that St. John took care of the Virgin there until her Assumption."

"My Lord, what a find!"

"Indeed. But don't become all bleary-eyed on me or have a stroke. Remember, it's still circumstantial evidence."

"It's impossible to think this is all an elaborate hoax. There are too many coincidences."

"Frankly, dear friend, I don't know what to think. Two men, one good and one bad, lost their lives during our little trip, which reminds me: a third man, who nearly lost his life, needs an Interpol and German federal police background check. I now suspect he was up to no good." *And was it Sister Denise I saw in the bank?*

*****

After leaving Bob's lab and before she went to the Yard to see Langston and collect her keys to the gallery, Esther received a call from Oxford from Oscar Willoughby.

"You sent me quite a puzzle," he said. "What you wrote differed a bit from the rubbing. Thank God I also had that."

"Hello to you too, Oscar."

"Sorry. I apologize for skipping pleasantries, but it's wonderfully exciting to give you this news. We formed a little team here to study your problem, my dear. We decided on the best translation for the inscription inside the ring."

"I'm waiting."

"Allowing for some uncertain linguistic choices and other assumptions, the inscription says the following: 'To my Lord and Savior, from M.'"

"Really? That's all? It seemed longer."

"Those words represent our best free translation, not a literal one. I'm having those minute metal samples also tested. By the way, where's the ring?"

"I hate to go into details—maybe at a later time—but the ring was on a saint's finger. That inscription doesn't make any sense, though. He might have been a holy man, but there's only one Lord and Savior in Christianity."

"Maybe 'Lord and Savior' is an honorific." He laughed. "Or maybe he was James Bond and the ring was given to him by his superior, M?"

"You have a strange sense of humor. Thanks for the deciphering. Let me know what the metallurgy test shows."

Oxford humor, she thought. *M indeed! Hmm. M.* She perched on her piano bench and made an ugly chord as she leaned back, resting her elbows on the keyboard. Possibilities swirled in her mind.

She waved the white flag and went to see Langston.

*****

"The prodigal daughter returns from abroad," George said, offering his hand in greeting. "You look no worse for your travels, Esther."

"You're right," said Esther. "Although sometimes trouble finds me. I don't flinch. I meet it head on. I'll give you an update. But first, how's my gallery doing?"

"The girls sold that monstrosity someone called a work of art," he informed her, finding her keys to the gallery in his out-box and handing them to her. "My wife says the gallery is in tip-top shape." He sat and she followed suit, sitting across from him. "Thanks to Anna, we know who the art thief is. He was working on commission tendered by a Russian oligarch. I'm sure we can't touch either one, but we passed the information on to Russian police and Interpol. He better be careful if he travels this way again, don't you think?" He winked at Esther. "Are you going to the gallery from here?"

"I thought I'd tell you about my adventures first."

"I'll confess I was worried. I knew about your kidnapping. You do get in some awful fixes, Esther."

"You don't know the half of it." At that moment, she recalled a discussion with Bastiann. *That other Mary! The Magdalene!* She jumped up, knocking Langston's desk lamp askew. "I need to phone Bastiann!"

"I guess I can arrange that. Do you want privacy?" She said yes. "Then use my phone. I'll go wander around a bit."

"When I'm through, I'll tell you the whole story about our adventures. Mostly mine, that is. Bastiann had his own before he arrived in Turkey to accompany me. I've concluded detectives can become fantastic archaeologists."

"You can also explain that comment."

Bastiann had his mobile turned off. She texted him a message beginning with the translation from Aramaic. Then she wrote: "I think M might be the Magdalene. That ring could have once belonged to Christ!"

Chapter Forty-Seven

Twenty-First Century, London

Esther entered her flat and saw the post stacked on her counter. *Probably ninety percent rubbish! What's the internet good for if companies keep sending you catalogs?* Reggie had done a good job sorting it, though. *Or was he snooping?*

She tossed all the catalogs in the waste bin and went to her piano bench and sat down.

The recurring flashbacks to her days in Berlin had bothered her. *Those were exciting times, full of danger and suspense. I felt alive.* She tried doing some do-it-yourself psychoanalysis. *Is my mind trying to tell me that making Bastiann number four will lead to my dying of boredom? Or that I will become a widow yet again?*

She often thought the first condition had been her father's fate. He had been an active man for a long time; then he wasn't. *Maybe it's genetics?*

She also knew many people in the twilight of their lives who had become bored. They would sit around and watch the telly or stare at walls. Her few hobbies, mostly playing the piano if she discounted sex and what she considered gourmet food and drink, would disappear when she became too feeble and had to sustain herself with porridge. *And forget about dancing a Viennese waltz with Bastiann!*

Ah, Bastiann! She knew more about his life than he knew about hers, yet he was so damn protective. Her passion for her paramour had mellowed into something wonderful. *What was that line from that musical bastardization of Pygmalion? Ah, yes.* She paraphrased it in her mind: *"I've become accustomed to his face."*

She smiled as she completed her psychoanalysis. Old age might be boring, but she knew with his company it would be much less so. *Maybe that's all one can ask for?*

She then laughed. *The poor man will have to live with the prospect of me returning to haunt him, for I'll surely go first!*

She exchanged that morbid thought for another as she rubbed the bronze plaque above the keyboard bearing the inscription, *Stanley E. Miller, Esq.* She began to play the piano version of Albinoni's famous Adagio.

*****

"What's your interest in this case?" said the Viennese detective.

Bastiann glanced at Sergio Moretti and his wife, Diana, standing beside him. He would never admit to the true reason: to meet the man who had once competed with Esther's count for her favors. He wasn't impressed by Sergio, but maybe the man would have been a striking man in his prime.

The official reason and excuse for his presence was to close the case on Bruno Toscano. *What had ever possessed Sergio's maid, Elise, to pass information to that slug?*

Elise was nervous. She became more so as the detective's colleague entered the interrogation room. The barrister the state provided her only seemed bored.

Her inquisitor read Elise her rights under Viennese law, which was more or less standard now across the E.U. He then said their conversation would be recorded. "Is that okay with you, sir?" he said to her barrister.

The man agreed. "I've already told her to answer your questions only on my cue."

"Let's start then. When did you first meet Bruno Toscano, *Fraulein*?"

The barrister agreed again.

"He approached me at a coffee shop. He knew *Frau* Moretti had purchased the armoire and wanted to know why."

"Did he pay you in advance for the information you gave him?"

Another nod from the barrister.

"Some. He matched that when I told him about the parchment and the painting."

"And he left it at that?"

The barrister waggled his index finger. "That's an open-ended question, Inspector," he said.

"I'll rephrase. Did you tell him about Mrs. Brookstone's visit?"

The nod came.

"Yes. He wanted to know who she was."

By the interrogation's end, the Viennese inspector had the complete story about Elise's duplicity.

"It's a minor lapse," Bastiann told the Morettis after the interrogation. "Nothing terribly sinister. Elise is poor, so the pittance Bruno offered seemed like a lot of money to her. I suggest you revoke the charges against her, even though what she did led to Esther's kidnapping."

"Does that mean we have to rehire her?" said Moretti's wife.

"While I'm sure she won't do anything like this again, that's up to you."

"What would you do?" said Sergio.

The detective there with the three of them interrupted the conversation. "Although you're all immigrants and she's one of us, you should still come down hard on her," he said before Bastiann could answer Sergio.

Bastiann studied the man's reflection in the one-way window for a moment. *What's that mean? Anti-immigrant feelings? Or police not wanting to waste their time? Am I over-reacting?*

He knew all about Europe's turn to the right with many countries no longer accepting refugees from the war-torn Middle East. The Mediterranean countries were likely the worst, but Austria had always been dancing around fascism ever since Hitler invaded the country and annexed it during the war. That dance had increased in tempo. Many Austrians were now against all immigrants, their policies not only limited to anti-Semitism. *Will the world ever learn?*

He imagined what Esther might say: *Let's call today's populism what it really is, fascism. Using the word populism as currently it's used is just disguising a wolf in sheep's clothing*. Or something of the sort. In any case, she would jump right in and call the detective out on his putdown of immigrants, for he knew she believed diversity was the very essence of democracy. Esther didn't suffer fools gladly, and she was outspoken in her opinions. Another thing he loved about her.

He sighed, glared at the cop for a moment, and then mentally shrugged it off. "I'd rehire her, but with less salary and on the condition of good behavior in the future. If she behaves properly, raise her salary in three months or so.

Esther told me she's competent, which is a good recommendation. Loyal employees are often hard to come by. Her alliance with Bruno appears to be her only negative during her employ."

The wife made a satisfied face at her husband. "Then that's what we'll do. I prefer that over training someone new. She's also a good companion when Sergio's out and about, leaving me alone as he often does."

Bastiann smiled at Sergio's wife and thought of Esther. *Why would Sergio ever leave this angel alone?*

*****

Esther's visit to her gallery the next morning was short, just long enough to confirm Langston's report. She had launched a tirade against a car that nearly hit her when she crossed the street, but soon realized it was wasted vitriol because there was no driver. The man in the rear seat, who had been reading *The Times*, waved his hands helplessly.

She was a user of technology, not an abuser. As she walked the block from her Jaguar to the gallery, she mused about how much technology had changed. *I wouldn't be a good spy for MI6 now!* Ever since the war, technology's importance had grown.

She walked into the gallery muttering but in control of her feelings so she would not take out her ire on Anna and Dorothy. They assured her all was well. No more art thieves had picked on the little gallery.

She spent just fifteen minutes there since she wanted to visit her handyman. *It's time I showed my appreciation for his actions!*

She found him at home in his modest house in one of London's working man suburbs. The ride in her Jaguar was long, but she didn't mind it. Harry was special. And the journey in London's traffic allowed her to see how far he had to go on public transportation to work at her gallery. Guilt accompanied her on that ride, even if her car wasn't new. *It's the quiet, steady types no one appreciates. Do I take him for granted?*

She parked in front of the tidy little house in the tidy little neighborhood. Like many British homes, there was a small but well-tended flower garden across the front of the house, except for where the pavestones were. They were like a meandering dotted line leading to the front entrance.

He answered the door with a big smile. "Esther, what a pleasant surprise."

She gave him a hug and the once over. "You don't look too worse for wear. How are your wounds doing?"

"Stitches are starting to itch, ma'am, and I can't scratch them, but don't just stand there. Please, come in. Dora, my employer is favoring us with a visit. Prepare the tea!"

The small but comfortable living room reminded Esther of her childhood. Their house had been modest too, with more religious icons on the walls. Harry made the introductions when his wife brought in the tea service, complete with scones.

"Sorry, Esther, we don't have any *baklava*."

"Oh, Harry, not with tea!" But she was chuffed that he had remembered her favorite pastry. "Scones will be fine."

"How many lumps?" said Dora.

Although it was only late morning, sharing the tea ceremony with Dora and Harry meant a lot to Esther. First, she was relieved Harry was well along the road to recovery. Second, the strange gap between employer and employee seemed to dissolve with the lumps of sugar in the tea and their conversation, which sparkled with Dora's Eliza Doolittle voice and Harry's Jamaican accent and turns of phrase. *Indeed, we are all equals here. Just the three of us chatting about how busy life is and how uncertain it can often be.* Harry told the story about the knife-wielding thief from his viewpoint. She then told him and Dora a bit about her adventures in Turkey.

"That Bruno sounds like a terribly evil man," Dora said in her Cockney voice. *We need Henry Higgins to change that accent,* Esther thought with a grin. From her, at that moment, it seemed charming. "I would have fainted in fear, Esther."

"Love, I think you would have come at him with a rolling pin," said Harry. "You did a good number on that purse snatcher in the Tube. Nearly castrated him, I dare say."

The woman's pale face turned crimson, matching her rosy cheeks. "I ruined a shoe. You shouldn't have mentioned that, Harry. It was rather unladylike of me."

Esther laughed. "Don't worry, Dora. I would have done the same thing." *And I did, even under the effects of chloroform!*

After a pleasant hour and a half, Esther bid goodbye and left to return to her gallery, sad with the thought her country didn't appreciate the strength immigrants brought to it. Once they had accepted Prince Harry's new duchess, too many of the English had returned to their usual distrust of foreigners. Her own Harry was the proof such an attitude was unwarranted ninety-nine percent of the time.

She soon put the visit out of mind once she returned to the gallery. She had to determine if her skills were up to the task of restoring a painting a client had asked her to restore, if possible. Normally she would have told the gentleman to go to a restoration shop, but she had sold him several paintings. He didn't purchase the one he wanted restored from her gallery, but she wanted to try to maintain his goodwill. *I suppose the rich search for bargains even for their art restoration. That's why they're rich.* She was careful with her money too. *Must be that Scotch blood in me!*

She had been a bit disappointed with the available gallery space when she purchased it. It had been a bargain—the old man who had owned it passed on and the relatives only wanted to split the proceeds as fast as possible. It came with a small stock of paintings on consignment, which is how she had met Silva. The relatives didn't want to bother with those either.

It was well located, but she didn't have much of a work area. Still, the area she had was better than nothing. She would have passed on the purchase if there hadn't been any at all. About two-thirds of the space was dedicated to displaying artworks for sale on consignment. She followed that usual business model. The ceiling was high enough so there was sufficient wall space in the showing area. There was also just enough room in the front for refreshment tables and folding chairs when she offered her showings on the first Sunday afternoon of each month. Her little lab also allowed her to putter a bit, testing authenticity of older paintings, if need be. She enjoyed that work more and more as time went on. *Perhaps Papa would be proud of me for using my hands so much, but he wouldn't understand my tool shop at all!*

Chapter Forty-Eight

Twenty-First Century, Munich

Inspector Kurt Geiszler was surprised at how gaunt Walther appeared when he met him for beers in Munich. He didn't consider him a close friend, but friends they had been. He appreciated his previous help, even if Kurt's crazy idea didn't produce anything of consequence. Plus, the museum's employee usually paid for the beer.

He had met Esther Brookstone when she was still at the Yard. Her case had ended with arrests in Austria back then. It wasn't unusual that he pursued crimes and criminals into other countries. The federal police force in Germany was a bit like the FBI in the U.S. in that way. That's how Esther's case had drawn him into Austria, with the local authorities' approval. It was only the other day he had helped an FBI agent heat up a trail gone cold.

He waited until he heard about Walther's return before suggesting they meet again. It would be a first, since Walther was usually the one to propose meeting, but the inspector figured he would be flattered and not suspicious. Kurt used the excuse that he wanted to hear about the man's adventures in Turkey.

He had been surprised when Esther called him and asked for a favor. He rang Interpol HQ in Lyon to start the investigation she requested. The results surprised and saddened him. He was already in Augsburg when he learned of Walther's return. The drive east to Munich was easy enough. However, confronting Walther was difficult.

"I've never been beaten like that," Kurt said after hearing about Walther's adventures in Turkey. "I suppose you heard Bruno Toscano paid the ultimate price for his villainy."

"I'll shed no tears for the man," said Walther. "Will you?"

"Considering his crimes, I would have preferred he rot in jail for the rest of his life, but I think Turkish justice would have been swift, so it's just as well." He eyed Walther as his drinking friend took another gulp of beer from his stein. "But now it's time for you to hear my story. You said you met my friend, Esther Brookstone. She asked me to initiate an investigation with Interpol. Would you like to hear the results?"

Walther drew a sad face in the moisture his stein had left on the tabletop. "Does it relate to Bruno's attacking me?"

"Not exactly, but it affects you nonetheless." Kurt removed folded papers from his sports coat and handed the sheets to Walther. "This is what Interpol discovered."

Kurt watched as Walther read the list of charges, his brow furrowing. When he finished, he looked up. "I suppose I need a barrister."

"Yes, you do. I asked Director Schuster the favor of letting me make the arrest." Kurt read Walther his rights. Most charges were German crimes considering who Walther's employer was. "With time off for good behavior, your jail time will only be a few years. I'm sorry."

Walther shook his head. "No, I'm the one who's sorry; sorry you betrayed our friendship and sorry I was caught. What made Brookstone suspect me?"

"Experience. She asked herself why Bruno would attack you. The man was stupid, after all, and had no reason to do so unless you were searching for the same thing he was. Interpol's investigation discovered you were at the auction where Bruno bid against *Frau* Moretti, but it also uncovered that long history of misusing the museum's funding. Your trip to Turkey was just one item on the list."

Walther frowned. "Will we remain friends?"

"Time will tell," said Kurt, pitying the man. "Again, I'm sorry, Walther."

Later that evening, Kurt's wife, Helga, who drove from Berlin to spend the weekend with him in Munich, turned over and studied him as he undressed for bed. Her reporter's instincts apparently kicked in because when he crawled into the soft hotel bed, she asked, "Do you want to talk about it?"

"I had to arrest a man who I thought was my friend. That's all. I'm sorry I'm late."

She put her finger to his lips. "You're never too late for me."

*****

Bastiann caught a plane from Vienna to London. On the flight, he received a message from Interpol HQ in Lyon. The German federal police had arrested Walther Beck for a series of crimes. The charges went back several years.

He respected Kurt Geiszler. He also grudgingly had to admit there were some good cops, like Erkan, in Turkey. He would have to avoid his Turkish stereotypes in the future. *There are good people everywhere. You only have to be lucky enough to meet them.*

All that prompted him to check his other messages. There was one from Hal: *Someone got to Manousakis. He didn't need a life jacket.*

Hal's crazy code for "found dead floating in the water." *Ernesto again?* Bastiann suppressed a shiver. If his guess was correct, being fired by the cartel leader was always quite permanent. His mind went back to that hotel room visit. He waved to the flight attendant and asked for whiskey.

After he landed, he caught a taxi at Heathrow and gave the driver a good tip when he arrived at his destination. As he stepped from the taxi, he saw Esther's gallery two storefronts down the block and grinned. *Always nice to surprise the old girl.*

One of her employees approached him like a vulture when he walked in. "You look like an important man who needs to buy a painting."

"I've been here before, Dorothy," he said.

She pulled her glasses from her skirt pocket and put them on. "Mr. Bastiann, please forgive me. This is such a surprise!"

"Yes, precisely the intention. Where's Esther?"

"In her tiny lab trying to decide if she can restore a religious painting. It's a bit moldy, I'm afraid."

"Should be a simple task for her," Bastiann said. "I'll find my way back. Where's Anna, by the way?"

"Lunch break. She does the first hour, I do the second."

He glanced at his watch. "It is that time, isn't it? The time change distracted me. Well, give her my regards. I heard she did a brave thing. Hopefully, Esther will accept my lunch invitation, whether it's an early or late lunch for her."

He walked to the rear of the gallery, through a narrow hallway, and spotted the door with "LAB" stenciled across the wood paneling. He knocked on it.

"I told you not to interrupt, Dorothy!"

"It's me, Esther."

He heard fast footsteps. Esther threw open the door and flew into his arms. After some lengthy kisses, she stepped back.

"Why didn't you ring me, you beast!"

"I was in a bit of a hurry to make a plane. But before then, I participated in an interrogation requiring the utmost discretion." *Because your old boyfriend was involved!* "You look a lot better than you did after all those adventures in Turkey."

"You received my text?"

"You'll have to tell me all about it at lunch."

*****

"I tell you, Gerry, that's exactly what happened. Two people are dead. That's a big deal!"

Gerald Prince made a face. "I'm sorry, but it all sounds like another one of your conspiracy theories and there's nothing in your story I can use as leverage to make her consent to doing the documentary."

"Idiot! You don't understand! This is a real conspiracy! I'm certain Brookstone is covering up something for the Vatican."

"Like what?"

"I don't know what, but there's something. Don't you want to find out? What kind of journalist are you?"

He shrugged. "A safe one, if I can even be called that. I produce documentaries, you know. I don't write for *The Guardian*." He tapped the table. "And it likely wouldn't matter if I did find out. If the Vatican is involved, our government's probably involved, and the last I heard, the government owns the BBC. Another ale?"

She stood, shaking her head. "Shove it up your arse."

He watched her leave. He hated when she became so obsessed with her damn conspiracies. He decided to check her website that evening. *She's most likely going to write about it.* Someday he would have to count how many conspiracy theories she had written about. He asked her to take down the one claiming the existence of an MI7, the service in charge of preventing religious crusades by ETs. *What a waste of energy!*

Chapter Forty-Nine

Twenty-First Century, London

At lunch, Esther and Bastiann had cheese, crackers, and white wine as appetizers. They snacked and sipped as Esther went through all the tests she had made. She studied the other customers as she talked, as she often did, a habit she had for many years.

She spotted the green woman—green snake tattoos on her neck and green spiked hair—sitting at the bar. The reflection of her face in the mirror was familiar. *Speaking of habits, Sister Denise? It can't be.* She decided her mind was playing tricks on her.

"None proving or disproving the authenticity of the artifacts," he said when she finished.

"It's enough circumstantial evidence to create a conundrum," she said. "What should we tell Inspector Erkan's colleague, Aslan Remzi? Who receives the relics? A museum in Turkey? The Vatican? A London museum?"

"Whoever receives them will run their own tests, I'm sure, but I'm not sure we have any solid commitment with Erkan's colleague. I suggest we determine who receives them by where the most people can see them, assuming they're proven authentic."

"Where the most people who would care to do so can see them, I think. We also must take into consideration they're Catholic relics along with their association with Botticelli."

Sebastien seemed to be lost in thought. "To change the topic, doesn't Henry the Eighth take London out of the football match with respect to the Vatican? You opined the Anglican Church would be Catholic if it weren't for him. The Vatican wouldn't see that as an argument for keeping the relics in London, considering their age and provenance."

Esther laughed. "What a memory! Catholics are indeed a minority here, right now, and most blokes care more about football than religious relics. Yet Turkey is so unsettled and might remain so for some time."

"That filters the choices down to some museum in France or Italy, to my way of thinking. May I suggest the Vatican's museum complex? They don't exhibit everything in their possession, but many scholars flock there to do their research, not just tourists."

"Langston gave me the same advice. Do you think Aslan Remzi would be okay with that?"

"Yes, but there's the problem of retrieving the relics from the Turkish bank and delivering them to the Vatican. The Turkish government might not allow that, even if Remzi consents. Christ is considered a Muslim prophet, after all."

"Hmm. And they also revere the Virgin. Let's table this discussion. I see our lunches coming."

*****

"You know," said Bastiann after lunch, "there's still a lot of historical vacuum to be filled. What was John doing all the time after the Virgin Mary was gone?"

"And what was he doing with the ring?" Esther said. "Did the Magdalene keep it after the Crucifixion?"

“Maybe she gave it to John for safekeeping. Or maybe the M was for mother.”

“I had the same thought,” she said, “but the Aramaic word for mother is *immah*. I don’t think she would have used her own name and ‘Lord and Savior’ together. No, I think the Magdalene gave that ring to Christ and then kept it after the Crucifixion. By the way, the metallurgical test was inconclusive. That particular alloy of gold and silver has been used to strengthen soft gold for centuries. We’d call it about 15 carat gold. The impurities don’t tell us much either, although the ring tests as almost pure gold and silver.”

“Okay, far too much information. Back to what John was doing all the time between taking care of Mary and his own burial. Was he a missionary trying to convert the ancient world to Christianity? And did he write the Book of Revelation?”

“We don’t have enough information to answer either of those questions, or many others,” said Esther. “My father was interested in proving John lived to a ripe old age and wrote the Book of Revelation. The description of a ‘younger brother named John’ in that apocalyptic dream could just be referring to someone he encountered during his travels. As we know, the John who wrote the Gospel had a brother named James, who was martyred, but the ‘brother’ might only be someone in a congregation this second John visited.”

“Any word from Turkey?’

“My plan is to fly back there and collect the relics and deliver them to the Vatican, assuming they’ll receive them. I told Remzi before leaving that’s what the Inspector would have wanted, setting the stage, as it were.”

“Not clear. What if he decides against that?”

Esther shrugged. “I’ll still have to go to Turkey and take the relics to some museum in that country. That would save a lot of bother with customs.” She smiled at him. “All that’s tomorrow. Let's use the night to convince ourselves our situation should be more permanent."

"You mean living together? We're doing that as much as possible already."

"But we're only doing it unofficially."

He considered that statement and then smiled. "I understand. Esther, will you marry me?"

She raised her glass of wine. It was her third. "Most certainly, but before I change my mind, let's plan for a wedding in Paris. It's a lovely spot for a wedding and honeymoon. I expect you to set everything up while I'm out of the country."

Chapter Fifty

Twenty-First Century, Vatican City

Esther was losing her patience. On her way to Turkey, she decided to see about the Vatican's interest in the relics she and Bastiann had found. If they weren't interested, she might turn them over to Erkan's colleague who would place them in some museum. Most likely in the capital, Ankara. After all, they were found in Turkey.

She was perched in an uncomfortable and rickety chair in a hallway facing a nondescript door, waiting for one of the museum's curators to see her. She spotted a nun passing at the end of the hallway at full speed. *Likely rushing to do some old priest's bidding.* Her father had been a misogynist; she imagined many old priests were even more so. *Is the Church ever going to change?*

She had been at a Catholic funeral mass once for a dear colleague who had died of pancreatic cancer. It pained her not to remember any more about the service other than the priest spewing nonsense about the role of women in the Church. *The Bible tells women they should be subservient to men. It was written by old men!*

She almost cheered in the theater when Eowyn killed the villain who couldn't be killed by any man in *The Return of the King. A brief bow to feminine power!* Guilt smacked her on the head for reminiscing about popular culture within Vatican City. *What's keeping this priest?*

*****

For someone involved in the process of determining the authenticity of religious art and relics, the young priest, Father Antolini, had the bearing of an Italian bureaucrat. *They've plagued the poor country forever, so why not the Vatican too?*

"Thank you for seeing me," Esther said.

"You're most welcome, *signora*."

They shook hands and studied each other for a few moments. "Have you considered my proposal?"

"I've studied your petition and to save both our time, our answer is no."

She frowned. "You mean 'your' answer is no. That seems odd. You owe me an explanation."

The priest brushed back a stray lock of blond hair and fidgeted a bit. "You're being a bit adversarial, *Signora* Brookstone. We don't need to provide an explanation."

"Maybe 'we' don't," she used her index fingers to form quotes, "but 'you' do. The museum will lose a great find. Another museum would jump at the chance."

He smiled, but his blue eyes remained cold. "I hear there are some fine museums in London. Why don't you approach them?"

"Because our find would mean more to your Church."

"Perhaps. If it's authentic." He spread the photos she had provided him on his desk. "We don't like to waste time on fakery. Please understand I can't make a decision based on some fuzzy photos."

"Father, they're enlargements of pictures taken with my mobile. I don't lie like some politicians. Every word of my story is true."

"Please, please. I'm not saying you're a liar. But you have to admit your story is incredible."

"Two men died. I admired one of them and called him my friend. He defended us and the relics from an evil man. Please don't let his life be wasted. Why can't you at least examine what I have stashed away at that bank?"

He rearranged the photos and placed his large hands on his desk next to the pile. "Such an investigation requires funding we prefer to spend on less dubious projects, and it should be done with scientific methods. We did that with the Shroud of Turin."

"You have the equipment right here to do the testing. All you need to do is bring the material here."

The priest thought a bit. "Why are you so zealous? You know there are many who would sow confusion among the faithful. Is that your agenda?"

She glared at him. "How dare you!" She then regretted losing her temper and hung her head. *His job is to put up roadblocks.* She raised her head and looked him right in the eye. "Maybe I'd like to provide the faithful with a pick-me-up after the Shroud. Isn't knowing about the saints' lives part of your purview?"

"It depends on the knowledge revealed."

"How about this? I'll keep quiet about the whole affair, but let me bring the material here. I think it belongs here because it will be safer. Perform your tests when you're ready. Let religious scholars determine what they will. History will be the judge of their decisions."

"Then there's no hurry. We will take our time, *signora*, be assured of that. I will change my no to a tentative yes. We will contact you."

"My contact information is on the form I filled out, but here's a business card."

He studied the card. "You own a gallery? Are you also a curator?"

"Yes, for the first, but maybe not in your sense for the second. I can recognize fakery, Father Antolini. You would know that if you had read the whole form corresponding to my proposal."

*****

On the plane back to London, she decided she would give the Vatican only a year. If she didn't hear from them by then, she'd make arrangements with Aslan Remzi. She smiled at the thought. If the relics ended at the Vatican museum, she'd create an international incident when Turkey tried to claim them. *Turks aren't so bad, Bastiann. Like in so many cases, it's the country's government and leaders who are difficult.*

She had personal worries that needed more attention. *Has he done anything about wedding arrangements?* She wasn't sure leaving them to him had been a good idea. She would ring him when the plane was taxiing after landing to see how preparations were going.

She leaned back in her seat and sighed, enjoying the precious moment to relax. A head popped up above the seat in front of her. "I saw you on the telly," the child said in a loud voice as if it needed to be announced to all the plane's passengers. "I told mommy that!"

Oh, good Lord! "Is your mum there with you, child?"

"She's napping. I need to talk to someone."

"If she's not already awake with that outburst, please wake her up and talk to her. I'm an old lady. I need a nap more than she does, I'm sure."

Son of Thunder

Chapter Fifty-One

Twenty-First Century, Lyon

"You clean up nicely," Bastiann said to Hal Leonard. The other Interpol agent fidgeted with his collar. "But you appear more nervous than I am."

Hal would be Bastiann's best man. Esther had wanted her old school chum, Natalie, to be her maid of honor, but she couldn't make the trip. The retired MI5 scientist who lived in her village was taking her to a show in London. She didn't want to cancel and wound the shy man's pride.

Bastiann knew Esther had never met that MI5 scientist. Her friend had given a good description, though, enough to make Bastiann a bit jealous when Esther had talked about him. But the Interpol agent thought Esther, the matchmaker, wanted her friend and the scientist to grow fond of each other. *That chap lost his chance with her. He had never known he had real competition!*

Bastiann was dressed in his ubiquitous three-piece gray suit while Hal was dressed in a navy blue suit he had just purchased. Identical red ties were the only bow to their teamwork in other affairs.

"Don't get me wrong," Hal said, "I'm honored to be your best man, but I've been avoiding weddings my whole life, especially my own."

"Always the playboy, but you're growing too old for that. Time for you to find someone to spend those retirement years with."

Bastiann grinned as Hal avoided that topic by countering with, "How's Esther holding up?"

"She's done this three times before, so I expect she's an old hand at it. She was a bit miffed about not having her Parisian wedding, but all was forgiven when she saw this lovely spot. She's still in a bit of a celebratory mood with the relics now going to the Vatican, assuming they act on their promise. Father Jean is also happy about that."

He flashed a smile at the old priest in the audience and gave a discreet wave. After he had queried the old man, Father Jean had convinced his sister to lend the estate's gardens and his study for the wedding. The wave was also for her and her husband. The sister had no problem with her brother not officiating. She was an atheist like Esther's previous husband, the count. *Sister and brother must have some lively philosophical discussions!*

"Quite some adventure," Hal said. "Do you believe any of its history? Or does it remain a legend?"

"The Vatican was interested, which says something. They'll be doing some testing themselves in their laboratories, I suppose. And Sergio Moretti is happy. His Botticelli quadrupled in value with the leaking of the story."

"You and Esther were lucky you weren't killed."

"Esther seems to carry an aura of luck about her." *She needs it! Trouble always seems to find her.*

"And quite a honeymoon you two have planned."

"As you Americans would say, we're going Dutch," Bastiann said with a grin. "We're each paying for a riverboat tour on the Danube that begins on land in Prague, goes to Venice, and then on to Budapest. The only way to travel in my opinion if you're not in a hurry and want to see places in a leisurely fashion."

"Any luck on subletting your flat?"

"Yes, but all bad. I'll have to change realtors. The current one is long on promises but short on completing them. I excused him at the start because there's not much commission in rentals, but now I think I'll have to fire him and find someone else. Or I can just keep the place until I retire from Interpol. Esther owns her place in London, after all."

"And has a castle in Scotland." Hal glanced at his watch. "Fashionably late, your Esther. Where's that damn limo?" He took his friend by the arm and leaned in to whisper. "I have never married, but I have one piece of advice for you, Mr. Groom."

"Let's hear it then."

*****

The bride and groom hadn't bothered to search for an Anglican priest in Lyon. A magistrate Bastiann knew there had agreed to perform a brief civil ceremony. The man had come in a tuxedo because the Interpol agent had forgotten to tell him the dress code.

Esther looked splendid in her powder blue power suit and beret, blouse with lace, white gloves, and pumps with reasonable heels. More like a fascinator, the hat perched jauntily on her auburn hair that she wore at shoulder length. Bastian smiled at his bride-to-be as she walked up the aisle on the arm of George Langston to the strains of Pachelbel's "Canon." *You look beautiful, my dear!*

There was also some live music. A contralto, who Father Jean's sister knew, sang Paul Simon's "Bridge over Troubled

Water" and "All I Ask of You" from Andrew Lloyd Weber's *Phantom of the Opera.* A cellist accompanied her. The two songs bookended the magistrate's homily that focused on autumnal love.

Both Esther and he had written some words, but they had kept them to themselves until then. To his surprise, she started with a verse from the Song of Solomon: "My beloved is mine and I am his; he browses among the lilies." She ad-libbed from there, following that lead. It was tame, unlike some of the Song, so he decided his words were just as appropriate, but he could see the magistrate, uncomfortable in his starched collar, becoming impatient, so he edited his spiel a bit to cut it short.

The usual pseudo-religious blathering common in civil weddings everywhere ended with his vows. He then placed the ring on her finger. She said hers and slipped a ring onto his. He glanced at the ring and then at her, eyebrows raised. "Take good care of it," she said in a whisper.

"You may now kiss the bride," said the magistrate.

He did so and everyone applauded, causing Esther to blush, but she was still smiling as they marched out together to Clarke's "Trumpet Voluntary."

*****

After the couple greeted everyone, including the avuncular Sergio Moretti and his young wife, Diana, Langston's wife—Langston was in the receiving line with the two newlyweds, Hal, and the magistrate—Kurt Geiszler and his reporter wife, and Bastiann's boss from Interpol, Karl Schuster, and his wife, the affair took a less serious turn and the fun began. The help had rolled back Father Jean's furniture against the walls and arranged serving tables in his study. Taking advantage of the manse's fine cooks, a buffet meal was placed on them with plenty of wine available. Multiple trays of French and Vietnamese dishes satisfied all tastes, and the small number of guests were able to dine comfortably at tables set up on the veranda.

The desserts were to die for. Esther's favorite, *baklava*, didn't go along with the wedding cake—made by the sister's chef—or the other French and Viennese pastries, but Bastiann had insisted on offering it. After dinner, most tables were removed to make a bit more room for dancing.

To Esther's surprise, Bastiann had ordered that the traditional first dance as bride and groom would be a Viennese waltz on the veranda. Father Jean played Strauss's "Roses from the South" through his study's music system as he had done with the Pachelbel and Clarke pieces. Its speakers broadcasted the music through the veranda doors of the priest's study. Bastiann managed to lead Esther through some respectable turns, even though the space for dancing was limited. Both of them avoided tripping on the mortared cracks between pavers, until everyone joined in as best as they could. Guests then danced the night away and chatted until everyone had so much drink they could neither talk nor dance.

After the celebration had muted a bit, Esther made the rounds and stopped to talk with Diana and Sergio. "Where are you displaying your new Botticelli in that huge house?" she asked Sergio.

"Always in the spy mode, aren't you?" he said. He put his arm around Esther and kissed her on the cheek. "You were a beautiful bride for Alberto and you're a beautiful one for Bastiann. He's lucky I saved your butt when you needed to flee East Berlin."

She laughed. "I would have found some other way out." She glanced at his wife. "Have you talked about our time there with Diana?"

"Mostly a bit of bragging," she said. "He never goes into details. I suspect he's forgotten them. Senility, you know."

"Does he still play with radios?"

"Hardly at all, but he won't let me throw away any of that electronic junk we have in our storeroom. There are even old vacuum valves in there!"

"I was in the administrative track when transistors became the fad," Sergio said. "And you never know when that so-called junk will come in handy, like when they discover all modern solid-state devices have electronic backdoors in them so the Chinese can do their spying." He paused before continuing. "As for your question, Esther—see, my lovely wife, I do have a good memory," he said, turning to her and then addressing Esther again. "We're donating the painting to the Uffizi Gallery. That way more people can appreciate it. By the way, we're sending you the parchment, but we're keeping that old armoire for one of our guest rooms."

*****

"Do you think everyone is having a good time?" Esther said later to Bastiann as they watched their guests. He noted that the contralto and the magistrate were becoming friendly. *Do weddings put everyone in a romantic mood?* He also noted that his best man and Philippa Bernard were sitting at one of the small tables, deep in conversation. He was happy she had been able to accept their invitation. She wasn't recovered enough to dance, but that didn't appear to bother Hal—or Philippa, for that matter.

"You needn't worry, Esther."

"I was only thinking they might not tell me because of some stupid sense of decorum. I don't like to be pandered to. Pampered, yes. Pandered, no."

"Esther, most everyone is here for you. Including me."

"Speaking of which, I'm jealous. You must have brushed up on the Viennese waltz with someone else. I wanted to try our hand at it in Grinzing, but we ran out of time."

"We can go back to Vienna sometime."

Later, as the newlyweds chatted with more of their friends, Bastiann received a text message. He called for silence and read aloud the message from NYPD homicide detective Rolando Castilblanco: "Dao-Ming and I wish the two of you the best. We consider both of you members of our international family along with Hal Leonard and everyone else present at your ceremony. Maybe we can all have a party at Esther's castle in Scotland sometime in the future."

"What a lovely thought," said Esther. Hal, who was legless from mixing all sorts of alcoholic beverages, led the applause, leaning on Philippa. Bastiann knew Leonard and Castilblanco were close and for good reason: Hal owed his life to the man.

No one heard Esther's whispered addition, "All the more reason to continue repairing the old place, love."

Bastiann shrugged. "I can't imagine Castilblanco feeling at home in the wilds of the Scottish moors. It's a far cry from New York City."

"Yet you seem to be comfortable there now when we go. Consider it our romantic summer cottage."

Bastiann remembered Hal's advice and only said, "Yes, dear."

Epilogue
Twenty-First Century, Ephesus

The small police car took the space the last tourist minibus just left. Aslan Remzi checked his watch. *Time for my evening's pilgrimage.* He left the car and walked along the Ephesian street.

Dusk was falling on the ancient ruins of Ephesus. He stopped walking when he came to the intersection between two old roads on Curete Street just down from the Heracles Gate. He looked toward the hills and smiled. Then he took a seat on a stone bench.

He surveilled the area to see if there were any tourists around and then glanced down at the ground in front of him.

"Don't worry, Mary," Aslan said. "If they return to the cave, they won't find his bones. He's no longer there. He's as safe as you are, there below. All these centuries we have guarded your final resting places. Your bones belong here, not at the Vatican."

Aslan had interviewed the fake nun. He didn't know any French nuns, but his sister was a nun who lived in Italy and talked about their lives there. He'd become suspicious when Sister Denise didn't act like one. He decided she was playing a role, but said nothing as she went to the aid of Inspector Erkan. He also decided to give her a break after a bit of sleuthing, first in French records and then in English ones. Erkan would have called it good police work; he called it avoiding a scene.

"Mary, wouldn't she be surprised to know there is something like a conspiracy?" He chuckled.

He looked around again, went to his knees, brushed clean the old stone with the iconic Christian representation of a fish, and returned to the bench.

For centuries his ancestors had guarded the Magdalene's grave beneath that Ephesian street. There was no mystery or conspiracy to it; it was only their traditional duty. Even St. John hadn't known she was buried there. The old man had most likely gone to his tomb wondering in what far land Mary walked... or was buried.

Like John, and before he returned to Ephesus, the Magdalene had come home—in her case, from the country where the huge rock guarded the entrance to the vast sea, to die where the Holy Mother of God had also spent her last days. That's how the legends went, passed on from generation to generation in his family, and he wasn't about to disbelieve them. In fact, he had sworn to his own father always to believe them.

When his oldest turned twelve, he would pass the story on to her and tell her how he moved the saint's remains, and to where. Then she would take the same oath. She would then pass the tale on to her oldest, *ad infinitum. Is it wrong not to tell the Holy Father in Rome?* He didn't know for sure, but he thought Mary's secret was one of those best kept secret. And now John's; the same could now be said about the location of the saint's bones.

He had known Inspector Erkan for so little time, but he missed him. He was a good cop and a good man. He hadn't seemed to value material things. Instead he valued justice and what was right. *If everyone did that, the world would be a different and better place.*

"You also understand material things aren't important, Mary," Aslan said in his soft voice. "You and John are nothing but bones now, and bones are material things. Where are your spirits? One of these days I'll find out. Until next time, *güle güle,* sweet lady."

Aslan walked to his car. Before entering his vehicle, he glanced at his watch. *I'll be late for dinner.*

Note from Steve:

You have just finished reading *Son of Thunder*, the sequel to *Rembrandt's Angel.* I hope you enjoyed it. Please write a review and post it, so that other readers and I can know your opinion. And I'm happy to hear from readers—use the contact page at the website below.

Besides *Rembrandt's Angel,* Esther and Bastiann have cameo roles in a few novels in the "Detectives Chen and Castilblanco Series"—Esther in *The Collector* and Bastiann in *Aristocrats and Assassins* and *Gaia and the Goliaths.*

You can read summaries, blurbs, and review extracts for all my books on my website, https://stevenmmoore.com, where there is also a list of free fiction you can download.

Below you will find questions for your book club or discussion group.

Around the world and to the stars! In libris libertas!

Son of Thunder

Ten Questions for Book Clubs and Discussion Groups

Sandro Botticelli has a low opinion of the priest, Leo, at times, yet calls him a friend other times. Are any of the painter's opinions genuine? Or is he just a man intent on having a good time in life?

Esther has retired from Scotland Yard, but she was also employed at MI6 during the Cold War. Do you think the government gives her just the first pension? If not, why is she silent about the second?

John has great admiration for the Magdalene. Do you think it's more than that?

Early Christians were persecuted by the Roman Empire. Do you think that's overstated in the novel?

Little is known about the places John visited, or whether he even visited them. Do you find the fictional account of his travels to preach the gospel too incredulous?

Do you think Esther should have left well enough alone after reading what was on the parchment?

More people than Bruno Toscano were interested in St. John's burial place. Discuss them all.

At times, Esther appears to be an elitist and other times not. What do you think of her opinions?

Do you think it was right for Esther to give the ring to Bastiann? Why do you think she did it?

This novel is a sequel to *Rembrandt's Angel.* If you read that novel, do you think she's a bit more subdued about her obsession in this novel compared to her obsession in that one? Or do you think she is becoming religious, as her ex-boss Langston suggests?

Notes, Disclaimers, and Acknowledgments

Needless to say, this novel is a departure from my usual mystery, thriller, and sci-fi stories. It's more historical fiction that weaves in facts, logical guesses, legend, and mostly pure, unsubstantiated extrapolation, to make a story that traverses many centuries. I had been dying to try it, and Esther and Bastiann seemed to be the perfect characters to feature in that blend.

Why St. John? Because it appears he lived a long life after the Assumption. I always wondered what he was doing all that time. I thought it was reasonable that he became a long-term missionary, much longer than Peter, Paul, and others, carrying the good news to the corners of the known world. And John was my favorite disciple, and his gospel is also my favorite. I tried to imagine this man, this disciple who Christ loved, and his many adventures. I hope I have done him justice.

While I mention John writing his gospel here (no one knows when he did this, or even if the disciple truly wrote it), there's enough controversy about his writing the Book of Revelation that I avoided adding to it. The two styles of writing do seem to be entirely different. (As portrayed in this novel, that could be attributed to the gospel being the earlier work.) I've also postulated the Magdalene was an early accomplice in what can only be called a revolution in the ancient world that continued until Emperor Constantine accepted Christianity.

I also wanted to prop up the Magdalene's reputation a bit. While not buying into Dan Brown's theories, it always seemed to me she got a bum rap from the early Church. Indeed, those other non-canonical gospels Father Jean

Laurent mentions paint different pictures of both the Magdalene and Judas. As I have John state in the novel, "Beware of those who would bend His message for their own purposes." Otherwise said, there is nothing that precludes early Christian leaders from promoting their own agendas—it's a common enough human failing—and excluding women as church leaders could be one of them.

All historical fiction creates narrative that fills in gaps in the historical records. That was one of my goals, as I stated above, but what I also wanted to accomplish in this novel was to make these figures from ancient history appear more human. We tend to make them more than that, but sometimes we need to celebrate their humanity in order to draw closer to them, persons we could have related to if we had been there to meet them. That's what all historical fiction does, but perhaps it's more important in the religious context.

I consulted many sources of opinions and texts of the gospels, both non-canonical and canonical, long before writing this novel simply because I was curious and interested—far too many sources to remember and list here. For the canonical ones, I agree with Father Jean: John is more original and captivating than the synoptic three. All four were already in use in early services in Rome and elsewhere. All four also mention the Magdalene, but her portrayal here as a financial backer of the movement and smart organizer is more loosely based on her gospel (presumably written by an admirer—the only version so far is a Coptic translation) and the gospel of Peter. Some of these non-canonical gospels influenced Christian traditions and iconography.

Much of the material I used is still often debated, particularly in the theological community, including St. John's caring for an ailing Virgin Mary, his final resting place, and even the legitimacy of the shrine to the Virgin near Ephesus (the latter is accepted by the Church). Maybe all that will change with further historical and archaeological investigation. If any experts wish to comment or correct me, they are welcome to shoot me an email using the contact page on my website.

Although some readers might disagree, I don't think there's anything in this novel to shake anyone's faith. Church canon was created by human beings after the Crucifixion, so both their faith and failings also went into the texts passed on and texts omitted from the scriptures and Church services. Leaders of the early Church made choices. Without having experienced the brutality of the Roman Empire, we can only guess at their reasons, but I haven't changed the basic message.

A final biblical note. The quotes I've taken from the Bible are from the King James version. The reason for this is simple: it is the version Esther would be familiar with since her father was a vicar. There are newer versions in modern English vernacular and in nearly every language still existing. Readers are invited to refer to their favorite versions using the chapter and verse indicated; the message remains the same.

Esther has enough faith to marvel at the wonders she and Bastiann uncover. As her old boss states, "You'd almost swear the old girl became religious." As a daughter of a cleric, she's as religious as many people, if not more so; it was her last husband, the count, who was the atheist. Both she and Bastiann are moved by the unfolding events in the novel. In fact, that's basically the story!

Of course, it's more Esther's. She's the one obsessed; first to disprove Botticelli was ever in Turkey, and second to find the tomb. Both Esther and the Magdalene—whom I imagined to also be a strong, smart woman—are amalgams of real women I've known. Dan Brown aside, this world would be a far better place with less testosterone and more women in control. Esther's poem at the start of the novel is mine, of course. It dates from my adolescence when I studied the world's great religions out of curiosity. (That includes Zen. My Detective Castilblanco has become a Buddhist as a bow to that questioning period in my life. For this novel, he's mentioned mostly as a participant in the wedding via a text message, an appropriate cameo for the internet age.)

I've most likely slighted poor Sandro Botticelli. His story is short here. As far as we know, he didn't travel far from Florence, but the "as far as we know" is key to my story. He didn't leave a plethora of notebooks like da Vinci. I only included Sandro because I needed a plot device to get art expert, Esther Brookstone, involved. I initially thought of da Vinci, but, after reading Isaacson's masterful *Leonardo da Vinci*, I had to conclude that Sandro fit better in the story. His friend, Bishop Leonardo da Padua, is completely fictional, but the church where Sandro was a parishioner is real, as are the Medici and Vespucci families. (Yes, America is named after Amerigo, and I postulated Sandro learned about map drawing from him.)

Besides Isaacson's work that not only described da Vinci but also described the milieu in which he worked, I'd like to mention specifically another "source." My old Latin American History professor I had at UC Santa Barbara. He was also a Jesuit scholar and served as a model for Father Jean, although the latter character is an amalgam of that professor and others I knew in Bogotá, Colombia, when I lived there and worked in academia.

The final motive for writing this sequel was both simple and two-fold: I wanted to answer questions about whether Esther and Bastiann ever tie the knot, and I wanted to say a bit about Esther's background in MI6 during the Cold War.

The latter is a bit of a prequel contained in a sequel, as it were, and shows another side of this smart, complex, and strong woman.

Many people contribute to making a manuscript into a novel. I would like to thank Carol Shetler for her editing/ beta-reading expertise; Michael James, chief editor, and Christine Horner, author support services, from the Penmore Press staff; and Lisa Arpino for her careful editing and suggestions for improving the manuscript.

Final thanks go to my wife, my constant and loving companion for thirty years, very best friend, and enthusiastic cheerleader. Without her, my writing life wouldn't be what it is. May Esther and Bastiann have as many years of joy together as we have had.

Steven M. Moore
Montclair, NJ
August 2018

About the Author

Steven M. Moore was born in California and has lived in various parts of the U.S. and Colombia, South America. He always wanted to be a storyteller but had to postpone that dream to work in academia and R&D as a scientist. His travels around Europe, South America, and the U.S., for work or pleasure, taught him a lot about the human condition and our wonderful human diversity; a learning process that began during his childhood in California's San Joaquin Valley. He and his wife now live in Montclair, NJ, just thirteen miles west of NYC's Lincoln Tunnel. Visit his website https://stevenmmoore.com, where you can communicate with him via the contact page there.

Steve is a member of International Thriller Writers.

If You Enjoyed This Book

Please write a review.

This is important to the author and helps to get the word out to others.

Visit

PENMORE PRESS

www.penmorepress.com

Rembrandt's Angel

by

Steven Moore

A Neo-Nazi conspiracy threatens Europe . . .

Esther Brookstone's life is at a crossroads. A Scotland Yard inspector who specializes in stolen art, she's reluctantly considering retirement. A three-time widow, she can't quite decide whether paramour and colleague Interpol Agent Bastiann van Coevorden should be husband number four. Decisions are put on hold while she and Bastiann set out to thwart a neo-Nazi conspiracy financed in part by artworks stolen during World War II. Among the stolen art is the masterpiece "An Angel with Titus' Features," a work Esther obsesses about recovering.

The case sends the intrepid pair on an international hunt spanning several European countries and the Amazon jungle. Evading capture and thwarting death, Esther and Bastiann prove time and again that adrenaline-spiked adventures aren't just for the young.

ÆGIR'S CURSE

BY
LEAH DEVLIN

A thousand years ago, the Viking colony of Vinland was ravaged by a swift-moving plague ... a curse inflicted by the sea god Ægir. The last surviving Norseman set the encampment and his longboat ablaze to ensure that the disease would die with him and his brethren.

In present-day Norway, a distinguished professor is found murdered, his priceless map of Vinland missing. The ensuing investigation leads to the reclusive world of Lindsey Nolan, a scientist and recovering alcoholic who has been sober for five years. Lindsey reluctantly agrees to help the detective who's hunting the murderer, but she has a bigger problem on her hands: a mysterious disease that's spreading like wildfire through the population of Woods Hole. As she races against a rising body count to discover the source of the plague, disturbing events threaten her hard-won sobriety—and her life. Will Lindsey be the next victim of Ægir's curse?

Leah Devlin is rapidly establishing herself as a writer of modern day mystery-thrillers. This story is as tight as a piano wire. Life at a seaside town in New England is full of treacherous undercurrents and peril, as residents are threatened by a menace from a thousand years ago. Murder, romance and deceit are a potent mix in this gripping novel, which I didn't want to put down.—James Boschert, author of the Talon Series and *Force 12 in German Bight*

BIG MOTHER

BY

MARC LIEBMAN

Big Mother 40 is a story well told and one in which aviation and special warfare veterans of the Vietnam conflict will identify, and about which they will tell their friends. Younger readers will enjoy the book simply as a great adventure.
– Michael Field, Captain USN (retired) Wings of Gold, Winter 2012 issue

Liebman skips macho combat images to plunk us into the deeper connections of war, from fear and courage to the truer realms of human relationships. His detail is authentic, and he lends even greater validity to the operations he describes with valuable author notes at the back of the book including a historic analysis of the time, military glossary and roster of characters. Despite the book's intensity and detail, the story is fast-paced. For a book you won't forget, you have to read BIG MOTHER 40.
Bonnie Toews, Military Writers Society of America, January 2013

CPSIA information can be obtained
at www.ICGtesting.com
Printed in the USA
JSHW022029260321
12970JS00001B/7